A NOVEL BASED ON THE LIFE OF

GIUSEPPE GARIBALDI

A MAN OF ACTION
SAVING LIBERTY

Rosanne Welch, PhD

THE **M**
MENTORIS
PROJECT

A Man of Action Saving Liberty is a work of fiction. Some incidents, dialogue, and characters are products of the author's imagination and are not to be construed as real. Where real-life historical figures appear, the situations, incidents, and dialogue concerning those persons are based on or inspired by actual events. In all other respects, any resemblance to actual persons, living or dead, events, or locales is entirely coincidental.

Barbera Foundation, Inc.
P.O. Box 1019
Temple City, CA 91780

Copyright © 2020 Barbera Foundation, Inc.
Cover front photo: Pictorial Press Ltd / Alamy Stock Photo
Cover back photo: istockphoto.com/benoitb
Cover design: Suzanne Turpin

More information at www.mentorisproject.org

ISBN: 978-1-947431-31-7

Library of Congress Control Number: 2020942205

All net proceeds from the sale of this book will be donated to Barbera Foundation, Inc. whose mission is to support educational initiatives that foster an appreciation of history and culture to encourage and inspire young people to create a stronger future.

The Mentoris Project is a series of novels and biographies about the lives of great men and women who have changed history through their contributions as scientists, inventors, explorers, thinkers, and creators. The Barbera Foundation sponsors this series in the hope that, like a mentor, each book will inspire the reader to discover how she or he can make a positive contribution to society.

Contents

Foreword

First and foremost, Mentor was a person. We tend to think of the word *mentor* as a noun (a mentor) or a verb (to mentor), but there is a very human dimension embedded in the term. Mentor appears in Homer's *Odyssey* as the old friend entrusted to care for Odysseus's household and his son Telemachus during the Trojan War. When years pass and Telemachus sets out to search for his missing father, the goddess Athena assumes the form of Mentor to accompany him. The human being welcomes a human form for counsel. From its very origins, becoming a mentor is a transcendent act; it carries with it something of the holy.

The Mentoris Project sets out on an Athena-like mission: We hope the books that form this series will be an inspiration to all those who are seekers, to those of the twenty-first century who are on their own odysseys, trying to find enduring principles that will guide them to a spiritual home. The stories that comprise the series are all deeply human. These books dramatize the lives of great men and women whose stories bridge the ancient and the modern, taking many forms, just as Athena did, but always holding up a light for those living today.

Whether in novel form or traditional biography, these books plumb the individual characters of our heroes' journeys.

The power of storytelling has always been to envelop the reader in a vivid and continuous dream, and to forge a link with the subject. Our goal is for that link to guide the reader home with a new inspiration.

What is a mentor? A guide, a moral compass, an inspiration. A friend who points you toward true north. We hope that the Mentoris Project will become that friend, and it will help us all transcend our daily lives with something that can only be called holy.

—Robert J. Barbera, President, Barbera Foundation
—Ken LaZebnik, Founding Editor, The Mentoris Project

"A tree is judged by the quality of the fruit it bears, and individuals are judged by the benefits they can bestow on their fellow human beings."

—Giuseppe Garibaldi

"At a time when the United States was fighting for the preservation of our own Union, Giuseppe Garibaldi's campaign for the unification of Italy inspired many around the world in their own struggles, including the thirty-ninth New York Infantry, also known as 'the Garibaldi Guard.' Today, the legacy of Garibaldi and all those who unified Italy lives on in the millions of American women and men of Italian descent who strengthen and enrich our nation."

—President Barack Obama,
Presidential Proclamation
150th Anniversary of the Unification of Italy

Chapter 1

CHILDHOOD IN PIEDMONT UNDER FRENCH RULE

On October 26, 1860, Giuseppe Garibaldi found himself as far from his childhood home as a man could be, having traveled around the world and back again in his fifty-three years, seeking a goal no man had yet accomplished: the unification of his beloved Italy. As he stood in his tent on the battlefield, he wondered . . . were the sacrifices worth this moment?

Fastening his trademark red shirt, he thought of those who had chosen to follow his cry "Rome or Die"—young men now buried in similar shirts in hillsides far from the country farms they had left behind.

Pulling a gray poncho over his head, he thought of friends around the world who might never know that their sacrifices had contributed to this impending moment.

As his fifteen-year-old daughter, Teresita, adjusted the black scarf around his neck, he looked into her eyes and thought of the woman he had lost on the way to this dream.

"Are you thinking of Mamma?" Teresita asked.

"Of my Mamma . . ." he said, remembering. "And of yours. And you. This dream—all my dreams—have been sustained by women all my life."

He paused. The moment was so precious that Teresita held her breath.

"I look into her eyes every time I look into yours," he said. "This was to be our shared triumph." How could he help but feel the presence of his beloved Anita on this of all days?

His only surviving daughter kissed him on the cheek. "This day still belongs to both of you," she said.

"'I am my beloved,'" he repeated. "That's what she said to me."

Teresita's fingers stopped in the middle of tying his scarf. He had never shared Anita's last words with their children.

"Now I say it of her. Forever," Giuseppe said, "I am my beloved."

The words brought a smile to Teresita's face, brightening her father's mood as he stepped from the tent and mounted his horse, groomed so meticulously that its coat shone like a mirror. He rode off, no longer only a child of French-held Nice, no longer the failed leader of the South American rebels of Rio Grande do Sul, no longer merely a candlemaker's apprentice in the turbulent times in the far-off United States. So much lost, yet so much gained in what still seemed so little time. He could barely believe it all himself.

At this moment, Giuseppe Garibaldi could claim himself the victor in a nearly twenty-year struggle over who should rule the now-scattered kingdoms of the once-powerful Roman Empire. It was almost impossible to believe the journey that had brought him to lead this legion, that had brought him from his birth in Piedmont to this encampment in Teano, that had brought him to this meeting with a king . . . impossible to believe that such a journey had begun at a small wooden desk nearly fifty years earlier.

"'Our fate cannot be taken from us; it is a . . .'" five-year-old Giuseppe faltered as he read aloud to his mother, Maria Rosa.

"Gift," she enunciated. "'Do not be afraid. Our fate cannot be taken from us; it is a gift.'" It was her favorite passage in her favorite book, *La Divina Commedia*. "Signor Alighieri's words are like music. A young gentleman is judged by how smoothly they flow off his tongue."

"Music is easy. Language is hard," the young boy said. "None of my friends have Italian, with one tutor, English with another, and French with another."

"You are not the other boys and they are not you." Maria Rosa, known to friends by her middle name, Nicoletta, never gave up—on anything. Including teaching her sons to read in Italian, a language the local French neighborhood of Nice did not respect.

At twenty-nine, Nicoletta had learned not to bother with what others thought. She followed her own ideas, gleaned from a life of studying the teachings of the Catholic Church, caring for the local poor, and keeping her four rambunctious young sons in line. That responsibility she took to heart by feeding their bodies with quality homegrown vegetables, and their minds with quality homegrown Italian literature. They read from Cicero to Dante, with a little of the English poet Percy Bysshe Shelley thrown in, as she was partial to his way with words—and his bent for romance.

"Let me tell you a story about living up to other people's ideals," she said.

Giuseppe had never been sure if her stories were meant to teach him how to live or distract him from his current desire, which right now was to stop sitting up so straight on such a hard chair and to stop reading such a difficult work as Dante. He listened intently, trying not to lose focus on his own goal in this conversation.

"There was a man walking a donkey through the countryside one day with his young son riding on top. They encountered a man who berated the father for allowing his son to ride while he walked, so the father and son switched positions with the child walking and the father riding."

"That is smart," Giuseppe said.

"Not according to the next man they met," Nicoletta said. "'Poor child!' the man sighed. He thought it awful that the father was riding and the son was made to walk, so do you know what they did next?"

Giuseppe thought for a moment. "I would ride together."

"Yes," his mother answered, smiling at his quick thinking. "Together, they continued until they met yet another man who cried, 'Oh, the poor beast! Two riding on top must be hard on such a weak creature.'"

"And the moral of the story?" Giuseppe asked.

"You must make your own decisions," Nicoletta said. "For never will everyone agree with you. So you study three languages because I've decided it is right for you."

"What if Signor Dante did not know my fate is to be a beggar?" Giuseppe teased, trying to avoid going back to work.

"Then you would have been born into the family of a beggar,

Peppino," Nicoletta said, using the family's nickname for him, "not into the family of a daring sea captain."

"I miss Papà," Giuseppe admitted. His father, Giovanni, known to friends by his middle name, Domenico, often left the family for months at a time to sail his ship, the *Santa Reparata*. On his rare nights at home, Domenico dazzled his sons with stories of his adventures at sea, from meeting pirates to speaking the exotic languages of the many ports where his ship docked.

"I miss him too," Nicoletta said, patting her son's head. "But that's why, if you study harder than other boys, you will be yet more than he and take a trade that keeps you on land. Be a doctor, a lawyer, or—can you imagine the honor—a priest . . ."

To that end, she had taught all her sons in turn to read Dante Alighieri, proud that far back in the 1300s he had written his *La Divina Commedia* in Italian when most others were still using Latin as the language of the educated classes. She also taught her sons to read the writings of Niccolò Machiavelli and Cesare Borgia, learned men of the Renaissance often considered the forefathers of the idea of a united Italy. Such unification was Nicoletta's dream before it was her son's.

"We are Italians—Nice did not always belong to France," she said, taking out a book of maps common in a sailor's home and deftly turning their reading lesson into one on history. "Our small city was once part of the great Holy Roman Empire." Giuseppe followed her finger as she traced around the whole of Italy, Sicily, Spain, and the northern coast of Africa, the entirely of the holdings of ancient Rome. Her delicate finger even encircled part of England.

"And now?" he asked eagerly.

"Now," she said dejectedly as finger traced a smaller circle. "Now we are part of France."

"Why?" Giuseppe asked.

"Men fight over land," she said, wondering how much of the world's evils one could—or should—explain to a five-year-old. "Men fight over differences, in language, in looks—"

"Why?" Giuseppe asked again, interrupting her against the rules because he was anxious to understand.

"It makes them feel *forte*. Strong," Nicoletta said. When she saw the gleam in her little boy's eyes, she said, "But that is not true strength."

"Then what is?" he asked, desperate to know the secrets to making his mother, and often-absent father, proud.

"Unity is strength. Diversity within unity is strength. We are always stronger together than apart," Nicoletta said, taking her son's hand and walking him outside to an old oak tree in the field beyond their home. "See this oak?" Together, they looked up through the woven branches, so thick that the leaves nearly blotted out the clear blue sky.

"Trees survive for generations not by destroying life around them but, like a family, by making a place where all can live together safely."

"Who lives in a tree?" he asked. "Not me."

"Sh, listen," she said. Giuseppe tried not to move or make a sound, a grand feat for a small, fidgety boy. Soon they heard rustling and his mother pointed as a weasel crawled out of his burrow under the tree root and ran off. Next they heard a tiny trilling sound and she pointed up to a lark as it landed on a high branch. "A calandra lark," she whispered. "To say you sing like such a bird is the greatest compliment. They sing so magically, many people keep them as pets."

"Can we keep him?" Giuseppe asked, eyes growing wider as he started forward.

"No," Nicoletta said, pulling him back. The bird took flight. "He is free and must be allowed to go where he pleases. But—" She paused to lift a leaf, and they spotted a cricket tucked underneath. "Keeping crickets brings good luck." Mamma carefully cupped the cricket in her hand and gestured for Giuseppe to make the same shape with his. Gently, she deposited the insect into his tiny hands.

As they walked home, Nicoletta hoped her son had learned the lesson. "Do you think you understand what real strength is, Peppino?"

"Yes, Mamma," he answered. "It's when everyone works together for the good of . . . everyone?"

"Good," she said. Then, as lessons were over for the day, she reverted to her favorite occupation. "Did I ever tell you the story of the *Castagno dei Cento Cavalli* in faraway Sicily?" she asked.

"No," Giuseppe said, slowing his normally quick pace so the story wouldn't be interrupted by a return home and the demands of his other brothers. He cherished this time alone with his mother.

"Well, the Tree of One Hundred Horses is far, far south, in the Kingdom of Sicily, near the mouth of a giant volcano named Etna. The tree was born many years ago."

"Before you?" Giuseppe asked, unintentionally making his mother laugh.

"Yes, before me. Before my mother and her mother, and her mother before her. Before even Jesus. Or Caesar. Once upon a time, a legion of one hundred knights were caught in a terrible thunderstorm. The rain would ruin their armor with rust. The mud from the flood would swallow their horses. But the Tree of a Hundred Horses sheltered them all under its bountiful branches. That is strength. That is unity."

"I will see this tree for myself someday," Giuseppe promised as he cradled his lucky cricket. "Perhaps it's just another wonderful story."

"*Chi non va, non vede*," Nicoletta said, quoting her favorite Italian proverb. "*Chi non vede, non sa*." Never one to miss a chance for a lesson, she asked Giuseppe, "Translate that into English for me and I will tell your tutor that you are ready for another lesson."

"'If you don't go, you won't see,'" Giuseppe translated, a skill that never failed to make his mother smile. "'If you don't see, you won't know.'"

A few years later, in the summer of 1819, on a day Nicoletta devoted to taking her sons to hone the swimming skills so necessary for a life at sea, Giuseppe had a chance to prove he had learned her lesson of strength and unity.

Nicoletta watched contentedly as Angelo, who was older by a year or so, and Michele, who was younger, ran along the pathway beside Giuseppe. The youngest, Felice, trailed behind not matter how hard he tried. The boys always raced to see who would touch water first. Today Giuseppe won, running into the waves until the water was deep enough for a dive. He disappeared into the incoming tide. The others followed shortly, as did Nicoletta after pausing to deposit their food baskets on the sand.

The shore teemed with other locals taking a break from the rising humidity; swimming, reading, and unpacking for *pranzare*, the midday meal. After some time in the water, Nicoletta returned to her baskets and began extracting cold meats wrapped in cloth and an assortment of whole fruits and vegetables waiting to be sliced. It was enough to satisfy the appetites her sons were creating as they chased each other across the waves.

As she unfolded a towel from around some bread, a shout rang out over the waves, snapping her to attention. Nicoletta's eyes scanned the water for the source of the sound. Others on the shore did the same, but no one moved. Nicoletta picked out where Felice splashed in the nearby tide pool, immune to adult worries. Out in the sea Angelo treaded water as he listened, then she saw Michele doing the same a few yards away. She continued scanning the water for Giuseppe. One of the swimmers dove toward a woman frantically splashing and Nicoletta quickly recognized Giuseppe, arms extended over his head, cutting like a jackknife through the water.

"No!" Nicoletta shouted over the sound of the sea as she watched her twelve-year-old swim farther and farther from shore, knowing how tired he must be. Angelo and Michele had begun to follow, but fell back at the urgency in their mother's voice. Whether Giuseppe could not hear her or chose to ignore her, she didn't know, but he continued swimming to the flailing woman as others on the beach stood up to watch.

"Who is it?" one neighbor asked.

"No one recognized her when she arrived," said another as he entered the water to help, but he was already so far behind Giuseppe that Nicoletta knew he would be of no use.

Giuseppe glanced back to shore to gauge how far back he would have to swim with this woman in tow and he began to worry. What if he couldn't do it? When he saw the others were too far out, he pushed himself one more time, grabbed the young woman under the arm, and began swimming back to shore.

After what seemed an eternity, Nicoletta felt the relief of knowing he was going to make it back. When they reached the spot where they could stand and walk back through the waves, others ran out to assist the woman. A quick conversation revealed she was traveling through town and had come to the beach alone to refresh herself.

Meanwhile, Angelo, Michele, and finally Felice ran out to Giuseppe along with a host of their local friends. Angelo slapped him on the back, hitting so hard, water shot out of Giuseppe's mouth. He fell to his knees, coughing up the rest of it.

Nicoletta hugged her son tightly. "What were you thinking?" she demanded.

"I—I didn't," Giuseppe began. He spoke in pauses as the words slowly formed in his mind. "I didn't see anyone else . . . ready . . . or trying . . . so . . ."

"So you thought you'd take care of it all," Nicoletta said, not scolding so much as releasing the quiet tension that had risen in her.

"I was trying to be a tree," Giuseppe finally articulated.

"A tree?" Angelo said, confused. "Trees can't swim!"

Nicoletta laughed at the confusion their inside joke caused Angelo, but quickly quieted at the sad look that crossed his face when he felt she was showing favoritism.

"Haven't I told you the story?" Nicoletta asked her other sons.

The boys shook their heads vehemently.

"Sit down and eat your lunches," she said, "and I will tell you all a story about a tree and a hundred horsemen." The boys began eating as the young woman Giuseppe had saved approached.

"*Grazie,*" she said, hesitantly placing a basket of food at Nicoletta's feet and turning to walk away.

"Join us," Nicoletta said, introducing herself in welcome.

The woman seemed hesitant. Giuseppe rose to shake her hand, his words tumbling so fast, she could barely understand his dialect. "We are always stronger together than apart," he said. "Stay, and my Mamma will tell you a wonderful story—of a grand tree, a thousand horses, a terrible storm, and the knights who survived."

The young woman sat beside Nicoletta and introduced herself as Giuseppina.

"What a lovely name," Nicoletta commented.

"It's mine too," said Giuseppe.

"What a coincidence. We were both named for St. Josaphat," Giuseppina said.

Nicoletta smiled and, always turning life experiences into lessons, asked, "What is St. Josaphat the patron saint of?"

Giuseppe smiled. "Unity."

It was a lesson Giuseppe would learn over and over in his youth.

Chapter 2

Time with his mother and brothers didn't last. Soon Giuseppe, like all young men from the newly created middle class, was sent to boarding school in Genoa, over 120 miles from his home in Nice. Nicoletta hoped he would study medicine or law, but he picked up a knack for navigation instead. A short year into his schooling, when the teachers refused to give lessons on navigation, Giuseppe and a small group of friends decided to test themselves.

One night, under cover of darkness, they commandeered a small local sailboat and headed toward Liguria, some forty miles west. They wanted to practice their seafaring skills and reenact the Battle of Actium, which they had been learning about in history class. Or perhaps that was merely the way they rationalized their actions. Naturally, fourteen-year-old Giuseppe took on the role of the famed General Octavian.

Giuseppe's best friend, Pietro Anzani, played Octavian's right-hand man, Admiral Marcus Agrippa.

During the actual Battle of Actium, in 31 BC, the 250 battleships commanded by Octavian and Agrippa overcame those under the control of Mark Anthony and Cleopatra, who famously died by double suicide when they lost. Octavian's success led to the beginning of the Roman Empire, whose influences were still felt throughout the world.

On their much smaller boat, Giuseppe and Pietro worked frantically to stay on course as a thunderstorm struck. Rising waves rocked the boat. Giuseppe gripped the wheel tight as Pietro wrestled with the sails.

"You said you knew how to steer!" Pietro shouted.

"You said you knew how to sail!" Giuseppe shouted back.

"Not in such a storm!" Pietro said, but the wind swallowed his words before they could reach Giuseppe. "You have to abandon course," Pietro said urgently. "Sail into the wind and save the ship!"

"Strike the mainsail!" Giuseppe ordered.

Pietro balked at the suggestion. "We'll be at the mercy of the waters!"

Rather than waste precious seconds explaining his plan to freeboard, Giuseppe abandoned the wheel and began using the rudder to steer. When Pietro realized they were going to make a mad run for a landing, he struck the mainsail. Even he knew a boat could not have two masters. Giuseppe fought to hold the rudder steady. In under a half an hour, they made land and scrambled out of the boat, happy to be alive.

The next day they were less happy as they were both expelled from school. Not precisely the victory Octavian and Agrippa had enjoyed, but a solid reminder that you can't always win every game in life, yet you have to learn how to keep going.

Nicoletta and Domenico interpreted Giuseppe's adventure as proof he should follow his father into a career at sea. Two years later, Giuseppe embarked on his first long voyage from January to July of 1824 aboard the Russian ship *Costanza*. Italians crewed the ship under the leadership of Captain Angelo Pesante, a man Domenico called "the best sea captain I have ever known."

On this trip, sixteen-year-old Giuseppe saw the Black Sea for the first time. It was also the first time he saw a palace. As they sailed through the Golden Horn to enter the narrow Bosporus Strait, Giuseppe couldn't take his eyes off the palace on the hill.

"The Turks still call it the New Palace, though 'twas built in the mid-1400s," Captain Pesante said, his eyes following Giuseppe's gaze. "To distinguish it from the Old Palace, over in Beyazıt Square. This one's been destroyed twice—by earthquake and fire—but they keep rebuilding. And over there is where their Grand Vizier meets with his council."

"How do you know so much?" Giuseppe asked. "Can you read Turkish?"

"Can't say that I can. Course, no one reads as much as you do, Garibaldi." Pesante smiled. Giuseppe had carried more books on board for the long journey than even the captain.

"I do all my work," Giuseppe started in defense.

"I know you do," Pesante said. "And it's good to have some way to pass the time on these long voyages 'sides knot-making. But don't forget, you learn as much from a life of traveling, and from all the old seamen telling tales 'bout their travels. Guess I'm one of those old ones now."

Giuseppe could sense his captain's pride in his life's work, so he kept feeding him questions. "Is it because of all the palaces that they have named this place the Golden Horn?" he asked.

"Don't know when men started calling this the Golden Horn—or why," Pesante said. "Could be all the riches coming into the harbor. Could be the shape of this inlet."

"Could it be the way this strong yellow light makes the water shine?" Giuseppe asked as they watched the sun set over the surrounding hillsides.

"You talk like a poet," Pesante said. "But words are good when men are far from home. They remind them they have something to return to. They remind them there is something more important than even the sea. Never forget that."

"I won't," promised Giuseppe.

The next year, Giuseppe joined his father's crew on the *Santa Reparata* as they traveled the Tyrrhenian Sea off the western coast of Italy, named for the Tyrrhenian people who may or may not have been the Etruscans of pre-Roman Italy. "Such are the mysteries of the world," Nicoletta had said when they studied the area in preparation for his journey. "We can only know what scholars can prove, and scholars can prove only that for which they find evidence. Perhaps you will be such a scholar one day," she had added, not yet sure she was happy with Giuseppe's choice to be a sailor.

Giuseppe might not have been ready for such a long voyage, but Domenico didn't want his son to miss Pope Leo XII's celebration of the Jubilee Year of 1825. The occasion marked a time for remission of sins and universal pardon during which prisoners could be freed and debts could be forgiven by God's earthly representatives at the Vatican. On that trip, Giuseppe served as a regular crewman and sailed to Rome, delivering a cargo of regional wine from Nice for the citywide festivities. The trip planted the seeds of his future mission, as he fell in love with the city that had once been the capitol of the Roman world. He dreamed of helping Rome take that honored place again someday.

As they approached Civitavecchia, the port of Rome, Domenico took a moment to join his son at the bow. "Imagine," he said, "this port has been here since Emperor Trajan built it in the second century."

"But now it too belongs to France," Giuseppe responded, echoing his mother.

"It has changed hands often," Domenico said. "After the Saracens nearly sacked the whole settlement, Pope Leo VII had a new city built farther up the hill."

"Such a line of Italian history. He was Leo VII, and over a thousand years later we are celebrating with Leo XII . . . at a port claimed by France." Giuseppe couldn't help but ask, "Why can't Italy be whole again?"

"The world changes constantly. I have often left the port of one country and returned to find it belonged to another," Domenico said. "Have faith in the future. I have traveled far from the home where I was born, and I imagine you and your generation will travel yet farther with all the new technology available."

"New technology?" Giuseppe said. "But Captain Pesante says you are the only captain who still keeps an astrolabe on board."

"There is technology and there is beauty, and not always do the two meet," Domenico said as they walked into the captain's quarters. He picked up the astrolabe that sat on his table amid more modern navigational equipment, including a telescope and a pendulum clock. "My father gave this to me. Papà told me that if the great writer Geoffrey Chaucer thought it was so important for his son to understand the astrolabe that he wrote a treatise on the star taker, then it was important for me—and for the sons I would have someday—to understand."

"All Mamma taught me about the astrolabe is that it was the name given to the child of Abelard and Heloise," Giuseppe said, disappointed. "Another French story."

"Those doomed French lovers are not the whole story of the astrolabe," Domenico said. "While European scholars were endlessly debating theology, the Arabs in Spain possessed a knowledge of the heavens, geography, and mathematics that Europeans could only envy." He handed the instrument to Giuseppe, who turned the astrolabe over in his hands. "Let this be a reminder that all cultures have contributed to your world, whether you know it or not."

Though they had only a short time to spend in Rome, Giuseppe became enamored with the history and the art that covered the ancient city. They saw the Colosseum and the *Fontana de Trevi*, where Domenico enjoyed educating his son in his own fashion. "The ancient Romans mastered the waters with their aqueducts, their fountains, and their baths. For over four hundred years, this fountain served as the Baths of Agrippa. Let it be a symbol of what man can do when he works and studies."

To honor Nicoletta, they made time to see the Protestant cemetery where the tragic poet Percy Bysshe Shelley's ashes were buried. Giuseppe read the headstone out loud: "Nothing of him that doth fade but doth suffer a sea-change into something rich and strange."

Giuseppe found his favorite spot standing in front of the equestrian statue of Marcus Aurelius on the *Campidoglio*, or Capitoline Hill, one of the Seven Hills of Rome, between the Forum and the Campus Martius.

"He was a great warrior," Domenico said as he and Giuseppe stood in the sun and admired the bronze work of the anonymous artist.

"But that's not what I see, Father," Giuseppe said. "He carries no weapons and wears no armor. To me, Aurelius is a bringer of peace rather than a military hero."

"Excellent point," Domenico agreed, "for this is how he saw himself and his reign."

"How do you know that?" Giuseppe asked.

"I have read the great emperor's *Meditations*," Domenico said. "It has kept my mind exercised on many a long voyage. I'll lend it to you for our return home."

Giuseppe beamed at this chance to be looked at by his own father as an equal in intellect, if not yet in naval knowledge. Years later he would remember this trip and this city in his memoirs, as having been "dear to me beyond all things."

If his first two voyages gave Giuseppe a love for life at sea, his next voyage nearly destroyed it. Anxious to crew a larger ship than the one owned by his father, Giuseppe signed aboard the *Cortese* with a crew of twenty that carried wine from Nice across the Black Sea. The men anticipated difficulties because they had left late and feared encountering too much ice to make the passage. Instead, one night as Giuseppe and a few other off-duty seamen slept below deck, the sound of a boarding ax broke through the cabin door and shocked them all awake.

Several Barbary pirates flooded into the small sleeping quarters and held the men at gunpoint. As the pirate gathering all the crew's belongings crept closer to Giuseppe's mat, his eyes fell on Giuseppe's small pile of books: *The Divine Comedy* and *The Prince*, which had accompanied him on his earlier voyages, and *The Battle of Benvenuto* by Francesco Domenico Guerrazzi, a new one his mother had gifted him before this journey.

The pirate ignored the books, preferring to snatch Giuseppe's dagger from beside his bed. It wasn't until the pirate grabbed the extra pair of socks next to Giuseppe's mat that Giuseppe noticed the man had no shoes and his clothes were filthy, the fabric nearly worn through.

When the man moved out of hearing distance, a nearby bunkmate whispered, "I thought all pirates were rich." This brought the echo of his mother's favorite proverb to Giuseppe's mind, "If you don't see, you won't know." As they were forced onto deck Giuseppe's eyes scanned his surroundings for a weapon, but the pirates had taken them all.

On deck they were met by a crew of other pirates staring them down from a brigantine that had lashed itself to the *Cortese* in the darkness. Some pointed muskets across the small expanse between ships, and others still wielded their crossbows, as the sea air was calm enough for their aim to be true. Many of them were coatless on this cold night.

Of all the pirate groups that stalked the Mediterranean, the Barbary pirates, named for the Berbers who inhabited the northwest shores of Africa, were the most feared. They operated from ports such as Algiers, Tunis, and Tripoli, which practiced state-supported piracy. By the late 1700s, they had become so fearsome that many European nations and the nascent United States agreed to pay them an annual ransom—or tribute—to ensure trading vessels were not attacked.

The lead pirate shouted at Giuseppe's captain and the captain shouted back, but they did not understand each other. The captain spoke only Italian and French, and Giuseppe realized the pirate spoke a mixture of English and what he assumed was Arabic. Never had his mother's lessons been so important. He could now speak—and translate—six languages well. He hesitantly stepped forward. Several of their captors pointed their muskets directly at him.

"Our captain does not speak English," Giuseppe said calmly in that language.

"But you do," challenged the pirate captain, who did not hesitate to repeat his order. "Your men will load your cargo onto our ship."

Giuseppe translated for his captain, who at first refused on orders from the French government. The pirate captain laughed and said, "Americans pay tributes. The British pay tributes. France leaves you to your fate. What loyalty do you owe them?"

Giuseppe's captain tried to hold firm, but the pirate captain continued, "My crew will kill you all and do it themselves."

Giuseppe translated this ultimatum back to his captain, who reluctantly gave the order to transfer all the wine and other cargo to the pirate ship.

In a few hours, it was done. But before the pirates left, they had one more demand. "My crew spent too much time on the open sea," the pirate captain told Giuseppe.

"As have we," Giuseppe replied, wondering where this would lead as he translated to his captain.

"We take all clothes on board," the pirate captain said.

"We carried only wine and foodstuffs to trade," Giuseppe said, not bothering to translate.

"We take all clothes," the pirate captain repeated, gesturing for the crew of the *Cortese* to undress. Giuseppe and his fellow crewmen looked to their captain to see how to respond. They were shocked to find the captain, having understood the gesture, had begun removing his coat. Obediently, the crew followed his lead.

With all their cargo and clothing now collected, Giuseppe and the crew watched the ragged pirates transform by donning the stolen garb, mostly handmade by their mothers, sisters, and sweethearts. When the pirate ship had floated out of earshot, the naked men gathered around their captain.

"If France has abandoned us, why hasn't the British navy stopped them?" Giuseppe asked. "They are said to be the greatest navy in Europe."

"Those contemptible Brits," the captain said angrily. "They realized the pirates did far more damage to their adversaries. Instead of crushing those thieves, they pay them tributes."

Such dishonorable behavior angered all the men, but there was no time to argue. The captain turned to the crewman who had fallen asleep on watch in the crow's nest as the pirate ship approached. Giuseppe saw the man was shivering, and not merely from being naked in the cold. He was frightened, as he should have been. They all knew the penalty for such dereliction of duty was keelhauling—dragging a man at the end of a rope beneath the hull of a ship. Most captains had stopped using this particular form of discipline—a holdover punishment from a century before—but not on the *Cortese*, which was famous for it. The crew knew they would be made to watch to deter them from any further breach of discipline.

Surviving the pirate attack might have been enough to turn Giuseppe away from a life on the sea, but witnessing his first keelhauling confirmed it. Giuseppe and several crew members left the ship when it docked in Constantinople to pick up new cargo. Few signed on again for the return to Nice on the *Cortese*. Giuseppe was too disheartened to remain at sea, or to serve under such a captain, even long enough for the return trip home. First he and several other sailors who had fallen ill from the cold needed to recover from the journey before they could sign on to another crew and head for home, but one day in hospital changed that plan.

Several local women tended to the healing sailors, but Luisa Sauvaigo, also from Nice, caught Giuseppe's attention the first day he arrived. Exceptional for her time, Luisa had learned to read, so she came each day to read to the men from her favorite books, among them *The Divine Comedy*. She would sit in a chair surrounded by crewmen and read aloud to them—but one day, she had left her book at home.

"That's okay, Signora Sauvaigo," a fellow recovering crewman said, gesturing to Giuseppe. "Peppino here has his own books. He collects 'em."

Luisa turned to Giuseppe and asked, "May I borrow one of your books to read to the others? It soothes them as they heal."

Still weak, Giuseppe merely nodded. But when Luisa chose the book his mother had bestowed up on him, *The Battle of Benvenuto*, he perked up. "Have you read Guerrazzi?" she asked.

Taken aback, Giuseppe blurted out, "He is a strong voice for a united Italy."

"My father supports his mission," Luisa ventured, knowing a woman should not present a political opinion in public, but nonetheless stimulated by their exchange. When none of their onlookers objected, she continued, "Papà even subscribes to the newspaper Guerrazzi started with Giuseppe Mazzini."

Giuseppe's interest sparked. He had never met a woman interested in politics besides his mother. "I have seen this newspaper, before I left. I wish I could help them in some way."

Luisa looked into Giuseppe's eyes and saw something within him that made her respond, "You will."

As the two conversed, they could not know that Guerrazzi would later be imprisoned for his radical activities in the Young Italy movement; in 1833, he was held for three months at Forte Stella in Portoferraio. Afterwards, he became a powerful liberal leader. But at this time, Guerrazzi was merely the beginning of a conversation that would carry two ambitious young people into their first serious relationship.

Under Luisa's care, Giuseppe regained his strength. Rather than go home to Nice or even return to sailing, which would require months away from Luisa at a time, Giuseppe settled in Constantinople. Luisa recommended him as a tutor for the local Timoni family, a wealthy household where she served as a nanny. For the next few years, Giuseppe divided his time between courting Luisa and tutoring the Timoni children in math and in the many languages he knew.

The two young people so far from home had much in common, but Luisa's father did not approve of their match. He wanted only men of higher professions to court Luisa, and tutors were not well paid. Eventually, the two could only spend time together while at work. So Luisa attended balls and dinners with other young men at night, and in the daytime she and her true love swapped thoughts on politics, philosophy, and the news of the day.

After reading all they could of Guerrazzi, they had turned to yet another new voice fighting for independence: Ciro Menotti. Alas, his words came to Giuseppe and Luisa in the form of a letter written to Menotti's wife on the eve of his execution. They heard about both the letter and the execution from a newly arrived ship's crew. Menotti had tried to free the Italian region of Modena from Austrian rule, but had been arrested and condemned to death by hanging. In an effort to send a message, Duke Francis IV held the execution on May 23, 1831, in the citadel of the very city Menotti had hoped to free. Menotti's followers made copies of the letter to inspire future insurrections. A friend in the port smuggled a copy to Giuseppe, who read it together with Luisa one day over the midday meal they were permitted to share away from their charges.

"'Dearest wife,'" Giuseppe read. "'May your virtue and your religion be with you and assist you in receiving this sheet of mine. These are the last words of your unhappy Cyrus—he will see you again in a blessed stay. Live for the children and be to them both father and mother. The last loving command that I impose on your heart is not to give in to sorrow—beat it, and think about who it is that advises you to do so.'"

Giuseppe continued reading, though his voice broke halfway through. As Luisa rested her chin on his shoulder, they finished reading silently and sat in contemplation, as if after a homily.

Giuseppe finally broke the silence. "Are there no heroes we can look to?" he asked.

"There is you," Luisa said sincerely. "And we'll name our first child for Menotti."

"I cannot even make your father accept me, a poor tutor," he said. "How can you already be naming our babies?"

"He will come around," Luisa said. "Once you are a commander, how can he deny it when you ask for my hand?"

"How could I command a regiment? And such a campaign . . . it would mean leaving you."

"I could go with you," Luisa said. "Wives follow their men into battle to cook and care for them. Some even share in the fight."

"I dream of a life like that, with you and I together in the fight. But don't we need to be married before you make such a sacrifice?" Giuseppe teasingly reminded. "Your papà still won't let this lowly tutor onto your dance card."

Luisa nodded sadly. They might dream of uniting Italy, but first they had to unite their own family. So, in 1832, at the age of twenty-five, Giuseppe earned his certification as a merchant navy captain. There was more money in the ferrying of cargo than there ever would be in the figuring of fractions.

Life as a sailor required Giuseppe to leave Luisa for long stretches of time, to reencounter pirates, and to once again survive. All this traveling across the countries of the Mediterranean cultivated Giuseppe's interest in who ruled them, how, and why. He wrote countless letters to Luisa, sent via boats returning from the various ports where he docked, telling her all about what he was reading. Her letters grew less frequent, a consequence Giuseppe tried to believe came from the difficulty of locating a ship in operation. So he wrote. And wrote. And what he could not commit to paper he held in his heart for his return visits. He had joined Mazzini's secret Young Italy movement and prepared to participate in Mazzini's planned insurrection in his home region of Piedmont. He dreamed of taking Luisa with him as his bride, but when he returned to Constantinople after nearly a year at sea, he found her father had married her off to a richer man. Worse yet, she had already become a mother.

"How could you allow your father to do this to us?" he begged of Luisa at their final meeting.

"I am his child," she explained. "I had to obey."

Heartbroken, in April 1833, Garibaldi left Constantinople on the schooner *Clorinda*, taking a shipment of oranges to Russia. If he could not be with Luisa, Giuseppe decided it was time to return to Nice and make their dream of a united Italy come true. Alone.

Chapter 3

No woman took Luisa's place in his heart, though Giuseppe was not alone for long. At five feet five with blond hair and blue eyes, Garibaldi was visually more Greek than Italian, but Italian women were drawn to him all the same, especially those who also supported a united Italy. Teresina Cassamiglia and her mother, Caterina Boscovich, who owned the Osteria del Colomba in Genoa, were among many women who helped Giuseppe. Ignoring the danger that could come from aiding and abetting revolutionaries, they housed Giuseppe at their inn between naval journeys and slyly sought out other potential converts to Mazzini's Young Italy to send his way. The mother and daughter delighted in introducing Giuseppe to other men in the area who might share their mutual goals.

Though many men such as Giuseppe successfully recruited thousands of secret followers to the Young Italy movement, Mazzini failed in his attempt to radicalize Tuscany, was arrested and escaped to France in 1833, all which made the work harder and harder. Worse, the knowledge of how many of Mazzini's followers had been executed by the young King Charles Albert of Piedmont overwhelmed several of Giuseppe's arguments for independence. He took great solace in telling the story of the noble act Mazzini's most trusted confidant, Jacopo Ruffini, chose. Rather than risk giving away other conspirator's names when tortured, Ruffini died by suicide in prison.

"I wish I could say I would be as bold," Teresina said to Giuseppe one day when the inn was empty. "To commit a mortal sin in the name of the country . . ."

"He did it in the name of loyalty," Giuseppe said. "To keep his friends safe. That is the nobility of it." But to be honest, even Giuseppe could not say how far he would go in the face of such torture.

To avoid being found, arrested, and executed, undercover revolutionaries communicated using aliases. Giuseppe had chosen to use two different surnames interchangeably—whether to accent his mission or perhaps to mock those on the other side, he never explained. For some meetings he used Cleombrotus, a Spartan king who led the ancient Spartan-Peloponnesian army against the Thebans in the Battle of Leuctra. For others he used Borel, a martyr to their cause. This kept Giuseppe's identity hidden and those men's names—and spirits—alive.

Today he was using Borel as he spoke to the newest sailor Caterina and Teresina steered his way. As always, Giuseppe began by buying the potential new recruit a drink. "All for Italy!" Giuseppe said boldly in place of *cent'anni*, or "one hundred years," the traditional phrase when toasting.

The young sailor paused but did not disagree with the sentiment. He clinked his glass, drank deeply, then asked, "Isn't that the motto of that Mazzini fellow, the one who caused all that commotion in Genoa last year?"

Pretending not to know Giuseppe, his co-conspirator Giovanni Battista Cuneo joined the conversation from the other end of the bar. "Commotion? Is it not worth a little commotion to gain what Mazzini's men call 'one independent, free republic—the only true foundation of Italian liberty'? Not a bad motto either, eh?"

"For God and the people. That's what Mazzini says," Giuseppe added. "What say you?"

"I say Mazzini's a revolutionary, trying to overturn the Congress of Vienna," the young man began. It was a litany Giuseppe had grown bored of hearing. Tirelessly optimistic, he tried to keep the sailor engaged in the conversation long enough to convert him.

"A Congress that did nothing but stabilize a few handpicked powers and crush the smaller nations of equal value," Giuseppe said.

"Our new friend here," Giovanni said, tipping his glass toward Giuseppe, "seems a proud Italian. Where were you born?"

"Catania," the young man said.

"Sicily and Italy were once—and again should—be brothers in arms. All should proclaim the unity and independence of Italy," Giuseppe insisted.

"To what purpose?" the young man asked.

Giovanni gave Giuseppe a look that urged caution. Spies were everywhere and arrests had become far too common. But Giuseppe, unable to squelch his desire for success, ignored his friend's advice and stated boldly, "It requires a fully united country to wage war against Austria. All for Italy!" Giuseppe again raised a glass.

The sailor paused. It was hard not to be swept away by Giuseppe's enthusiasm, but finally pragmatism won out. "I prefer *cent'anni*. Health to you for one hundred years," the sailor said as he raised his glass, happy for another toast. "But you can keep your mottos." He tossed some coins on the bar and walked out.

"You risk everything by being so bold," Giovanni said angrily as the door swung shut. "Men have already been arrested—and executed—for this work."

"It's taking too long," Giuseppe said.

"You are impatient, my friend," Caterina said as she replenished their drinks.

"Mazzini has already failed once in Genoa," Giuseppe said. "He can't afford to fail again."

"If our plan fails, we too can be sentenced to death," Giovanni said.

"And you can escape as Mazzini did, to fight another day," Teresina said, collecting their glasses.

"I can't bear the idea of being forced to leave my country," Giuseppe said.

"At least you can fight for your cause," Teresina said. "All we women can do is cook and serve."

"Women are most important to the support of this venture. Hunger makes the world move," Giuseppe said with a smile as he dipped a piece of bread in a dish of olive oil.

"You're saying that to make me feel better," Teresina said, shrugging off the compliment.

"No," Giuseppe assured her, "Emperor Napoleon himself said it to Saint Helena. In the last collection of his letters they published, he wrote, 'Such is the influence of the belly.'"

"Then let us get back to work," Caterina said, urging Teresina back to the kitchen to help prepare the noon meal.

"I wish I could give more," Teresina whispered to Giuseppe before she left, echoing the sentiments Luisa had once spoken to him before he had lost her. The memory of Luisa, and the realization that he could not feel for Teresina the way she felt about him, put Giuseppe in a melancholy place for the rest of the afternoon. The mood served as a harbinger for one of the lowest years of his life.

In early February 1834, the military caught Mazzini's men in their second attempt at beginning an insurrection. Heeding a warning, the authorities arrested the men as they crossed the French border between Savoy and Switzerland. Mazzini had again avoided capture and ordered other forces around the country to attempt their takeovers anyway. When he received his orders, Giuseppe echoed Luisa once more, for she was ever on his mind. "I obey" was his simple reply.

On February 11, Giuseppe appeared at the appointed meeting place for the local forces, Piazza Sarzano near the Port of Genoa, dressed as a peasant so he would not draw attention. Expecting three hundred men, Giuseppe found himself nearly alone. Across the piazza he spotted a lone man reading a newspaper on a bench beside the Chiesa di San Salvatore, which sat at the center of the piazza.

Giuseppe slowly walked over to the man and said innocuously, "*Buona sera.*" The man lowered his paper and responded in kind. Encouraged, Giuseppe asked quietly, "Have you been alone here all evening? Have you seen no one at all?"

The man ignored the comment and instead looked to the lunette above the entrance portal to the church. He said loudly, as if he hoped to be overheard, "I see you too admire this beautiful fresco. Did you know Giuseppe Paganelli created it on the occasion of the consecration of the church in 1773?"

The man, though he appeared quite young, had a husky voice, hoarse and so stilted. He left his newspaper on the bench, approached Giuseppe, and whispered, "All is discovered." He looked meaningfully at the paper he had left behind and hustled off.

Giuseppe picked up the paper and saw his own name printed there for the first time, but it was in a sentence of death. He was twenty-six years old.

Having been identified as a leader of Young Italy, though he had not yet officially joined, a Genoese court had sentenced Garibaldi to death in absentia for high military treason and "tending to induce the royal troops to revolt and overthrow the government of his majesty." The edict read: "The council of war, invoking divine aid, condemns by default Garibaldi to the penalty of ignominious death, and declares him to be exposed to public vengeance as an enemy of the country and the state, subject to all the pains and penalties imposed by the royal laws against bandits of the first catalogue in which the condemned is placed."

Giuseppe didn't know which way to turn. The plan had been to storm the city, board a ship, and overtake it to sail to new ports and instigate more rebellions. The fact that he had signed on to that ship's crew using his own name so that his previous experience would ensure his acceptance meant he could not report for duty now. It would guarantee his own arrest. But by not reporting, he became guilty of being absent without leave—so he was trapped in the city. No matter his choice, Giuseppe understood he was a wanted man and he would have to leave the city—possibly even the country—or risk death. He returned quickly to the Osteria del Colomba, where Caterina and Teresina took him into hiding.

"I don't want to put you in danger," Giuseppe said as they showed him to a small cubbyhole behind one of the wine racks in the back.

"This is our chance to do more than cook," Teresina replied.

"Where is Giovanni?" Giuseppe asked.

"Safe," Caterina said. "Better no one knows more." She didn't want to say "in case you are captured," but it was implied.

Giuseppe stayed in hiding for four days. He heard soldiers question Teresina, but she pretended to be hurt by Giuseppe's disappearance.

"He promised we'd marry in spring," she said with a catch in her voice. "Can you find him for me?"

Caterina went so far as to offer the kind soldiers a free meal, showing no need to hurry them along, but their orders were more pressing than the smell of her focaccia bread.

When they were gone, Teresina came to the cubby with a new set of clothes for Giuseppe.

"You can thank Natalina Pozzo," she said.

"The greengrocer's daughter?" Giuseppe asked.

"Yes," Teresina said. "Her brother left them behind when he was arrested and she wants to help in any way she can. In fact, tonight you will stay in her home."

"I knew this was dangerous for you," he said, ready to leave immediately.

"The soldiers believe any lie a crying woman gives them," Teresina said. "You are safe, but Mamma believes you are safer moving about."

"I must go—I must return to Nice," he said, pulling on the boots Natalina had provided.

"How will you find your way without a guide?" Teresina asked.

"Cassiopeia has guided me across oceans," Giuseppe assured her. "I trust the stars to guide me across mountains as well." Remembering his father's astrolabe and all the lessons he had been taught about navigation, he knew he could find his way home.

That night he stayed with Natalina and consoled her over the fate her brother would surely face once his trial ended. Then he fled across the border toward home, alone once again.

After ten days of hiding by day and hiking by night, Giuseppe reached his family home only to find it under watch. Doubling back, he approached the home of his Aunt Concetta, who mistook him for a beggar by his tattered clothes. Once she recognized him, she brought him inside and fed him as he hadn't eaten more than the almonds he had gathered as he walked on his journey. Then she sent word to her sister that her son was home.

Nicoletta and Domenico embraced their son when they arrived at Concetta's home after they received her coded message. They brought him a new set of clothes and more food.

"Can you still love a son who's earned himself a death sentence?" Giuseppe said, using dark humor to release the tension he felt hanging between them.

"We will love you forever," Nicoletta said wholeheartedly. But a glance at Domenico's face revealed a lower level of appreciation for his son's activities.

"Yes," Domenico said, "but be careful. While I agree with your goals, you must remember this puts the whole family in danger."

Giuseppe could tell they were holding something from him. Finally, Aunt Concetta admitted, "The Tuscan police arrested Felice on his way to work last week."

"He is fine," Nicoletta said quickly, as much to relieve Giuseppe as to convince herself that her youngest son would be safe. "They released him, but warned him to tell them if you approach him for help."

"My brother has nothing to do with my work! None of them do," Giuseppe reassured his parents.

"Do you think they care? They arrested a ship's captain named Giuseppe Giribaldi, with an I, on the eighth," his father said, "and a man using your alias, Giuseppe Borel, yesterday."

"I can't stay here any longer," Giuseppe said. "I can't bring them to your door."

Exhausted, he fell asleep on the straw mat in Aunt Concetta's kitchen. In the morning, he washed his own clothes before leaving, a habit he kept all his life.

"You don't have to do that," Aunt Concetta said.

"The women in my life have done enough for me," Giuseppe said.

Despite his parents' pleas, Giuseppe headed out to Marseilles the next day. Using the new alias of Giuseppe Pane, he hoped to slip past the gendarmerie at the border, but being on high alert, they arrested him. Prepared for this possibility, Giuseppe made a break for the woods and lost the soldiers. He stayed for a night or two under the cover of the dense trees before venturing into town and entering another inn, where he had spotted a female proprietor he hoped might welcome him.

Not only did Camille Dubois welcome him, but she protected him almost better than Caterina and Teresina had. She hired Giuseppe, and soon his ability to tell stories and engage others in conversation became a draw for more customers and more profits. If she ever suspected Giuseppe was a fugitive, she did not let on. Frankly, if anyone asked her then or later, she would have said the inn was better off with him than without him.

Though forced to live in hiding, Giuseppe thrived in Marseilles. There, he formally joined the Young Europe movement, dedicated to liberty, humanity, equality, and progress for the entire continent. But his time in the city could not last.

Word came that on May 28, 1834, Mazzini had been arrested in Solothurn and exiled from Switzerland. He moved to Paris, where he was again imprisoned in July. He was released only after promising he would move to England. Even so, other arrests were in the offing, so Giuseppe began working as a seaman again, signing on to a crew as Giuseppe Pane. His plan was to find a new home where he could recruit men without living in hiding. By traveling to the various cities aboard a ship, he could discover such a place for himself. Giuseppe sent word to his family via Aunt Concetta. Unexpectedly, Nicoletta sneaked into the Marseilles to see him between voyages, knowing that after one such voyage he might never return.

Nicoletta's visit coincided with a citywide epidemic of cholera, the second of this still relatively new disease. Doctors didn't yet know how to treat it or how it was transmitted, so the local authorities ordered quarantines across the city. Vessels flew a yellow quarantine flag if any crew members or passengers showed signs of the disease, such as excessive vomiting followed by deep, unquenchable thirst. No one aboard these vessels would be allowed ashore for over a month, until the disease had run its course—or until those infected had died. Having friends on a ship cleared of disease that was headed back to Nice, Giuseppe smuggled his mother aboard.

"Come home with me," she pleaded as Giuseppe's friends showed them where she could hide.

"I can't," Giuseppe said. "I am too well recognized in Nice."

"Then take another ship, quickly, to a place where this plague cannot follow," she begged.

"I still have friends in the city and they need my help," he said. "Blame my mother for teaching me that strength comes when everyone works together for the good of . . . everyone." He kissed her on the cheek and left the boat. Standing on the pier, he watched the boat disappear over the horizon, wondering if he would live to see his mother again.

In the city, yet another friend set up an ambulance service, ferrying those who were sick to hospitals and those who had died to cemeteries. Giuseppe quickly signed up as a driver by day. By night he guarded patients, a necessary task as some citizens—those who succumbed to fear over faith—sometimes stormed the homes of those inflicted, planning to kill them to eradicate the disease.

No known cure for cholera existed besides rubbing camphor oil on the body, so Giuseppe dutifully followed local custom, for all the good it seemed to do. Some revived, others died, with little belief that any cure actually helped.

His public participation in the epidemic raised his profile among local authorities, and soon questions arose about his background. When the outbreak dissipated, Giuseppe Pane joined the *Nautonnier*, headed to Rio de Janiero, Brazil, where his friend Giovanni had already emigrated.

Giuseppe left Marseilles on September 8, 1835, arriving in a yet another new country in time for Christmas. But by then, Giovanni had moved to Montevideo, Uruguay, nearly 1,500 miles south, to found a free weekly newspaper for local Italians.

Giuseppe was once again alone. His dream of uniting his birth country began to seem impossible. How could he instigate change? How could he rouse his countrymen from so far away?

Chapter 4

1835 – 1837
SURVIVING THE FARRAPOS (RAGAMUFFIN) WAR

Giuseppe soon realized Brazil had much in common with the separated kingdoms of Italy. Once dominated by over two thousand indigenous tribes, Brazil had undergone great governmental and societal change since explorer Pedro Álvares Cabral landed in 1500 and claimed the area for the Portuguese Empire. Colonization decimated many of those tribes while others assimilated into Spanish culture, which contributed to steady Spanish rule for three hundred years.

In 1807, the year of Giuseppe's birth, Napoleon's forces had invaded Portugal. The prince regent, John VI, who governed the country on behalf of his unstable mother, Maria I, ordered the transfer of the Portuguese royal court to Brazil before he could be deposed. In November of that year, the royal family and its court of nearly fifteen thousand people traveled from the Spanish capital of Lisbon to the Brazilian town of Rio de Janeiro, which Prince John then claimed as the new capital of the empire. By turning the colonial capital into a seat of government, he opened the ports to foreign shipping and otherwise conducted the country's business as if he were still in Spain. The other powerful European countries disapproved of moving a capital to a colony, so Prince John returned to Lisbon in 1821 and left his son, Prince Pedro, as regent of what he renamed the Kingdom of Brazil.

By the time Giuseppe arrived in Rio Grande do Sul in 1835, the provinces' dissatisfaction with the central power had given rise to several small, localized rebellions. This history Giuseppe had to learn in order to understand his new neighbors and to choose a side to defend. All served to remind him of how much he wanted to affect change in his own homeland. But for now, he had to conduct such business from afar.

To fend off the loneliness of being a stranger in a strange land—and to stay connected to the movement for an independent Italy and keep his eye ever on the long-term goal— Giuseppe turned to writing. He sent a constant stream of letters to the Young Italy members now scattered around the globe. On October 17, 1836, he wrote a coded letter to Giovanni Battista Cuneo in Montevideo:

> *Brother, this is merely to tell you of our arrival here on the 15th, and that the daughter of our caulker is lovely, beautiful—of the kind of beauty which your ardent fancy paints; and that I am over head and ears in love with her. Assuredly, if I were not so out of practice, I should rub up our tools, grown rusty by disuse; but, alas! We shall go on doing nothing, as usual.*

> *Money, money is what we want; and with that in Italy we*

should also find beauties. The thought that we get poorer and poorer every day is not a lively one, is it, my brother? Patience.

Giuseppe had decided that the most feasible plan of fomenting Italian independence would be to secure a vessel, land in some part of Italy, and raise the flag of insurrection. The "daughter" of the letter served as a code word for such a boat. Luckily, in South America, Giuseppe found thousands of Italians displaced, as he was, by the revolutions of the last two decades. They were ripe for a leader to help their homeland earn its independence, and many men vied for that title alongside Giuseppe. His friend Giovanni worked on the cause from Uruguay while an already established émigré, Giuseppe Stefano Grondona, seemed to have a grip on Rio de Janeiro, and he did not appreciate any challenge to his power.

Grondona had gained a reputation by being expelled in 1823 by Pedro I for his revolutionary ideas. Exiled to Montevideo, Uruguay, Grondona returned to Rio de Janeiro in 1834 when Mazzini asked him to found the Italian Philanthropic Society, which would funnel needed monies to the Young Italy movement. When Giuseppe arrived in the city, Mazzini asked him to organize the election of the group's president, which Grondona won handily. Still, the two men did not get along.

"The job of a president is to unify, not divide," Giuseppe protested over coffee with two of his main supporters, both refugees: Giacomo Picasso, a barber, and Luigi Rossetti, a sailor originally from Genoa.

"Give him time," the more patient Luigi suggested. Luigi had been instrumental in locating the boat Giuseppe mentioned in his letters and understood the need for funds before they lost the opportunity to own it. "Raising funds takes time."

"I can only shave so many beards," Giacomo laughed as he rubbed his own. "It will take time to collect enough for the kind of boat we need, but when we do, Mazzini—"

"Pippo," Giuseppe corrected, giving Mazzini's code name so that others in the bar would not catch on to the true meaning of their conversation.

"Pippo," Giacomo restated. "Pippo will side with us. In the meantime, he likes Grondona. He trusts him. I don't know why. If he heard the way the man disparages everyone, even those who voted for him, Pippo would not be so trusting."

"How can we convince him our plan is more likely to succeed?" Giuseppe asked, cutting to the quick.

"We have to convince those around us to follow us instead," Giacomo insisted.

"It won't be easy," Giuseppe said. "Grondona has the most gossamer character that could exist in this world."

"People love him because he is providing what they want now. Here, in their new lives in South America," Luigi said.

"Precisely the problem," Giuseppe said, before dropping into a whisper. "We are here to recruit men to return to Italy to fight for its freedom. Not to be pampered while living here."

"There are problems here," Giacomo said. "Are these Brazilians not also my brothers?" He raised his glass in the tradition the three had begun of toasting to their brotherhood.

"Brothers for life!" the three young men promised in unison as they clinked glasses.

"Some other refugees have married and had children," Luigi said. "Their children are Brazilian. They will likely stay."

"Someone here needs to fight for them too," Giuseppe realized. "Freedom for some can only help spread the idea of freedom for all."

How this philosophy would play out, Giuseppe wondered as he wrote of these issues to Giovanni in Montevideo. They added to more melancholy. Something was missing in Giuseppe's life beyond a united home country. He missed his family. He missed his hometown. He missed Luisa.

Recruiting refugees away from Grondona proved harder than they hoped. In the face of lack of funds and of explicit instructions from leaders overseas, the friends had to make a living. Luigi bought an older ship much in need of repair. With Giuseppe as the captain, he and Luigi repaired it and took up trading and passenger travel between nearby ports. It allowed them to support themselves, but only at first. They named the ship *Mazzini* as a talisman, but even then, Giuseppe wrote dejectedly to Giovanni at the start of this new venture that it felt like taking a step backward. "My voyages are more remunerative than in the beginning; still, I am bent on you know what. Write to me when there is anything going on; trading muddles my brain," he wrote.

Slowly, their trading route allowed Giuseppe and Luigi to spread the word of their plan to return to Italy as revolutionaries. Away from Grondona's influence, they began amassing lists of men ready to return with them. The obstacle this time came from a need to offer leadership and loyalty to revolutionaries in this new country.

As they could not yet return to Italy, the two became embroiled in the cause of creating the Republic of Rio Grande do Sul, a region of Brazil that wanted to separate from Brazil in 1835. Named the Ragamuffin War for the fringed leather worn by the gaucho farmers who began it, winning this war became a cause close to Giuseppe's heart.

Because Uruguay had recently won its own independence from Brazil, in 1827, many Uruguayans joined this new cause in the hope of uniting with Rio Grande do Sul to form a yet more powerful state. Luigi too had invested in a printer in order to publish pro-rebel pamphlets and Giacomo continued raising funds. Giovanni had mastered the art of using the press to rally support for the cause. Giuseppe knew his talents focused on naval activities and leadership—what could his contribution be, he wondered.

Then a new voice arose, that of another Italian refugee, Count Livio Zambeccari. He had been taken prisoner at an early battle on the small island of Fanfa, fighting on the side of the new president of the rebels, Bento Goncalves. Giuseppe visited the count in prison to offer his support and his service.

"I am here because South America has become my second home," Livio explained. "I love Italy the way one loves his mother as she has been granted to him as a gift, but I love South America the way one loves the wife he has chosen." He looked at Giuseppe, sitting across the wooden table in the prison courtyard. "Why would *you* go to war to win liberty for a people you do not yet know?"

Giuseppe grew thoughtful. "My mother, both in flesh and in country, taught me to strive to be of value in this world. To help those who need my help. If my home country does not listen to my cries, if they are not yet ready for freedom, then I cannot continue to scatter my seeds on rocky ground. I must wait for those that landed on good soil to bear fruit."

"I sense the sadness in your soul," the count responded. "I also realize that love for your home will draw you from us—someday. But today is not that day. Until then, if you choose to be of service, who am I to deny you?"

The men created a plan for Count Livio, in the name of president Goncalves, to authorize Giuseppe to take the *Mazzini* and a crew of fourteen men and engage in battle with any ships of the Brazilian Imperial Navy they encountered along the continent's eastern coastline. Giuseppe agreed and rose to leave, but the prisoner had one more thing to say.

"While I admire your love for country, do not let it blind you to the need for other forms of love in this short life we lead. To be a soldier is honorable. To be a husband, to be a father— that is to be human. The land will not remember you, but the ones you love will."

"Having been raised in a family full of love, I hear you," Giuseppe said. "But how could I take such risks if I owed my industry to a family, to a wife? No, I'm destined to do this work. But I'm destined to do it alone."

With Giuseppe's help, the nascent navy began gathering both ships and men, whom he enticed by promising, "With me, you will challenge an empire and be the first to raise a flag of emancipation off these shores!" As captain of the *Mazzini*, Giuseppe succeeded in capturing a few other vessels, including one he renamed *Luisa*.

During one journey along the coast, Giuseppe found himself once again in the eye of a storm. Refusing to lose the *Luisa*, he recalled the wild ride he and Pietro had taken back in their boarding school days. Once again, as if in a dream, rising waves rocked the boat. Giuseppe gripped the wheel tightly and shouted to his crew, "Strike the mainsail completely!"

Like Pietro, they balked at such a wild suggestion. He ordered again, "Strike the mainsail!"

Giuseppe abandoned the wheel and began using the rudder to steer. One of his Italian recruits broke ranks and struck the mainsail. Giuseppe fought to hold the rudder steady and, just as in his youth, brought them all to land safely, earning a trust and loyalty required to build the army he would need to return to Italy. For now, though, he reconfirmed his dedication to this current battle. It was only just beginning.

The next voyage did not go as well. This time, they encountered two Uruguayan gunboats, which refused to recognize the flag of Rio Grande do Sul and instead claimed the *Luisa* to be harboring pirates. The gunboats fired incessantly on the *Luisa*, whose guns were nowhere near as powerful nor her gunners yet as trained. Wounded men began falling all around Giuseppe. As he bent to staunch the blood flow from the leg of a nearby crewman, a bullet struck Giuseppe in his neck and lodged between his ear and his throat. Valiantly, his men fought on while Pasquale Lodola, his copilot, dragged Giuseppe's body away from the barrage of bullets.

When Giuseppe finally regained consciousness, he saw the gunboats were retreating thanks to the continued attack of his crew. Pasquale immediately turned his attention to docking the *Luisa* at the nearest port, in Gualeguay, Argentina, so a local surgeon could tend to the wounded, including extracting the bullet from Giuseppe's neck.

Dr. Ramon de l'Arca, a native of Sicily, had been living in Argentina for over a decade. He hadn't been sure which side to take in the revolution of Rio Grande do Sul. "Until I met you," he said once Giuseppe had healed enough to speak.

"Why me?" Giuseppe asked.

"I saw the way the men love you," de l'Arca said. "They will follow you and fight for you anywhere. Which means Rio

Grande has a chance—but more important to me, it means Sicily has a chance to once again be part of the greatest empire of the world."

"We share the same dream," Giuseppe said.

"Yet only one of us has the power to make it come true," de l'Arca said. "You must heal quickly and leave this place." The urgency in the doctor's voice caused Giuseppe to look more closely at his surroundings. The doctor had covered all the windows.

"The locals celebrated our arrival," Giuseppe said. It was one of the few things he remembered from his semi-conscious state as his men carried him from the *Luisa*. The townspeople who had gathered to watch the gunboats fight began cheering as his men entered the port.

"That sentiment is not shared by the authorities," de l'Arca said.

"Is my crew safe?" Giuseppe asked, rising from his mat.

"Yesterday, the army arrested those of your crew who survived the battle," the doctor reluctantly said. "This morning, they seized your ship. Soldiers surround my house, ready to take you to prison when I tell them it is safe for you to travel."

Giuseppe was a wanted man again.

From that moment on, everything became a blur of pain. With the help of a local who promised he could guide him out of the city, Giuseppe, not yet well enough to travel, left the house in the middle of the night. He and the guide rode flat out for many miles before stopping to rest the horses, and themselves. As soon as they dismounted, a squad of Argentinian soldiers surrounded them.

"You never intended me to survive," Giuseppe said.

"Rebels don't deserve to survive," said the guide as he remounted his horse and rode off, leaving Giuseppe to be arrested, tied to a horse, and driven back to Gualeguay. There, Giuseppe came face-to-face with Mayor Leonardo Millan, who called for him to be tortured in punishment for siding with rebels. For several hours, Giuseppe hung by his wrists from the high beam of a doorway in the public square, his feet dangling just inches above the ground.

Thankfully, Giuseppe had more supporters in the crowd of onlookers than Mayor Millan calculated. First, some women brought Giuseppe water as he sweated in the sun. Then their men, many who believed in the rebels' cause, began calling for an end to this punishment. Fearful of a riot, Millan behaved as Pontius Pilate once had—by having Giuseppe cut down and transferred to a neighboring city for further punishment. Unbeknownst to Millan, he had chosen to send Giuseppe to a fellow mayor who did not share his distaste of the rebels. Giuseppe was pardoned and allowed to return to Rio Grande do Sul, where he arrived to a hero's welcome.

Giuseppe could not enjoy the celebrations, however, because he knew how much work there still was to do. The nascent republic named him the commander of its navy, which now comprised four vessels. Many Italian friends from the past gathered to help in this new venture, including Eduardo Mutru, whom he had known as a young boy in Nice, and Luigi Carniglia, a friend from his short stint at boarding school. Both men joined him on his new vessel, *Rio Pardo*, along with twenty-eight other men, some Italian, some Brazilian.

Before granting them time to prepare their ships, armed

imperial vessels blocked the harbor. Giuseppe came up with a plan to transport the vessels over land some fifty miles to the Tramandaí River. He ordered the building of two specialized carts, which, when pulled by two hundred oxen, made the journey a success. The four ships sailed into the sea a few miles above the blockade and headed north to spread the revolution to Santa Catarina, which adjoined Rio Grande do Sul.

Sometimes it seemed as if even the weather had taken sides with the imperial army. On this voyage another storm arose, but it proved far stronger than the last, whipping the waves into a violent, raging wall of water. Wave after wave rolled over the deck, each time sweeping more and more men overboard. Some were climbing the masts and clinging to them in the hopes of staying alive. From the wheel, Giuseppe scanned the coast, desperate for a cove to slide into and wait out the storm. Suddenly, one of the larger waves rose above him, dashed to the deck, and swept him away, along with the men who had been at his side for so long—Eduardo and Luigi—and the boat heeled over to starboard.

Tossed into the tide, the men grabbed for any piece of flotsam within their reach to keep themselves afloat. To his left, Giuseppe saw Eduardo clutching for one of the stays from a broken mast. The rope kept flicking just out of his reach. A dislodged oar came within Giuseppe's reach and he tossed it to Eduardo, who took it and made for the shore. To Giuseppe's right, he found Luigi sinking with the weight of his waterlogged coat. Giuseppe swam closer and tried to help his friend out of the coat as another wave came up and submerged them both, forcing Giuseppe to lose his hold. When he rose again from the depths, he saw neither Eduardo nor Luigi. He had no choice but to swim to shore before he lost the last of his strength.

Giuseppe arrived to find that of the thirty men on board, sixteen were unaccounted for, including all the Italians. He sat and scanned the tide, hoping to see some sign of life, some swimmer he could reach on time, as he had with Giuseppina all those years ago, but none appeared. Instead, thunder and lightning continued through the night. Exhaustion overtook him.

In the morning, in the wake of their tragedy, Giuseppe rallied the men. They had to walk toward town to connect with the Rio Grandean army. There was no time for recovery, as the imperial navy had begun bombarding the city. The army commander reassigned them to another vessel with a mission of attacking the much larger imperial navy. Giuseppe knew his men were too spent to engage in a battle, so he lured two enemy vessels into a series of canals to the south of the city, where he knew rebel soldiers waited in hiding. Giuseppe's strategic ambush helped capture the two ships without forcing his weary men to engage in a long, drawn-out battle.

Once again, Giuseppe could not enjoy the next day's celebrations, because he knew how much had been lost. When he docked in the port of Laguna, Giuseppe stayed on board. At thirty-two, he felt old enough to be a father to all the men who had survived. He knew they needed a rest, so he gave them shore leave. He didn't believe he could or would ever rest again.

Alone on deck, Giuseppe looked out over the hillsides of Santa Catarina, another land he had never known and for which he was willing to risk his life. As he paced, he found himself recalling the words of Count Livio: "The land will not remember you, but the ones you love will." Giuseppe felt his chance for such a life had been lost, but he hoped the young men who followed him could have what he did not. Perhaps, as was true of soldiers going back to the days of ancient Rome, the young men would meet young women in the towns they captured and carry them home to Rome.

It was a nice dream for the others. For himself, Giuseppe believed this Ragamuffin War had become the unplanned testing ground he needed to see if he had the talents and the drive to pursue that all-encompassing dream of uniting Italy. He felt the experience had taught him the qualities to command men. He felt that if he committed himself to use those skills to help oppressed people wherever he found them, that would be enough to consume his life.

As he swept the hillside with his telescope, ever watchful for unexpected attacks, his eyes fell upon a young woman riding horseback along the ridge, a long braid of dark hair trailing in the wind behind her.

"*Colpo di fulmine*," Giuseppe muttered. The thunderbolt struck. One look at her and suddenly Giuseppe knew he would never be alone again.

Chapter 5

MEETING ANITA AND FALLING IN LOVE

On the hillside, the same loneliness had filled Aninha Ribeiro da Silva for most of her young life. She had ridden to the bluff that morning to see for herself the ships of this glorious rebel navy, come to create a new nation. Freedom fascinated her. Having watched two older sisters married off to men they didn't choose but forced themselves to like, Aninha had begged her father not to let that be her fate. Sensing her strength and sorry for the sadness of his other daughters, he promised she would be able to choose her own husband. But when he died from a fall four years ago, that promise died with him. Her mother, desperate to avoid poverty, agreed to the proposal of a much older, but financially secure, man in town.

At the age of fourteen, Aninha wed the local cobbler, Manuel Duarte de Aguiar, a belligerent, violent womanizer. After four years of marriage, Aguiar had joined the imperial army and demanded Aninha travel with him, washing his uniforms and making his meals as other camp wives did. She declined, pleading that her mother would be destitute without her.

Spending the last few months on her own had been rejuvenating. She worked for a local couple, Henrique and Miguela, who owned a shop in town. They spent most of their days at the shop, leaving Aninha alone to clean and cook, which began to feel like the only freedom she would ever know. No one wishes for war, but Aninha confessed to her local priest that sometimes she wished this one would last longer.

After staring out at the ships for a while and wondering what it was like to move about in the world as you please, she headed back to begin the evening meal.

Meanwhile, Giuseppe had unlatched the dinghy and headed ashore to find this sudden focus of his future. Upon landing, he climbed the hillside to the outskirts of Laguna, finding only a few houses in the immediate vicinity. Short, one-story affairs, most homes glowed with the warm orange of old adobe brick. Lavender-colored bougainvillea crawled up their sides and over each terra-cotta roof.

Giuseppe approached the first local he found, who happened to be Henrique, sweeping the stoop outside his shop door. Thrilled to meet one of the victorious rebels, Henrique invited Giuseppe into his home for coffee. There, as if in a dream, he found the woman he had seen on the hillside preparing the afternoon coffee.

Henrique saw Giuseppe's shocked face. "Signor Garibaldi, this is my cook, Aninha," he said, politely introducing them. Neither spoke, not even the banal niceties one expects when meeting a stranger, because neither Giuseppe nor Aninha felt like strangers in that moment.

"Aninha, we owe this gentleman thanks," Henrique said, trying to break the awkwardness that filled the room. "He is part of the glorious brigade that . . ." He trailed off when he realized neither of the two were looking at him at all. Their eyes had locked to each other's with an intensity Henrique recognized—that's how he had looked at Miguela the first time he saw her. Immediately, elation and anguish mixed in his mind as he knew something the commander did not.

Giuseppe broke the silence first. Because he had only begun learning Portuguese, as it confused his Spanish and Italian quite a bit, he spoke from the heart in Italian. "*Devi essere mio*," he said.

Neither Aninha nor Henrique spoke Italian, so they were not sure what Giuseppe had said. Henrique looked back at him blankly but Aninha smiled. Instinctively, she understood his emotion and responded in the saddest tone, "And you ought to be mine."

Henrique discreetly left the two together. He knew they had much to say and feared he would only destroy such a beautiful moment of human connection by telling Giuseppe that Aninha was already married. That would be for her to say.

Still in the dark about such reality, Giuseppe began talking. "For too long," he said, "I have felt alone in the world. Of all the friends who have fought by my side, many are gone . . ."

"So too for me," Aninha said, recalling with love the faces of her father and younger brothers.

Giuseppe took her hands in his. "I need a heart to love me—to share this itinerant life."

"As do I," Aninha said. "I need someone who loves me and seeks to be my partner, not my owner." She looked into Giuseppe's eyes and saw all her own love and loneliness reflecting back. She could never lie to him. "But fate is a cruel mistress and . . . And I am already taken in marriage."

The echo of his mother's lessons in Dante filled his head. "Our fate cannot be taken from us; it is a gift," he said. But at that moment, he was no longer sure such gifts were meant for him. He left the home, devastated.

Yet for each of the following days as Giuseppe's crew took shore leave, he too came to town, partially to meet with Laguna's military and civilian leaders to plan their next maneuvers, and partially to see Aninha. He held long talks with Henrique and Miguela about her husband's behavior and his abandonment of her.

"Such a gentle woman should not be bound to such a man," Henrique said. "Believe me, I have seen how he treats such a treasure."

"I can't hear these things," Giuseppe said. "I would run off with her in a moment, but it will destroy her reputation forever."

Giuseppe and Aninha debated these issues together as they slowly began walking or riding along the hillside trails over the next few weeks, learning more about the other and pondering the obstacle of her marriage. Divorce was impossible. Annulment seemed impossible. Uniting Italy seemed impossible. Was every goal he set for himself to be, in the end, impossible? Here she was, the perfect soulmate, and a cruel twist of timing kept them from each other despite all they had in common.

"I am no less devoted than you are to the people's right to freedom," she swore on one of their walks. "I dream of fighting by your side."

"I believe you," Giuseppe said. "But I love you too much to hurt you more than I have already. I hope you love me enough to help me say goodbye."

Giuseppe could evoke the words but not the action. He kissed Aninha goodbye. She kissed back. And he returned day after day.

Before they could act on any decisions about their own future—if they were allowed to have one—several of Giuseppe's men came down with pneumonia and had to be taken to the local hospital, where Aninha volunteered with the other women of the town. One afternoon, as she fed a soldier who had lost an arm in the last battle, she attempted to soothe him with a story about the town. "We have magic here," she said, trying to draw the young man out. "Have you heard of the wonder of the way our dolphins and our fishermen work together?"

The young man looked at Aninha with sadness, but also curiosity, so she continued. "Every spring, a family of dolphins drive the fish toward our beach, where the fishermen stand along the shallow waters in wait. Then one dolphin rolls over and the fishermen know it is time to throw out their nets. The fishermen catch what they need and the dolphins feed on the fish who wiggle from the nets. A successful union, no?"

With her vivacity and gentle smile, Aninha finally succeeded in getting the soldier to speak. "How is that possible?" he asked.

"I do not know when it started or how it works," she

admitted while bringing spoonfuls of hearty shrimp soup to his lips. "To me, it serves as a sign that we are all one on this earth. When you are well, I will take you to see—"

Aninha cut herself off as she saw her patient smile broadly. He no longer looked into her eyes but over her shoulder. She turned her head, careful not to spill his soup, to see Giuseppe standing behind her. He had been silently taking in her story, as he did his mother's stories long ago. Of course he had fallen in love with a storyteller.

Aninha looked back at the young soldier, who was saluting his commander. When the other men on the ward realized their commander had arrived, they all began saluting. Some even attempted to stand despite their weakened conditions. Aninha couldn't help but be impressed.

"No need to pay attention to me, sailors," Giuseppe said. "Save all your attention for this angel who has come to soothe your souls, something we all need more than the repair of our wounds."

When duty called him to report back on board and prepare his men for the next voyage, Giuseppe waited for Aninha to finish her ministrations so he could walk her home. He said he had to stop seeing her.

"Why?" Aninha asked.

"I love you too much to hurt you."

"We have different definitions of hurt," Aninha said. "Manuel hurt my body and I survived. I'm not sure I could survive the wound to my soul if I lost you."

"Then I will have to be strong for the both of us," Giuseppe said, kissing her hand for what he thought would be one last time. As he rode back to his ship, Aninha watched him go with her mind in another place.

Aboard the newly christened *Rio Pardo*, Giuseppe tried to forget her by focusing on the charts of the lagoon in preparation for the fight he knew was coming. Scouts heard the imperial army intended to blockade the port and retake the town. Giuseppe took command of three gunboats assigned to defend the harbor. But as he studied the charts, he found himself wishing Aninha were at his side instead of the two captains of the other gunboats. He had assigned the *Seival* to John Griggs, a North American of Irish origin, who had joined the Rio Grandeans for love of liberty, and the *Casapava* to Lorenzo, another Italian learning the art of war with dreams of uniting Italy.

By nightfall, the men had a plan. But so did Aninha.

At midnight, the sailor manning the crow's nest called, "Skiff off starboard bow!"

The cabin boy knocked on Giuseppe's cabin door, which opened immediately, as he had not fallen asleep. Together, they headed to the bow. Two gunmen at the starboard took aim and awaited Giuseppe's signal to fire, but instead he halted them. "Only on my word," he said.

Then he shouted to the skiff, "This is the *Rio Pardo*, a member of the commissioned navy of Rio Grande do Sul. State your business."

"Freedom," Aninha called as she rowed closer. "I intend to join this rebellion to fight with you for my people."

"Stand down," a shocked Giuseppe ordered the gunmen. "And drop the hook ladder." He knew he ought to be angry, but he could not stop the joy that flooded his heart at the sight of her.

In minutes, Aninha had reached the ladder and climbed

aboard, carrying a small satchel of clothing that Giuseppe took from her as she swung onto deck as if she belonged there.

The crew milled around, unsure how to behave with this unexpected guest. A few may have known Aninha's full story, but most did not. Ever vigilant for her reputation, Giuseppe introduced her to them as his wife, Anita.

"Anita?" she repeated, questioning in her eyes.

"Aninha belongs to the past," he whispered as he hugged her. "Anita belongs to our future." Neither knew the name meant many things in many cultures, but for Catholics, Anita derived from the Hannah of the Bible, and had come to mean grace and kindness in a leader.

"Our future," Anita said, and she never looked back. It was October 23, 1839.

In a few days it was as if she had always lived at sea, which was a blessing because the battle was only just beginning. To beat the greater odds of the larger navy, Giuseppe designed risky strategies. He assigned a smaller vessel in his fleet to sail out of the port toward Rio Grande do Sul with weapons in view. Imperial blockaders followed, allowing a clear passage for Giuseppe's fleet to exit the harbor and be safe on the open sea.

In her few days on board, Anita learned all she could about the working procedures on a gunboat, from tying knots to raising the rebel flag to firing weapons. She had an affinity for it all, as if she too had been born into a seafaring family.

"No, my father was a farmer. A gaucho," she said to the sailor who complimented her affinity. Then she added with a knowing smile, "But my children will be born of the sea." She returned to her practice with tying knots as the sailor moved to the galley to check on the evening meal.

At night, she and Giuseppe talked of all the things that people in love find fascinating about each other. They tried to tell their whole life stories in the short time they shared alone each night.

"Are you happy you came to Brazil?" she asked one night as he pulled off his boots.

"Yes," he said slowly. "Yes, because it brought me you. And yes, because this is the land that has taught me I have what it takes to command men . . . And yes, because here I have decided that if my own land rebukes me, I commit myself to use those skills to help those who are oppressed wherever I find them."

"But you still intend to return to Italy one day?" she asked.

"Yes," he said. "But now I know I will not return alone."

Giuseppe and Anita cherished those quiet moments, but they were not to be quiet for long. Their small cluster of boats had reached a rebel-held harbor in Santos, São Paulo, where they girded themselves for the battle to come. Barely one night into their stay, an Imperial corvette appeared. The smallest class of warship, corvettes served on coastal patrol and were a particularly fast attack craft. This one immediately gave chase for two full days, forcing Giuseppe's small navy back down the coast toward Laguna.

Through quick maneuvers, Giuseppe lost the corvette as they approached the island of Abrigo and quickly turned the tide by capturing two Brazilian sloops, which they planned to offer to the rebel army still stationed in Laguna. The *Casapava* had stayed behind to keep watch for enemy ships; the *Seival* had sprung a leak, so it followed the *Rio Pardo* slowly.

Still, as victors, they headed back only to be met by a Brazilian brig-schooner off the coast of the city of Imbituba. The crewman in the crow's nest shouted the news and all looked to Giuseppe to respond. He looked across the deck at Anita, whose eyes beamed both faith and belief in him, giving birth to a wild idea. "Attack!" Giuseppe shouted.

"One solid boat, one damaged boat, and a few captured schooners against their navy?" his boatswain questioned.

"Only we know the *Seival* is damaged," Giuseppe said. He ordered the cannon on the *Seival* to be dismounted and placed on a promontory on the eastern side of the bay during the night as the *Rio Pardo* anchored at the bottom of the bay. In the morning, all hands aboard manned guns, including Anita, who began the attack by firing the first volley against the nearest enemy ship. Seeing her fierce pride in their cause, the other men joined in with even more energy and resolve.

As they blasted their way out of the bottleneck with the guns on board, the cannon on land followed. Confused, the enemy changed the focus of some of their fire toward whatever ghost boats must be backing up Giuseppe's *Rio Pardo*. Anita kept up a constant stream of encouragement to the men. They fought while also ministering triage to those wounded by return fire, even to the point of dragging their bodies out of the line of further fire while she bandaged them.

Knowing it wouldn't be long before the enemy realized the trick Giuseppe played to increase the size of his squadron, he needed to contact reinforcements on land, under the command of Colonel David Canabarro.

Not able to lose one ounce of manpower and in under-standing that a messenger might use this assignment to run away, Giuseppe turned to the only person on board he could trust implicitly.

"Of course, I will go to Colonel Canabarro," Anita said, resting her hand on his forearm.

"But you must promise to take this message and then stay on land until this is over," Giuseppe demanded.

Saying nothing, Anita plucked the paper from his hands. She quickly headed toward a skiff. Giuseppe kissed her as she descended the ladder into the skiff, which she would pilot alone in order not to waste any manpower.

"Promise you will stay safe!" he called.

She pretended the waves blocked his words and simply waved back with a smile. Such a promise was impossible to make in the midst of war. Giuseppe watched until her skiff disap-peared in the mist closer to shore. He hoped she would be safe and simultaneously marveled that he had been blessed enough to find such a woman to share his life.

A few hours later, against Giuseppe's wishes, Anita returned to the ship, but with disheartening news. At forty-four, a full decade older than Giuseppe, Canabarro served as his superior, but did not seem able to place the same trust in his men as Giuseppe. Canabarro found the losses too high and the enemy too numerous to continue the fight. His letter refused more troops for Giuseppe, believing the fight to be hopeless.

"The fool!" Giuseppe decried when he read the response. "Without reinforcements, it will be hopeless! How can I tell these men—*my* men—that they die for nothing?"

"It is never for nothing," Anita said. "Each battle, win or

lose, contributes to the whole. Each man plays his part. They know that. And if they don't, we'll prove it to them by how we honor those who go before us."

"Then we must withdraw now," Giuseppe said. "Salvage all the ammunition and men we can."

In minutes, Anita began ordering the unloading of the ammunition into skiffs, each one piloted by a wounded man who himself needed salvaging back on land. On Giuseppe's order, the same took place on the other boats in their small flotilla. Anita oversaw the gentle wrapping in old sails of those who had died so they could be given proper rites of burial at sea once the *Rio Pardo* could break free of the bay.

"Now what, captain?" she asked when she could turn her attention to the next task. Darkness was falling, further aiding their mission.

"Now you will take a skiff to land," he began, "where I will meet you when—"

"No," Anita interrupted. "I am my beloved. I go where he goes."

"I'm to do the last duty a captain ever wants to take on," he said, dissuading her.

Without knowing—or needing to know—the nature of the duty, Anita insisted, "We will do it together." So they untied the last of the skiffs and sailed across to the *Seival* to come face-to-face with the sacrifice of war.

On the deck of the *Seival*, they found Captain Griggs cut in two by enemy fire, yet his face retained its natural ruddy complexion so that he seemed as if still alive. Together, Giuseppe and Anita wrapped his body and allowed him the ultimate honor of burial at sea. As he slipped underwater, she sang a hymn she'd known since childhood, and Giuseppe carved his name and the date—November 15, 1839—onto a plank. Then he yanked it off to carry away before he and Anita set fire to the ship so the enemy could not put it to use against them.

On shore, they tended to their wounded by the flickering light of the burning *Seival*. They thanked the heavens for a fog that kept the enemy ships from completely understanding the severity of their situation. Anita performed triage alongside local women who came to their aid. Some men were beyond help, wanting only someone to hear their last words to carry back to their families. Others required such rudimentary stitching up as could be done by the tools at hand, with no hope of avoiding the infection that would likely set in later. Still others had escaped with barely a scratch. "Such is the fate of war," Giuseppe said to Anita as they worked.

The fog kept up all the next day as they buried those who died despite Anita's ministrations. She stood beside Giuseppe as he nailed the board bearing John Griggs's name on it to a tree overlooking the other graves. "*Dopo una salita c'è sempre una discesa*," she said in condolence.

"After a great climb, there is a great descent? I feel all my life I have been likewise climbing and descending, climbing and descending . . ." he said. Then he tried to change the subject, "You sound like my mother with all her proverbs."

"It is an honor to be compared to her," Anita said. "I hope we meet someday."

"You will," Giuseppe said. He knew their only chance to avoid capture when the Imperial ships landed would be to march double time until they caught up with the rear guard, commanded by General Teixeira, on the way to Santa Vitória.

"I need you to know that, among the many sufferings of my stormy life, I have not been without happy moments. I count this chance to march, with my wife at my side, as one of them."

"I am my beloved. I go where he goes," Anita said.

At dusk, she and all the men began the march. Anita and Giuseppe refused any benefit the other men did not have, so they all walked or rode the available horses in turn and shared their rations, or lack of them, as they went. Those who could still walk propped up companions who couldn't do it alone and for whom there weren't enough horses. The next few weeks would take them down beaches and up hillsides, hoping to return to Rio Grande do Sul, where they could recruit and regroup.

As word spread of their battle moving to land, some of the other soldiers' wives and families came to travel with their men. Women and children cooked so the soldiers could be free to train. But none of the other women were allowed to take part in the planning and strategizing with the men. Only Anita.

Chapter 6

FATHERHOOD AND WAR IN FOREIGN LANDS

"Do you knit as you sleep as well?" Giuseppe teased Anita for her swift progress. She knitted as she alternated between walking and riding horseback.

For herself she had fashioned a red wool cape over a white peasant blouse that billowed around her neck. After finishing the last stitch on the poncho she had designed for him, she handed it proudly to Giuseppe. He draped it over his head and across his shoulders. The varying colors of the stripes across the chest gave the piece a distinguished look that made Anita smile.

"You look like my father," Anita said. Remembering her father's advice, she added, "They say young couples should look to their partner's parents to see the pattern of who they will be with someday."

"But not all my men will have wives as talented as you," he said as he kissed her. "And you are far too busy to knit them all such luxury, yet soldiers need uniforms to bind them."

"Not to mention to help them avoid shooting their own

men in the midst of battle," Anita agreed. "We will find something that suits them all."

"Though we are a poor band with little finances?" Giuseppe asked.

"God will provide," Anita said.

By mid-December 1839, the troops met up with Teixeira's division at Santa Vitória, on the border between Rio Grande and Santa Catarina. Giuseppe and Teixeira were tasked with devising a new strategy because, instead of pursuing Giuseppe's men, the enemy had awaited the arrival of two fresh divisions of troops and moved to attack the more mountainous regions of Rio Grande do Sul. That left the men no choice but to support the area's rebel population with Giuseppe commanding the infantry and Teixeira the cavalry. The larger choice they faced was one the South American rebels had been grappling with since the start of this war. Giuseppe used this moment to nudge them forward.

"We cannot accept slaves into our ranks," Teixeira insisted. Since the beginning of the war, enslaved Afro-Brazilians had run from Brazil and its slaveocracy, hoping to fight for Rio Grande do Sul, then join the new republic and create a home that disavowed slavery. Though rebelling against Brazil, many Rio Grandean leaders still believed in the sanctity of private property, so they neither condoned recruiting runaways nor cared to arm or train Afro-Brazilians.

"We must," Giuseppe insisted. "No one will fight for freedom more than those who are not free. They have the most to lose if we lose, so they will be more dedicated and more disciplined than half the others who come along for the thrill of battle and disappear when they see the baseness and the blood."

"Many of those recruits we have relied on will not take kindly to seeing black men in their ranks," Teixeira countered.

"But they have fought side by side with such men before," Giuseppe said. He knew that in past conflicts it had been an acceptable option for rich men to send their slaves to fight in place of their sons. "This time they won't be fighting in their master's place, but for their own freedom, as it should always have been."

Whether Teixeira finally capitulated to Giuseppe's point because of the younger man's tenacity, or because of the fact that their camp became overrun with Afro-Brazilian men demanding to join, Giuseppe could not say. All he knew was that when the battle began, though greatly outnumbered, these newest troops managed to repel the Imperial divisions with the help of the locals. Anita found herself moving between manning her own gun and helping the other women bandage wounded men who fell around her.

The minute the hard fighting ended and they knew they had succeeded in defending the town, Giuseppe and his men rejoiced, as did the local townspeople. Though poor farmers, the locals came out with food to share and offered clothing to those whose shirts or pants were damaged by bullets or blood—or both. In awe of Anita, the women of the town gifted her a new set of clothes. The local cobbler fashioned a pair of boots that fit her better than the men's pair she had been walking in for many miles.

Rather than stay to rest, Giuseppe and Teixeira knew they had to keep their men moving to stay ahead of the opposing army. For the next ten days they marched from town to town, raising the Rio Grande flag with the help of locals at each stop. As they marched, they collected more runaway Afro-Brazilians, who underwent training on the move. Proving themselves to be good with horses and with guns, these men became nicknamed the Black Lancers.

On Christmas Eve, Giuseppe's division arrived triumphantly in Lages, Santa Catarina. That night, Anita and Giuseppe attended midnight mass at Our Lady of the Prazeres, dedicated to the Virgin Mary and the Immaculate Conception. Though it was the holiest night of the year for a Catholic, Anita did not take Communion. Only Giuseppe knew what this meant. He kissed her as she knelt and prayed to Mary to forgive her, and he prayed for the right to marry this woman who had done so much for her people, for his men, and for him.

The peace of the holy day was not to last, however, as Teixeira decided the best move required attacking the enemy army on two fronts. Giuseppe disagreed.

"We are but a small band to begin with," Giuseppe argued respectfully, knowing Teixeira outranked him both in military position and by being a native of Brazil. "To separate is to weaken our power, and perhaps our morale. When the men see the numbers who have joined the fight, it fills them with pride."

"Believe me," Teixeira said, "I have used this strategy before. Attacking them in two areas will keep one from coming to reinforce the other. It will also deceive them into thinking we are more than we are."

"That worked with the cannon on the hill," Giuseppe said. "But even then, superior numbers destroyed the advantage."

Sadly, Teixeira, too insecure in his position to listen to another man's advice, ordered that he and Giuseppe split their forces. So Giuseppe, Anita, and their divisions headed north while Teixeira and his men headed south.

Relying on those of his troops native to the region, Giuseppe learned they could follow some shortcuts. On that inland route, they camped under the cover of the verdant Curitibanos forest-land, including the pine tree and the *Araucaria*, an evergreen conifer with stiff, sharp leaves particular to the region.

They moved as stealthily as such a contingent of men, horses, and ammunition wagons could move. One morning, between the cities of inland Curitibanos and coastal Forquilhas, the much more numerous troops of the Imperial army attacked their meager numbers, highlighting Teixeira's faulted strategy. Giuseppe led his troops from horseback in the front lines; due to the death of the munitions officer on the march, Anita commanded the rear guard, taking charge of protecting and allo-cating all weapons and ammunition for the attack.

Before parting, they shared a hurried embrace. "Stay safe," Giuseppe begged. "For your sake and—" He couldn't yet say it out loud.

"I will," Anita promised before riding to the head of the troops who stood guard over the wagonloads of weapons, rations, and livestock, including the horses they needed to refresh the cavalry and the cattle they needed for food. The men saluted her as she took up position, aimed her musket, and shouted to the men to prepare their weapons. Then they waited, listening intently to the sounds of battle all around them, ready to die for their dream.

At the front of the battle, Giuseppe and his men faced Colonel Mello Albuquerque, whom Giuseppe recognized as a better strategist than Teixeira when he saw that Albuquerque had split his own force into four squads. Surrounded, Giuseppe sent a scout to recall Teixeira's men. As hours ticked by, the soldier did not return with word. Giuseppe had no way of knowing if he had survived through enemy lines. On his own, with diminished forces as the enemy closed in, Giuseppe knew their only chance lay in extracting his troops, retreating, and reforming to attack another day.

To do that, he needed to aggressively strike Albuquerque's center line and attempt to break through. That meant pushing forward, farther and farther from his supply chain—and from Anita. Giuseppe ordered his men to climb the hillside, taking cover among the forest's rocks and thick foliage. Men would be safe there and could conceivably fend off the enemy's larger force until reinforcements arrived or they managed to tire Albuquerque's men.

As they ascended, Giuseppe sent a scout to the rearguard to ask Anita to join them. She refused. Though mounted on a fresh horse that would ensure she could catch up to Giuseppe's line, she would not leave her infantry men behind. "Our mission is to protect the supplies," she told the scout. Frightened of delivering this message to Giuseppe, the scout turned back alone.

One section of Albuquerque's men arrived in the rear guard, and Anita and the troops fought fiercely. With no time to reach the extra ammunition, they resorted to using their swords. The fighting was so hard that Anita couldn't serve as nursemaid to any of the men who fell around her.

When a concerted volley of bullets burst into their midst, one blasted through Anita's hat, inches above her head. Still, she rode among the troops and urged them onward, until another bullet pierced her rearing horse. The horse fell to his side, dropping her to the ground from a height of more than five feet. Instinctively, she rolled over and out of his way as he came down. She had but a moment to soothe the beast by running her hand down his mane. Wishing she had a bullet left to put him out of his misery, she kissed his cheek before racing off into the blinding smoke.

"Anita!" Giuseppe called in vain as he and his men reached the top of the hillside. His eyes brightened as he saw the scout returning, but darkened when he saw he was alone. Giuseppe crossed himself and pushed forward, praying a rosary under his breath for Anita's safety. The Battle of Curitibanos, which later would also be known as the Battle of Forquilhas, was the first time Giuseppe and Anita were separated since she had joined the rebels.

As she slashed at the deep green foliage and tried to run through the dense, gigantic bamboo leaves decaying on the ground, Anita grew tired, but she knew she could not rest. Then she saw them: five members of Albuquerque's force making camp no more than ten yards ahead of her. She turned to run, but they were upon her in a moment. She tried her best to hide her condition—not wanting to appear vulnerable nor give them anything to use against her—by pulling her hat close to her eyes and wrapping her poncho twice around her middle.

The first soldier to reach her yanked the sword from her hand and knocked her to the ground. She silently thanked heaven for the soft bed of decaying leaves. He tied her hands behind her back and yanked her back up. Only then did he look in her face and shout, "It's a woman!"

Unsure of what to do, the men decided to bring her to their captain, Goncalves Padilha, who also had no idea what to do with a female prisoner. So, they rode on horseback to hand her off to Albuquerque in his camp on the other side of the Marombas River.

"What sort of man allows a woman in your condition to partake in such dangerous affairs of men?" Albuquerque asked with no trace of insult, but Anita read beneath his words.

"A man dedicated to uniting all people," she said. "A man dedicated to helping oppressed people. A man—"

"Enough!" Albuquerque cut her off. "I know of this Garibaldi and his reputation. Where you see mercy, I see a mercenary sent to destroy my country—"

"It is my country too," Anita said. "And the people of Rio Grande do Sul demand the freedom to make their own way. As it was when the North American colonies rebelled against England, it shall be for Rio Grande."

"A difference in perspective," Albuquerque said. "Neither of us know the outcome of our sacrifices, but for now we must play our parts. I am the victor. And you, I'm sorry to say, signorina, must play the part of the widow, for we have word that your husband fell in battle."

It took all she had not to react, not to offer this man the pleasure of the response he expected from a weak and wailing woman. In her heart, Anita felt it could not be true. Her mind began racing to find a way to use their trickery to her advantage.

On the hillside, Giuseppe and his surviving men continued fighting the dwindling section of Albuquerque's troops. Taking the hill had been a successful strategy. From this vantage point, he could even see Teixeira's men trouncing another section in the adjacent valley. Once they had vanquished Albuquerque's men, the next tactical move would be to retreat, but he was loath to leave until he knew what had become of Anita.

"Are you *sure* you saw her taken away on horseback?" Giuseppe asked the scout.

"They will not harm a woman," he sputtered.

Giuseppe had no choice but to begin the retreat for the safety of his men while he continued praying for the sake of his beloved. They descended the hill in darkness and marched back to Lajes for supplies and support. It was a miserable march, worsened by the fact that the animals they needed for food had been confiscated when Anita's troops were surrounded. Along the way, Giuseppe and his men lived on roots they dug up or on raw bamboo shoots they chewed after shucking off the husks. They could not spare time to boil the shoots to ease digestion and remove the bitterness. After four days of this diet, the men were becoming too weak to walk.

In his mind, Giuseppe had turned the scout's phrase "They will not harm a woman" into a prayer.

On the fifth day, they broke free of the forest and found a settler's cabin in the clearing. The farmer, a supporter of Rio Grandean independence, allowed them to camp in his fields and provided two of his own stock of steers for them to butcher and roast. Of course, not having had so much real meat in some time meant that several men overate and paid the price later, but all were satiated and ready for the next leg of their journey.

Anita spent those same four days in the enemy camp, sharing short rations with those of her troops who were captured with her, nursing those in need, and planning her escape. Each day she asked for proof that Giuseppe had died and each day she was told a different version of how he fell in battle. Finally, she inveigled on Albuquerque to allow her to search the battlefield herself, using the ploy that as a widow she was owed the right to provide her deceased husband a proper burial.

On the fifth morning, a soldier escorted her to the battlefield to search among the decaying bodies from both battalions. There, she found friend after friend among the dead, men she had mended, men with whom she had shared family stories, men whose wives and girlfriends she knew still waited back home for those who would never return. She held back tears but she did not hold back stories, talking constantly to wear down her one guard who had seated himself below a bamboo stalk to avoid looking at his own possible future. Eventually, in the heat of the sun and the continued monotone of Anita's voice, he fell asleep. She waited an agonizingly long time to make sure her movements were no longer being detected. Then she moved toward his horse and began leading the animal away by its reins.

They picked their way among the dead until they reached the edge of the battlefield. There, Anita mounted the horse and began to trot, then gallop, back toward the hillside where she had last seen Giuseppe.

When she reached the area, she found all were gone but the dead. Again she looked for Giuseppe, but to her relief she could not find him. She followed the tracks up and over the hillside, but now she could hear the hoof beats of Albuquerque's men. Her poor soldier guard had finally awoken and had to admit he'd been deceived by a woman and lost his charge. If captured again, she knew there would be no second chance. So, she spurred her horse onward, finally coming to the Canoas River. She had no idea of its depth.

Then she saw a native butterfly of brilliant orange outlined in black strokes land on the rocks at the water's edge. It hopped from rock to rock, then glided on the air over the water as if beckoning Anita to follow, promising to show the way. Even though her stolen horse did not seem keen to take her lead, she plunged in and headed toward the opposite shore. But once they reached a third of the way across, the horse panicked and refused to move further. Anita urged him forward to no avail. She looked behind her to see the soldiers had gathered at the river's edge, waiting for her horse to turn and deliver her back to their control. Instead, she abandoned the horse and began to swim, reaching the opposite side as the soldiers argued over whether to follow. Before they could come to a consensus, she disappeared in the forestland on the other side.

Two days later, Giuseppe and his men had reached the outskirts of Lajes, where they stopped at the farm of another supporter. The man apologized, as all he could supply them with was a few bushels of beets, carrots, and cabbages. He had sent off the majority of his broccoli, cauliflower, and spinach to the city markets. Still, Giuseppe thanked him profusely; vegetables had been sadly lacking in their diets. The men moved to roast the food or eat it raw across the evening.

Night fell as they lay down in his field for one more night of rest before reaching the city. There, they could regroup with Teixeira's divisions and prepare for the next battle, wherever it might come. Just as he was falling into yet another fitful sleep, Giuseppe saw a figure in the corner of his eye slowly walking out of the woods. Something about it moved him. He stood up to help, then began running as he realized who it was. Anita.

He fell to his knees, apologizing so sincerely until she could take no more.

"I chose this path," Anita said. "I chose you. I would have it no other way."

"You are the greatest gift of my life," Giuseppe said, walking her back to their men.

"There is a greater gift coming," she answered.

Soon to come, however, was greater sorrow. After regrouping, the rebels headed to São José do Norte, where Giuseppe knew they had to take control of the lagoon to ensure future success by keeping the supply lines open. But Imperial forces had merged there, understanding the same theory.

"All we can do is try," Giuseppe said.

"It seems risky." Anita said matter-of-factly what the others had danced around.

"Yes," Giuseppe admitted, "yet it is the only way. If we let the Imperialists entrench in this city, we will never move forward."

"The biggest problem is our lack of numbers," Teixeira said. Normally uncomfortable with a woman in the discussion, he had come to respect Anita after her capture and subsequent successful escape. "Too many leave when their families need them for harvest."

"Too many have no understanding of the need for military discipline," Giuseppe said.

"It is the Italian troops who stay," Anita said in gratitude, "when it is not even their country they save."

"To them," Giuseppe began. "To me. To all of us, this is the fire in which we shall be forged before we can light a flame of freedom in our homeland."

"You are capable of understanding a greater goal," Anita said.

"Most men are not," Teixeira said, subconsciously including himself in that list.

"All we can do is try," Giuseppe reiterated. "And use all that is on our side: the dark of night, the love of land that lives in the hearts of those men who have stayed with us, our own strategy . . ."

"And?" Anita prodded.

"And the sad fact that so many have gone so long without proper rations that they will push forward ever harder when they know the stores of São José do Norte will belong to the victor," Giuseppe said.

"I hope you are right," Teixeira said, "for I fear this battle will decide the fate of this rebellion."

Sadly, the battle proved decisive for the Imperialists. Through Giuseppe's leadership, his men were able to breach the city walls and hold three of the four strategic fronts. At the fourth front, Anita and those men still in possession of horses awaited the cavalry of General Canabarro before continuing, but Canabarro failed to arrive. Then the lack of discipline did their troops in, as Giuseppe had predicted.

Feeling victory at hand, many of the most haggard men stepped out of their squads to loot the town, hoping to bring something of value back to their families, or merely wishing to render this bastion of Imperialist support useless. Now with an open shot for the Imperial army to win back a couple of those fronts, Giuseppe had to call in the tattered remnants of his own cavalry to attack.

Giuseppe joined them at the city gates, where he and Anita led the men into the city. But they spent more time disrupting the looters and corralling them back into order than they did fighting against the arriving Imperial troops. The battle was a loss. Only forty or so of Giuseppe's troops survived the onslaught and retreated to a hacienda in the nearby town of San Simon. Meanwhile, the Imperialists reestablished control of São José do Norte, the beginning of the end of the rebellion.

Just as one dream was ending, another began. In the barn of the hacienda on September 16, 1840, a rebel-allied farm-wife helped bring Giuseppe and Anita's baby into the world. The sadness of the loss of their military campaign paled when they saw that a skull deformity had been created in the child due to Anita's fall from her horse during her escape.

They named him Menotti in honor of Giuseppe's respect for the Italian freedom fighter Ciro Menotti, whose letter to his wife on the eve of his execution had so impressed Giuseppe years earlier. He murmured Menotti's words to Anita as she rested after the birth, "'Dearest wife, may your virtue and your religion be with you. Always.'"

To the child, Giuseppe whispered, "You, my son, are the best blend of Brazil and Italy, and you shall be a fighter for both."

Giuseppe proved prescient again, as Menotti would not be defined by his deformity. He would grow to become a freedom fighter alongside his father, earn the rank of general, and help with the reunification of Italy—but that would be nearly twenty years in the future. For now, the more pressing matter of being able to provide for his family weighed heavily on Giuseppe.

Chapter 7

1841 – 1842
MARRIAGE IN MONTEVIDEO:
RAISING A FAMILY AND A LEGION

As a freedom fighter, Giuseppe had lived a long time on army rations and promises of payment when the war was won. While this suited the life of a single soldier, it would not do now that he had a child to care for. He also wanted to marry Anita properly, but in the wilds of the Brazilian forests, they had no word from the outside world of the whereabouts of her first husband, Manuel, which made seeking an annulment impossible.

He confided this to his friend from his earliest days as an exile in Montevideo, Luigi Rossetti, who happily helped Giuseppe uphold Italian tradition in this land so far away from their shared homeland. Without request, Luigi, who still owned the small trading concern in that city, loaned Giuseppe enough funds to buy the necessities for the child, as well as a brightly colored handkerchief, a small present for Anita.

"Where did you find such fine needlework?" Anita, a seamstress herself, asked as she fingered the perfect stitches along the seams. They sat together in the young family's small field tent, sharing camp coffee and their dreams for uniting Italy.

"We bought it off another Italian émigré, just off the boat at the port," Luigi said, relishing the memory of meeting another of their compatriots.

"That's not all he offered us," Giuseppe said with a twinkle in his eye. He took up a guitar that leaned against the canvas wall and began to strum "Va Pensiero," a new song they had heard on the docks, sung by the newly arrived Italian sailors. He sang quietly, so as not to wake Menotti: "*O, mia patria, sì bella e perduta! O, membranza, sì cara e fatal!*" ("Oh, my country, so beautiful and lost! Oh, remembrance, so dear and so fatal!")

Luigi joined in with a voice that was strong and true: "*Le memorie nel petto raccendi, ci favella del tempo che fu!*" ("Rekindle our bosom's memories, and speak to us of times gone by!")

Anita hummed along, turning the opera into a lullaby for Menotti, who breathed gently as she rocked him.

"It is an opera by a new composer, another accomplished Giuseppe," Luigi said, gesturing to his friend across the room. "Just not that one."

"Must I do everything?" Giuseppe asked facetiously as he readjusted his fingers on the strings.

"This Giuseppe is Giuseppe Verdi, and the opera tells how King Nabucco conquered and exiled the Jewish people," Luigi explained as Giuseppe found the right chord and finished the song. "*O t'ispiri il Signore un concento che ne infonda al patire virtù.*" ("Or let the Lord inspire you a harmony of voices that may instill virtue to suffering.")

"To me—" Giuseppe said slowly, parsing the thought as he went. "To me, it reminds me of Italy."

"Everything reminds you of Italy," Anita teased, making Luigi laugh heartily.

"Wait until we take you home, dear lady," Luigi said. "I will show you Genoa, home to the greatest sailor who ever lived."

All this talk made Anita feel the pull across the ocean. "I go where you go—you're my home," she said to Giuseppe.

"But are you not the bold Brazilian Madonna who fights for freedom beside her beloved?" Luigi teased.

"Our child is part Italian, so I am part Italian," she said, using the foot pedal beside her chair to rock the baby in a hammock that hung from the tent poles, typical in a one-room Italian peasant home, copied in this traveling tent by Giuseppe's ingenuity.

"I had hoped to do for your homeland what I wish to do for my own," Giuseppe said, trying to keep his mind off the impending loss of the rebels of Rio Grande.

"We have one more chance, my friend," Luigi reminded him. Giuseppe was loath to leave Anita and Menotti so soon, despite his loyalty to the rebels, yet he knew if he expected discipline in his own soldiers, he must offer it to his superiors. He and Luigi had been assigned to join General Canabarro's command, leading over 1,800 men to what would be Giuseppe's final battle in this war.

Because she could not wield a gun in one hand and a child in the other, Anita followed with the other camp wives, despite Giuseppe's pleas that she stay behind until the baby was weaned. Instead, she rode with the three-month-old Menotti on the saddle in front of her. When the troops came to a stream swollen by recent rains, Anita turned her poncho so the hood was in front and wrapped Menotti inside it so she could keep the wet child warm with her body heat.

In this battle, Canabarro, Giuseppe, and Luigi faced a new and far more vicious foe in the form of Colonel Francisco Pedro de Abreu—nicknamed the Mouringue because he put so many women in mourning, or the Relentless Enemy by others, for being both respected and feared as a man of surprises.

Both nicknames suited him in this encounter as, with more men and more access to reinforcements, Mouringue plowed down most of Giuseppe's troops. In one agonizing moment, Giuseppe, busy fighting for his own life, watched three Imperial soldiers engage Luigi. His dear friend fought valiantly with his sword until one of them slid the end of a spear between Luigi's ribs, causing him to fall into the mud at his horse's feet. Devastated at the loss of such an old and valued friend, only the thought of Anita and Menotti back at camp kept Giuseppe on his feet and fighting for his own life.

When their entire company fell into retreat, he and two other soldiers lifted Luigi's body onto Giuseppe's horse. They carried him to the next valley, where he was buried. Anita and Giuseppe prayed over Luigi's grave as she tied her handkerchief to the wooden cross that served as headstone. "Such a man must never be forgotten," Giuseppe whispered. "When I return to Italy . . ." He could not finish, not yet ready to imagine returning without Luigi.

"When *we* return to Italy," Anita said, "we will visit Genoa and tell them all of his sacrifice." She reached out to hold Giuseppe's hand. "But for now, we will tell Menotti. Every night," Anita promised. She kept that promise so well that, later in life, those stories fueled Menotti's desire to complete his godfather's task.

Giuseppe could not dwell on this loss for long. President Bento Gonçalves had begun peace talks with the Imperialists and knew those men who had been loyal to him might pay a price. When he capitulated on behalf of Rio Grande do Sul, Gonçalves gave Giuseppe and Anita nine hundred head of cattle in thanks and payment for their service. At his bidding, they drove the herd south and settled in safety in Montevideo, Uruguay.

During the grueling two-hundred-mile journey to their new yet still temporary home, they lost a number of cattle to starvation, as the land offered little water that time of year. Giuseppe and the cowhands he had hired for the trip had to slaughter the weakest to save the value of their hides, which he sold upon their arrival in Montevideo.

"It won't hold us very long," Giuseppe confessed.

"We don't need that much," Anita said. "I'm happy we can be together. That's all I want."

Yet Giuseppe sensed a lie behind her words. He knew in his heart that she wanted something else, something he was determined to give her.

He sent letters to other people who knew her husband to see if they could apply for an annulment. Finally, he learned that Manuel had died on the battlefield in one of the last skirmishes of the Rio Grandean war. It happened while Giuseppe, Anita, and their cattle trekked to Uruguay. While he felt guilty rejoicing at the death of one man, war had forced him to witness many losses—so this one loss of a man who had been abusive to a woman he loved brought less guilt than it might have in his younger years. It was impossible not to rejoice, as this news paved the way for the day when he and Anita finally stood before a priest of their new parish, dedicated to San Francesco d'Assisi, and vowed to love each other. "Till death do us part," they said nearly in unison. It was March 26, 1842.

While word of Manuel's death brought muted happiness, since that they lived in a port city again, other news came easily to them. Hence, word also came that Giuseppe's father, Domenico, had died on March 3, 1841.

Now that they lived in a parish and had married, they could attend to another matter of great religious importance to Anita: Menotti was baptized. They gave him Domenico as his Christian name, as there was no Saint Menotti.

Attending to another important matter, Giuseppe sought out a proper job for a father and husband. He had cause to thank his mother, whom he hadn't seen in eight years, for all the training in his childhood. Long prepared by Dante and other readings, poetry writing, and navigational calculations, Giuseppe became a schoolmaster to support his family. Father Paolo Semedei, a Corsican priest and fellow exiled Italian, gladly hired Giuseppe to teach literature, algebra, geometry, and French to the young men of the town.

This picture of domesticity did not last, however, as tensions rose between Uruguay and its former mother country, Argentina. The city came under siege by order of Juan Manuel de Rosas, the Argentine dictator, who wanted to recapture the whole country.

Rosas sent a flotilla of ships commanded by the English immigrant William Brown to Montevideo to bottle up access to the smaller rivers that flowed into the River Plate. The Paraná and the Uruguay Rivers served as crucial trade routes out of the country and into Paraguay, which provided both livestock and products as wide-ranging as cotton, tobacco, coffee, and sugarcane.

Once again, those in need of military leadership came to Giuseppe to ask for aid. This time, many who volunteered to help Uruguay were from its Italian immigrant population, and most shared Giuseppe's future goal, making the appeal ever more difficult to ignore. Not many men volunteered to lead such a dangerous mission of sailing over a thousand kilometers inside enemy territory—certainly not many with Giuseppe's record of successful strategies at sea against formidable opponents. He accepted a command in the nascent Uruguayan navy.

He didn't know how to tell Anita he had taken on a new mission that she, despite her bravura performance on both earlier naval missions, could not follow.

"I wouldn't stop you if I could," she said when he broke the news. "But I have learned that when liberty calls, you can't help but hear."

"These men need me," Giuseppe said. "We share the same goals for now. And for the future."

"Then you must go to secure the chance for us to all go together in the future," she said. She presented Menotti so Giuseppe could kiss the child's forehead. Anita's optimism nourished Giuseppe, though he knew that in leaving her, he was leaving his support system when he needed it most.

In command of the Uruguayan fleet, Giuseppe put his strategic talents to work by fooling the enemy from the start.

While they suspected him to lead his three main ships—the *Constitucion*, with Giuseppe on board, followed by the *Pereyra* and the *Procida*—up the larger Uruguay River, he instead followed the smaller Paraná. To further throw off Commander Brown's spies, he made sure to find pilots whose major experience came from working the Uruguay River and trusted they would be of enough quality to manage an unknown river when he changed their route midway through the mission.

At first it worked; Brown sent five of his ships up the Uruguay. That allowed Giuseppe's fleet a two-week head start. Short of monetary support, and therefore of rations, the crew had to land whenever they saw herds of animals, and slaughter them to feed the legion. If that wasn't slow going enough, often the wind died down and soldiers had to disembark and pull the craft along by ropes, usually a job reserved for oxen. Still, they felt fortified. Then Brown's fleet caught up and bottled them up in a local harbor. The Battle of Arroyo Grande began December 6, 1842.

Soon, the *Constitucion* ran low on munitions while smaller ships in the fleet began taking on water. "We shall have to surrender!" shouted Giuseppe's first mate as he bandaged a wounded man. Countless other wounded men lay scattered across the deck.

"Not while there is still gunpowder and there are still men of honor," Giuseppe ordered. Though when munitions began to run out, he saw they could do no more. To be captured would destroy all the morale the young country had mustered, so he ordered the evacuation of the men, the wounded, and the remaining rations from all ships. Skiffs began making trips back and forth between ships and land as Giuseppe smashed chains to pieces to fill the cannons and hold off Brown's forces. Other men joined him in solidarity. Finally, with the small band of men who had stayed behind to load the skiffs, there was nothing left to do but once again set fire to the ship and take the last skiff to shore.

No one stayed in the port for long as they marched, carrying the wounded by makeshift stretchers, into the nearby town of Aguas Corrientes. There, the locals feted them in gratitude. Though they had lost the battle against Brown, they had won the war for the hearts of the people. Both local and international papers wrote of Giuseppe as the hero of the freedom-loving Uruguayans, and the national paper praised him for saving the young republic's honor. Yet, as with each engagement and each subsequent loss, Giuseppe assuaged his feelings of failure with the fact that he was learning more and more of what he would need to succeed in the single-minded goal of his life: a united Italy.

Anita read the words of praise at home in Montevideo, small comfort to a woman who had been living on her own for nearly a year, missing her husband and raising her son on stories of a heroic father. Soon, Menotti would have the chance to see both his parents in action once Giuseppe's forces returned to Montevideo. They would defend it against the Great Siege laid out by Rosas in cahoots with Manuel Oribe, Uruguay's former president who hoped to regain power. Montevideo—being the capital of Uruguay and directly across the River Plate from Buenos Aires, Argentina's capital—became a natural first target in what became known as the Guerra Grande, or Uruguayan Civil War, between the two powers.

∼

There were four thousand Italian families in Montevideo at the time. When the city was under siege, Giuseppe put together a force of Italians to defend the city. Following the attention generated by the newspapers, hundreds of those Italians joined Giuseppe's forces with a two-fold promise: they would fight for freedom for Uruguay and use this fight as a training ground so they could all return to Italy and unite their own beloved country. Among them Count Giovanni Livraghi stood out as a man ruled by the same passion Giuseppe had to unite Italy. They talked of it often over campfires and as they rode across this land still foreign to them both.

Known as the Italian Legion, they slowly outfitted themselves in what would become their iconic look both in South America and later when they would march through Italy in 1860 as the Expedition of the Thousand. With Anita's influence, Giuseppe's men took on the look of Brazilian gauchos, like her father and the ragamuffins he had defended. The look would grow to include hand-knitted ponchos for the cold nights, sombreros to protect from the sun on long marches, red shirts Giuseppe procured from a stock destined for slaughterhouse workers in Buenos Aires, and leather boots from wherever and whenever they could find them, which sometimes meant from fallen enemies they found on the battlefields they marched past. The shirts would become their calling card and all the Italian Legions who followed Giuseppe became known as Redshirts. They eventually adopted a black flag that represented Italy in mourning, with a volcano at the center that symbolized the dormant power in their homeland.

First, Giuseppe took charge of reestablishing the Uruguayan navy while higher powers handled the politics of the siege. Being home to an exorbitant number of foreign subjects, mostly from Britain and France, the Argentine military could not bombard

Montevideo without incurring anger from those citizens' home countries. Similarly, the Argentine navy could not inhibit trade from those countries via a blockade, as that would harm subjects of England's Queen Victoria and France's King Louis Philippe. Due to the intricacies of these issues, the Great Siege of Montevideo continued from 1843 to 1851, officially the longest siege of the entire Uruguayan Civil War.

The local leaders needed to take bold action to survive, and Giuseppe argued for the boldest.

"You have to offer freedom!" he urged General Melchor Pacheco y Obes, now in charge of defending the city. Though born in Buenos Aires, Pacheco sided with the Uruguayan rebels and joined their cause. He rose quickly through the ranks thanks to his cultured education and leadership skills.

"To slaves?" Pacheco asked.

"To men who will fight," Giuseppe, now promoted to the rank of colonel, said. Count Livraghi added a bit of history, "Slaves fought hard with Spartacus." Giuseppe saw that his friend played on Pacheco's bias toward men of culture. Though not as classically educated as Pacheco, Giuseppe's lifelong habit of reading served him well against such a man as he offered, "Othello served as a great general."

"Slaves of that era were not the same," Pacheco countered. "Victors enslaved prisoners of war, already men of accomplishments. Of course, they could command counterattacks. These slaves here are no more than savages saved from the jungles of Africa."

"You may treat men as animals, but that does not make them animals," Giusppe said.

Count Livraghi added, "Such men fought hard for Teixeira at Lajes."

Then Giuseppe finished with, "They fought for both the British in New England *and* the Americans in their revolution. We need them to fight in ours."

An intelligent man, Pacheco accepted Giuseppe's logical argument over a lifetime of misplaced bias and offered freedom and eventual citizenship to any enslaved men who joined them. In a short time, such men numbered nearly five thousand new soldiers for the rebels. Once again, Giuseppe's strategy and his leadership both on land and at sea would help turn the tide of someone else's war.

Sure enough, though it took a few years, the city of Montevideo survived its Great Siege after a series of successful military engagements involving the freed men, Giuseppe, and his legion. Together Giuseppe's Italian Legion achieved three major victories in 1846. After the Battle of San Antonio del Santo in February 1846, Giuseppe earned the promotion to general.

All that time at war left little to spend in the peace and comfort of his own family, which grew to include two daughters, Rosita in 1843 and Teresita in 1845. Far from home, Giuseppe was in the midst of battle, though in later years neither he nor Count Livraghi could not remember which one, when he received a letter from Anita's doctor via the Uruguayan Minister of War. Giuseppe ripped it open as Count Livraghi gestured for the messenger—Giuseppe's right-hand man, Andrea Aguyar—to take a seat in case the letter required an immediate return response. Thanks to Giuseppe and Count Livraghi, Aguyar was one of the formerly enslaved men now fighting for freedom alongside then. He and Giuseppe had bonded over their life goals and over the care and feeding of a three-legged mutt they named Guerillo, saved and adopted by their squad after being hit by a stray bullet. Guerillo, named for the guerilla-style warfare for which he served as a mascot, could often be found running alongside one of the men's horses or, as now, curled under Giuseppe's camp desk.

The three men braced themselves to hear harsh news about other fronts in the war. Neither was prepared for the devastating personal news that came instead. Little Rosita had died before her second birthday.

"When?" Aguyar asked.

"More than two weeks ago," Giuseppe said in a daze. "My poor beloved, all alone at such a time." He stared straight ahead, unable to comprehend the sorrow Anita must have faced.

"Even if you had been there—" Aguyar began, instinctually attempting to assuage his friend's conscience.

"Even if you had, there was nothing you could have done," Livraghi concluded.

"I could have held Rosita before she passed," Giuseppe snapped. "I could have held Anita as our first daughter passed. I could have . . ." But it was clear in the doctor's letter: there was nothing anyone could have done. Giuseppe wished to return home to help Anita through her mourning, and it was as if fate decided that was right. The final Argentinian attacks on Montevideo drove Giuseppe back to protect his family and friends.

This time, as in their first years together, while Giuseppe, Aguyar, Livraghi, and the Italian Legion fought back the formidable Argentinians, Anita organized women in Montevideo to build fortifications, distribute food, and raise money. She managed this while in mourning for one child, caring for two others, and carrying yet another. They welcomed their second son, Ricciotti, in 1847. This series of victories, along with the desire to leave this place of loss and the arrival of a new child, renewed Giuseppe's hope for returning to his beloved home country. With the bonuses bestowed upon him from a grateful nation, Giuseppe made plans for his family—and his legion—to return to Italy.

Chapter 8

1848
RETURN TO ITALY

Political changes in the various kingdoms on the Italian Peninsula convinced Giuseppe and many members of his Italian Legion that now was the time to return. It was the time they had been waiting for to use the skills they had obtained in their battles for South American freedom to support unity in their homeland. In September 1846, Pope Pius IX—who would serve for thirty-one years, longer than any other elected pope—was elected after serving as the bishop of Imola. Formerly known as Cardinal Giovanni Maria Mastai-Ferretti, he had supported reformist ideas in the past. In his new position, which included being governor of the Papal States, he granted general amnesty for political prisoners and released a new constitution allowing, for the first time in history, more secular participation in the states' government.

It was particularly encouraging that a few kings, including King Charles Albert of the Kingdom of Sardinia, offered constitutions to their subjects. King Ferdinand II of the Two Sicilies refused such progress until revolution broke out in Palermo. Then, on March 4, 1848, to curb such violence in his own region, Charles Albert offered freedom of the press, a right made all the more necessary to good government based on the way the Americans had embraced it in the years following their own revolution. Finally, after the outbreak of revolt in Lombardy, Charles Albert declared war on Austria on March 23 of that year.

The Industrial Revolution helped the cause of unification as well. Consolidated countries such as England and Belgium enjoyed the benefits of modern technology, including the building of railroads for transporting goods, which expanded their profits and their power. A new generation of Italians realized that if they continued using this ancient idea of city-states, Italy might never enter the new era, instead further declining in status after having once been the greatest empire of the ancient world.

Meanwhile, Giuseppe Mazzini, of the Young Italy movement, had been busy in his exile in France. He was publishing articles about the Italian Legion's exploits in South America, fanning the flames of their fame on the continent so that the people clamored for Giuseppe's return. On April 15, 1848, Giuseppe stood on the dock alongside Aguyar, knowing that if he didn't accept this invitation, there might not be another.

"Is now the time?" Aguyar asked as they approached the ship with their trunks and their soldier packs, the three-legged Guerillo racing to keep up with them.

"With all Mazzini has written," Giuseppe said, still partly convincing himself, "and with dearest hope that Pope Pius IX is finally on our side, yes."

"We must at least try," Count Livraghi agreed.

"Italy must become a republic so that its citizens may always be Italians," Giuseppe said.

He had already corresponded with Charles Albert to offer his services, but Aguyar knew the king had turned them down. "To have your loyalty questioned by a man who gained his place in this world through nothing more than being born to the right mother," Aguyar said.

"I was born to the right mother," Giuseppe said in defense of Nicoletta. "Perhaps not the right mother to make me a king, but the right mother to prepare me to handle men like this one. Once he sees how we repel the Austrians in Milan, he will beg us to come to his aid." Due to Charles Albert's declaration of war on Austria, Giuseppe and his followers planned to offer assistance to the provisional government of Milan, which had rebelled against its Austrian occupiers.

Giuseppe looked ahead at all the dockworkers and called them by a word he had picked up in Portuguese: *estivador*—or *stevedore*, those in charge of unloading cargo. The hustle and bustle reminded him of the cold day last December when he had accompanied Anita to the same dock. She had held Ricciotti in her arms and Menotti by the hand while Giuseppe carried the three-year-old Teresita, holding on to her until the last moment when Anita and the children had to mount the gangway so the ship could depart.

"It's time," Giuseppe said, kissing Teresita on her forehead and handing her to Anita.

"If not for the safety of the children, I would stay with you," she said as she embraced Giuseppe and pushed Menotti forward to hug and kiss his father.

"Say '*Ciao*, Papà,'" Anita coached the eight-year-old, who was still unclear on the idea that they were leaving the only land he had ever known.

"*Ciao*, Papà," Menotti said obediently. Giuseppe lifted the boy off the ground and swung him around in circles, smiling together.

They had decided that Anita would travel on a separate ship so as not to arrive with armed men, nor with Giuseppe, who still carried a death sentence from his earlier activities toward unification. She planned to take the children to Giuseppe's mother, Nicoletta, in Nice so they would have a stable home. She would then join Giuseppe as he battled for Italy.

Giuseppe held a letter detailing Anita's arrival in the port of Genoa in March. After eight winter weeks at sea, three thousand supporters who had read of her exploits for the cause in Mazzini's articles had greeted her ship. Some of the most exuberant of them rowed out in their family fishing boats with all their children on board to welcome the wife and children of their hero. "*Viva* Garibaldi!" they shouted.

"'Ah, if you knew how the name Garibaldi is loved and longed for in all of Italy, especially in Genoa!'" Giuseppe read proudly to Aguyar, though they both already knew the letter by heart.

When Aguyar saw the trunks had been carried on board the *Speranza*, he gently nudged Giuseppe from his memory. "General, it's time."

"Yes," Giuseppe said. He looked back at the land that he too would likely never see again and marveled at the loyalty of a wife, and now a friend like Aguyar, who would leave their homeland to help unite his.

~

By the time they arrived in June, the political climate had changed again and early victories were soon followed by a series of defeats. The *Speranza* sailed to Nice to reunite Giuseppe with his family as he gathered the updates needed to plan his next move. Between the men who had sailed with him from Uruguay, including Count Livraghi, and the Italians who immediately joined him in Nice, there were 150 men at Giuseppe's disposal. That number soon rose to over 3,700 men. Even Mazzini signed up in the rank of ensign, due to his far less military experience. On July 14, the Milanese army appointed Giuseppe to general, as he had recruited so many to the effort of overthrowing the Austrians. Known as the Anzani Battalion, Giacomo Medici was their commander.

Before they could join the fight, Charles Albert's army failed at the First Battle of Custoza on July 23 to 25, 1848. Much criticized for this debacle, and for his preoccupation with annexing Lombardy-Venetia to his own kingdom, the king lost the chance to follow and destroy the weakened Austrians.

Giuseppe's battalion was marching to its first posting in Bergamo, Switzerland, propelled by anticipation. Having loved both reading and history his whole life, Giuseppe knew how powerful it would be to remind the men of the great success the Lombard league had in defeating the Holy Roman Emperor Frederick Barbarossa at the Battle of Legnano in 1167. "Bergamo will be the Pontida of the present generation, and God will bring us a Legnano!" he vowed with a shout.

After Charles Albert's defeat, they were recalled to Milan to shore up the city's defenses. But before they arrived, the king signed an armistice with the Austrians, ending the war in his region. This frustrated Giuseppe and his men, because it resulted in many deserting the battalion and the cause. Giuseppe commandeered two passing steamboats and headed to the only other region still actively at war with Austria, the Province of Varese, with those soldiers he retained.

To rally the men, Giuseppe had them sing a new song, "Fratelli d'Italia" ("Brothers of Italy"). Written in the autumn of 1847 in Genoa by Goffredo Mameli and Michele Novaro, the song told the story of a fractured Italy and the men ready to die to unite her:

> *Let us unite, let us love one another,*
> *For union and love*
> *Reveal to the people*
> *The ways of the Lord.*
> *Let us swear to set free*
> *The land of our birth:*
> *United by God,*
> *Who can overcome us?*

After singing it on land and on sea, "Fratelli d'Italia" soon became their anthem. It did the work music does by knitting people from faraway places into one cohesive unit.

When they landed again just outside the city of Luino, the battalion encountered an Austrian regiment. It took only an hour for Giuseppe's cavalry troops to dispatch the Austrians with Giuseppe and Aguyar at the front of the attack. Lessons they had learned from the gauchos of South America gave them an edge over the staid and traditional tactics of the Austrians. Taken by the way Aguyar used his lasso to collect horses running loose after their riders had been wounded, Giuseppe used his roping skills to pull enemy soldiers off their horses. It led to an all-out rout and the Austrians dispersed and ran.

"Did you see the looks in their eyes when you roped the first rider?" Giuseppe said as he and Aguyar settled the men in for a well-earned sleep at the camp that night.

"I don't understand why none of them carry their own ropes," Aguyar said, adjusting a few of the ponchos he was improvising into an awning to keep the harsh morning sun from their eyes when they woke.

"It's not European," Count Livraghi said. Despite years in Uruguay he still preferred the customs of his homeland.

"*Chi non va, non vede. Chi non vede, non sa.*" Giuseppe said. Aguyar had been picking up Italian but looked to Giuseppe for the proper translation. "'If you don't go, you don't see. If you don't see, you don't know.' It's something my mother said to me a long time ago. Who knew how true it would prove to be?"

Aguyar took his saddle off his horse and placed it at the head of Giuseppe's sleeping space. "Get some rest, my friend," he said. "Commander Medici made it my duty to see that you are always rested."

"Who gives the orders around here?" Giuseppe said with a smile.

"In this case," Aguyar said, "I do, whether it be safe for me to do so or not."

While some members of the Black Lancers had joined Giuseppe and Aguyar, Aguyar was still one of the few men of color on this expedition. He was unsure of how the locals would take watching him work as an equal with Giuseppe.

"My friend," Count Livraghi said. "Here in Italy, we are used to being visited by men who look like you."

"Why, San Filippo of Agira had skin far darker than yours," Giuseppe said. "Born of a Syrian father in Thrace, he went to Sicily to preach and they made him a saint. That's how our people will treat you for all you are doing to unite them."

The next morning, the Austrians returned with reinforcements under the command of General Konstantin d'Aspre. The son of a war hero from the French Revolution, d'Aspre had much to prove. Giuseppe saved the Anzani Battalion by splitting it into multiple parts, all of which successfully crossed the shores of Lake Lugano, over the border in Switzerland. There, they were given refuge at the estate of the Marchese Gaspare de Rosales and Contessa Maria Cigalini dal Verme, Milanese nobles who had a love affair similar to Giuseppe and Anita. Rosales and Cigalini had met when she was already married but because they shared so much, including their political desires for a united Italy, they ran away together, staying one step away from the Austrian authorities who then had jurisdiction over such personal actions as infidelity. Maria divorced her husband and she and Rosales had two children. They had turned their home in Milan into the headquarters for Mazzini's Young Italy movement, but when the Austrians came too close to that city, they had taken refuge in their estate on Lake Lugano.

Forced to concede due to a lack of manpower, munitions, and other government support, Giuseppe dug down deep to keep his morale high. All over the regions of Italy, supporters sang his praises in thanks for his bravery and loyalty. Yet, while he still believed even failure taught important lessons, at forty-one years old, he worried failure might be the only legacy he would leave for his children.

≈

Due to the king's armistice, Giuseppe traveled to see his family in Nice under an assumed name, Giuseppe Risso. Aguyar accompanied him by playing up his ethnicity to pose as Risso's valet. Knowing he could not stay in one place for long, Giuseppe and Anita traveled back to Genoa on the invitation of several revolutionaries who wanted his advice on their next move. Unsure of how they would be received, they left the children with Nicoletta.

"A mother should not leave her children," Nicoletta argued.

"And a wife should not leave her husband," Anita responded.

"Even Solomon would admit Anita cannot be cut in two," Giuseppe said, trying to bridge the gap between the two most important women in his life. He held his mother's hands and added, "I want the children to know you, to hear your stories, so they will come to love you as I do."

The day of their departure was filled with tearful goodbyes, but all knew it was the best choice for them as a family. All along their travel route, locals called upon Giuseppe to make speeches and rally them to the cause of unifying the kingdoms. In Genoa, thousands came to hear him give his strongest call: "Rise up with the strengths of the rights you do not hold, of the blood you have shed, in the glorious name of Italy! Place your faith not in symbols but in justice! He who wants to win can win!"

So enthralled by Giuseppe's words were the people from the Kingdom of Two Sicilies that they pleaded with him to bring his Redshirts to Palermo and defend them against King Ferdinand II. The people had given Ferdinand the nasty nickname of King Bomba for attacking the Sicilian port city of Messina, which they knew meant he would march west to their city soon. Remembering his mother's many stories about the island of Sicily, Giuseppe accepted this invitation and spent a few weeks gathering more troops.

On October 24, 1848, Giuseppe, Anita, Aguyar, Livraghi and a contingent of some seventy or more volunteer Redshirts boarded the *Pharamond*, which headed south on the Ligurian Sea toward Palermo. "Now, perhaps I will see this *Castagno dei Cento Cavalli*, and when I return I can stand witness to the truth of your proverbs to my own children," Giuseppe wrote to his mother.

Upon a short rest stop in Livorno, fresh news of violence in the Independent Republic of Venice changed their course. Many local men wanted to help the Venetians defend their sovereignty, rather than continue to sail far south to Sicily. In solidarity, Giuseppe led them east to Florence, collecting more men along the way. These new volunteers ranged in age from fourteen to forty and had left behind occupations such as shopkeepers, teachers, artists, and ditch diggers. Some had even been guilty of crimes in their hometowns and used the legion to escape, but after spending time with Giuseppe's men, some of their number discovered a deeper desire to be useful to their countrymen.

At this point, they decided Anita must return to Nice. Skirting the Papal States, which were still under French control, would be too dangerous. Uninterested in becoming part of a united Italy, the pope did not support Giuseppe and his forces, which raised the stakes of their travels. Both agreed children should never lose both parents.

Marching north into Bologna, a new leader asked to join Giuseppe's cause: Father Ugo Bassi. With him, he brought more men from the region.

Always the more practical of Giuseppe's lieutenants, Aguyar

asked the priest, "How do I know we can trust your men? We are on the march with no time for training."

"You are an example of why you can trust us," Bassi said.

"How?" Giuseppe asked.

"If General Garibaldi has entrusted so much of his safety to a former slave," Bassi said, "it will bond my men to both of you, for very few of them are yet willing to see a slave in that manner. Once you treat a slave as a man, you tell all former slaves they have a chance at a full life. Those men will follow you forever."

Giuseppe gladly handed Bassi position as chaplain of the Legion. That November, together they crossed the Apennine Mountains, where snow reached their knees, making the hero's welcome they received in the town truly gratifying. Still, they had no time to revel in the town's embrace; they needed to make for Ravenna, where they planned for what had become a force of five hundred to sail to Venice.

But once again, violence prevented their next move. Word reached Giuseppe that Pellegrino Rossi, the new prime minister of the Papal States who had been appointed by Pope Pius IX, had been stabbed to death as he entered Parliament on November 15. Fearing the loss of the Papal States, Pope Pius abandoned his residence at the Quirinal Palace in Rome to the more fortified Vatican. The Swiss Guards were disarmed, making the pope a prisoner in his new palace. Giuseppe took this as a sign that those in Rome who had been agitating for unity were winning, so he turned Rome into the new—and final—destination for his Italian Legion.

Still feeling himself a stranger in this new land, Aguyar asked, "In all this land, why is Rome the key? Why not Venice? Or Milan?"

Memories of being in Rome with his father for the jubilee flooded Giuseppe's mind as he tried to explain. "Italy will not truly exist as a nation until her flag, symbolizing the unity and freedom of the former Roman Empire, flies from the Capitol in Rome."

"Then we will see it fly," Aguyar promised as they continued preparations for the journey.

Their ongoing problem lay in securing provisions for the Legion on yet another long march. Giuseppe solved that the only way he could: he asked the men if they would be willing to transfer their loyalties from him to the provisional government formed in Rome after the pope departed, which would finally enable them to receive a regular salary to provide for their families. As a regiment, they agreed to become the fighting force of Roman unification, and so they began the journey to a new home many of them had never seen.

On December 8, they reached Cesena, near the Adriatic Coast some two hundred miles from Rome. There, they received word that in Rome, the government had accepted their offer and the townspeople awaited them with enthusiasm. Giuseppe, Aguyar, Livraghi, and Colonel Angelo Masina—who had become a new leader among them by bringing a battalion of cavalrymen to the Legion—headed for Rome to sign the papers and scout out the situation in the city.

At his first stop along the way, Giuseppe made sure to purchase rosary beads to send home to his mother because he would not be there for Christmas. Then he sent a message to Anita, asking her to come to Rome with the children.

When he finally arrived in Rome, he entered the ancient city still in awe, just as he had as a boy of fifteen. This time he showed Aguyar the ruins of the once-great center of an empire.

They stopped at the Villa Doria Pamphili, near the Porta San Pancrazio, one of the ancient walls of Rome that leads to the ancient road of the Via Aurelia.

"This Rome is a modern city. It is hard to imagine," Giuseppe said, "the time before Innocent X became pope and aspired to a grander and more expansive villa. His changes obliterated what this might have been in ancient times."

"A simpler family farm, perhaps," Aguyar suggested.

Giuseppe pulled a book, Pliny the Elder's *Natural History*, out of his satchel. He had read as many of Pliny's *History* books as he could over his sea voyages. Pliny had been an honored naval commander and author, two things Giuseppe hoped to accomplish himself. Covering topics such as astronomy, mathematics, geography, anthropology, zoology, botany, and more, the collection had grown to thirty-seven books before Pliny died while attempting to rescue, by ship, a friend and his family from the eruption of Mount Vesuvius.

Looking out over the vastness of the Villa Doria Pamphili, Giuseppe began reading aloud, though he knew much of the book by heart: "'In the whole world, wherever the vault of heaven turns, there is no land so well adorned with all that wins nature's crown as Italy, the ruler and the second mother of the world.'" He looked out across the large expanse of garden and thought quietly for a few minutes. "I want Italians to be Italians again. Like Romans were Romans in Pliny's time. Coming to each other's rescue, no matter the odds."

"I understand now," Aguyar said. "I understand why we're here." Then he turned and walked back to the horses they had left in the garden.

When they reached their hotel, they found a crowd of locals and a guard of honor standing outside. Clearly, word of Giuseppe's approach to the city had spread. Many asked to carry him to the Capitol on their shoulders.

Livraghi laughed at the whole situation. "I am a man with a title and yet it is you they want to worship."

"No," Giuseppe said to them all. "Not while the fight still rages. Not while our fellow Italians cannot lay claim to the whole of their homeland."

Worried by the outpouring of adoration for a man they did not know well, local authorities first made Giuseppe the general of his legion to calm the crowds by giving them what they had been chanting for half the day. Then, in fear of having given him too much power, they elected him Deputy of the Constituent Assembly of the local city of Macerata. He would have to stow away the tools of a soldier as he practiced the tools of a politician.

Chapter 9

1849
ALL ROADS LEAD TO ROME

Within weeks of Christmas, Anita and the children arrived on the daily coach to the city of Rieti. In this town north of Rome, Giuseppe billeted with his legion on the grounds of a local palace. The first day was filled with reunions between Giuseppe and his children, the children and Aguyar, and then the children and all the soldiers who had known them since birth. Along the way, Anita took Communion with Father Bassi, examined the livery stable to see what care the horses were being given, and met the medical staff for the Legion. It wasn't until evening, when the children were put to sleep in the room next to Giuseppe and Anita's in the main house, that the two could finally talk.

"What you have done is a marvel," Anita said.

"But it still needs your touch," Giuseppe said. Even after all this time apart, the couple could finish each other's sentences. "Do you want to see the cavalry drill?"

"I am sure the horses are fine," Anita said. "It's the men I worry about. You have a doctor but no nursing staff."

"Then we shall have one," Giuseppe declared as they drifted off to sleep, finally in each other's arms once again.

Over the next week, Anita organized and recruited nurses from the local Benedictine convent. Bassi facilitated the first meeting between Abbess Heloise and Anita, and they became dear friends and colleagues while creating a field hospital for the camp. Though they were not currently in battle, the men still fought the bacteria that claimed many a soldier on a daily basis: influenza, pneumonia, and malaria.

In the hospital, Anita met Margaret Fuller, an American journalist who had been sent to Italy by the *New York Tribune* in 1846 as its first foreign correspondent. Fuller also found herself offering nursing assistance wherever needed.

"Why fight for a country not your own?" Anita asked as they made the rounds in their wards.

"I suppose that's a question you could be asking yourself," Margaret responded, knowing Anita was Brazilian by birth and accent.

"I am my beloved," Anita said, the response she always gave when asked why she joined this cause so far from her own homeland. "You became involved in this battle before marrying an Italian."

"True," Margaret said. She took a moment to phrase her answer in Italian, because neither spoke the other's native language. As a writer, this task of articulating her thoughts perfectly took more time in her second language. Finally, Margaret said, "There is something of this fight for freedom that hearkens me back to what our founding fathers—and founding mothers—must have felt when they created America. I missed fighting for that great cause, so I can't help but contribute to this one."

Anita invited Margaret to celebrate the holidays with them so Giuseppe could meet her Italian husband, the revolutionary Giovanni Angelo Ossoli, and their beautiful baby boy, Angelino, who was just learning to walk. The Garibaldi children kept the child busy at play while their parents discussed the fast-moving events of the day. Margaret had met Mazzini during his exile in England, shortly after she crossed the Atlantic. A supporter of Mazzini's cause, she met many of his followers, including her husband, a marquis who had been disinherited of both title and monies by his family because of his involvement with Mazzini.

"But why did they not support uniting all Italians?" Giuseppe asked.

"They do not trust revolution," Ossoli said. "As it so often upends in *statu quo res erant ante bellum*."

"In America we've cut that phrase back to the crisp 'status quo,'" Margaret said. "It's one thing I love about the Italian language. The elegance and romance—the musicality of the words."

"And I find English fascinating, as it suits the English people so well by getting straight to the point," Giuseppe said. "I would like to write a book someday."

"You've certainly led a life worthy of telling," Ossoli said. Though it sounded almost too reverent, his sincerity could not be questioned.

"What are you writing now?" Giuseppe asked Margaret, who lit up at the mention of her work.

"A book about the history of the Roman Republic," she said.

"I began it almost the minute I arrived in Florence last year and proposed the idea to my British publisher. Of course, still stung from the loss of the colonies, he rejected it. So, now I have a letter in to my American publisher. While I love my first book, I believe this work may be my most important. It will be something good that may survive my troubled existence."

Giuseppe raised his eyebrows at the tone of Margaret's statement, but Anita gave him that look close couples share that told him not to verbalize his thought. It might make their guest uncomfortable. As the couple took their leave of the Garibaldis' for the evening, Margaret offered Anita a copy of her first book, *Woman in the Nineteenth Century*, as a token of gratitude for their burgeoning new friendship. "I put a good deal of my true self in it, as if—suppose I went away now, then the measure of my footprint would be left on earth," she said, her voice holding yet more melancholy.

Later that evening, Anita clarified things as Giuseppe helped her clear the table.

"Margaret and Giovanni were not able to marry before Angelino was born," Anita said, recognizing this shared experience as why the two women had been drawn to each other.

"But I sense the love they have for each other is as strong as that which I share with you," Giuseppe said, hugging Anita tightly before they headed off to bed.

While Anita, the abbess, and Margaret managed the soldiers' medical care, Giuseppe and Livraghi rode into Rome to attend the National Assembly with the dream of seeing Rome finally declared a republic.

Having a bit more experience with government, Livraghi

warned, "Politics takes longer than battle and requires a different set of talents and strategies."

The morning he departed, Giuseppe pondered how it would feel to finally meet one of his idols, Francesco Domenico Guerrazzi. He had written *The Battle of Benvenuto*, the book Giuseppe had read over and over with his first love, Luisa. In 1848, Guerrazzi had been appointed minister, with some idea of mediating between the reformers and Grand Duke Leopold II of Tuscany. Now he would be in Rome to do just that, and instead of being merely a dreamer, Giuseppe had made himself a participant in these long hoped-for reforms.

"You and he are equals now," Anita reassured him. "You may work in different ways, ways that are mysterious to each other, but you share the same goal. That will be the tie that binds you as friends and colleagues."

"You sound so like . . . like someone I once knew," Giuseppe began, silencing himself before mentioning Luisa's name. This conversation reminded him of the many engaging debates he had held over Guerrazzi's techniques with Luisa so long ago. Though the two young lovers had been separated by the unkindness of her father back then, Giuseppe held a space in his heart for all they had shared.

"You can speak to me of the women in your past," Anita said. "It will help me to know you more."

So Giuseppe told Anita all about Luisa and how her father had married her off while Giuseppe was away at sea. "I feel a bit guilty, because it was Luisa who promised to name my first son Menotti, after reading that beautiful letter he wrote his beloved wife on the eve of his execution," he said.

"No need to ever feel guilty," Anita said. "Menotti is now the name I associate with our beloved son. I feel no jealousy about Luisa, only sadness that she lost the chance to live this life with you. To raise her own Menotti, her own Teresita, her own Ricciotti." She paused. Anita wanted to add Rosita to that list, but could not bring herself to say the lost child's name yet. Nor could Giuseppe. Instead, they held each other in silence.

Finally, on February 9, 1849, Giuseppe convinced the Assembly to declare Rome a republic by delivering the same kind of rousing speech to his constituents that he had learned to make on the battlefield. Many in the Assembly did not want to insult the pope, who had the support of the French, though they wanted to take back control of the Papal States. Likewise, many in the Assembly did not want to send soldiers to defend the Kingdom of the Two Sicilies, which was still fighting the Austrian occupation.

Despite the beginnings of rheumatism, which required him to be carried into the Assembly hall, Giuseppe stood long enough to implore his colleagues to unity. "Sicily's cause and Venice's cause *are* Italy's cause!" he said. "This new Rome of the people *must* send men to fight Italy's only true enemy, Austria. Not because Austria will be on our doorstep once it destroys the north, but because we are, and have always been, brothers."

Giuseppe's words were magnified by Mazzini's arrival from France. He came ready to raise the support needed to defend the nation. "There are not five Italys, or four Italys, or three. There is only one Italy," Mazzini said. "And the destiny of Rome and the destiny of Italy are the destiny of the world."

After the decision to become a republic took hold, Giuseppe joined the Assembly in calling upon Guerrazzi to form a triumvirate to run the provisional government, a choice made because it mimicked the ancient Roman Republic form of government. Giuseppe Mazzoni and Giuseppe Montanelli from Tuscany joined Guerrazzi. Tasked with managing the creation of a constitution to define this new government, the men inevitably clashed. Mazzoni and Montanelli wanted a confederation of Italian states, rather than uniting them all as one nation. What they agreed on included enshrining freedom of the press and abolishing capital punishment, and insisting all religions be practiced freely because the Papal States had only allowed Catholicism or Judaism. To smooth over followers of the pope, they promised his continued right to govern the Catholic Church.

Despite that promise in their constitution, Pope Pius IX—upon hearing word of the new government in the Papal States, which had been his domain—responded from his exile by excommunicating all Assembly members. Giuseppe knew this would be a blow to his mother, but it was something over which he had no power. What Giuseppe could control was his legion, now grown to several thousand, and he feared their courage would soon be called upon by this tentative new republic.

This became more of a reality when, on March 12, 1849, seeking to vindicate his past failures, King Charles Albert broke the armistice he had created with Austria. He called up his Piedmontese army to fight the Austrians, and Giuseppe put his men into extra training sessions in preparation for being called to march to Tuscany. Events began unraveling faster than the leaders in Rome could respond. The Austrians promptly defeated Charles Albert's men in battle at Novara, a city west of Milan, on March 23. The grand duke abdicated his throne in favor of his son, Victor Emmanuel II, in the hope that he might secure better terms from Austria. Then Charles Albert went into exile in Portugal, where he died four months later.

≈

Before Giuseppe moved his men from Rieti to Rome to support the Republic against a rumored French force sent by Louis Napoleon—a force expected to be superior in strength and supplies to the thousand men of the Italian Legion—he and Anita had a long talk.

"It's time," Giuseppe said.

"I know," Anita admitted. "I've known for a long time."

"You must take the children back to my mother," he said. "I don't want them to go any more than you do. We've had so little time to be a family. I promise you, when this is over—"

"Let us make no promises until it is over," Anita interrupted. "For now, we will send the children home. I will stay."

"I'll stay too, father," Menotti said, entering the room.

"Not yet, my son," Giuseppe said. "Your day on the battlefield will come, but you will be a man then."

"And your Mamma and Papà will be proud of you, Meno," Anita said. "But for now I will stay and you will escort your sisters back to safety. That's your job as their oldest brother. I will stay."

It was Giuseppe's turn to interrupt, but he took one look at her face and knew he would lose.

Anita sent the children back to Nicoletta in Nice, then followed Giuseppe to support him in defending the fragile Roman Republic. To better manage the situation, or as a sign of a failing new government, citizens nominated Guerrazzi as dictator on March 27. Two days later, the Assembly appointed Mazzini as a member of a triumvirate of the new republic, though Mazzini soon became the true leader of the government, as he showed good administrative capabilities in social reforms.

Soon enough, the rumor of French aggression proved true.

Envoys from the new government sent to Paris returned with word from the newly elected President Louis Napoleon, who would become Emperor Napoleon III. Because Napoleon had participated in an insurrection against the pope in 1831, the envoys had hoped he would now take their side. But under intense pressure from the French Catholics who had voted for him, Napoleon instead sent troops to restore the pope to power.

A force of eight to ten thousand French troops under General Charles Oudinot quickly followed the envoys. Worse yet, Catholic Spain sent four thousand men to Gaeta to defend the pope in his refuge. A French staff officer rode to Rome to meet Mazzini and demand the new republic allow the pope to return and retake power.

Giuseppe stood with Count Livraghi in the Roman Assembly with his men when Mazzini reported on this message. His heart thrilled to their thunderous shouts of "Guerra! Guerra!"

"We need to answer their call," Mazzini said, approaching Giuseppe. "But in all honesty, no one else wants the responsibility of ordering you and your legion into battle."

"I know," Giuseppe said. "But I also know that you are a man who does not shirk your responsibility."

"Nor do you," Mazzini said. "But we both know the army coming against you is triple the number you command. I do not wish to send men to their deaths."

"Nor do I. That's why we are a volunteer army, fighting for the love of Italy. Any man who chooses to may leave, yet few ever do."

"Even though so many came with you from across the ocean?" Mazzini asked.

"The love of freedom has no borders," Giuseppe said. "Nor should the Italian people any longer."

General Pietro Roselli, commander-in-chief of the Republic's army, which numbered nearly ten thousand, supported the inclusion of Giuseppe's men into his regular army. He offered to turn the Italian Legion into his advance guard, with Giuseppe in command.

"If you will take the charge," Mazzini said.

Count Livraghi almost answered for his friend, but held back. This obligation belonged to Giuseppe and Giuseppe alone.

Giuseppe nodded to Mazzini, his back stiff and straight. "I obey," he said. Then the two men left the Assembly to prepare.

Margaret's dashing husband Giovanni Angelo Ossili joined Giuseppe's legion, as did fifteen-year-old Achille Cantoni, who became part of the military corps nicknamed the Hunters of the Alps. Unexpectedly, a well-known Dutch artist named Jan Philip Koelman also approached Giuseppe one day with a request to volunteer.

"But you are an artist, sir," Giuseppe said. "You should not risk injury to your hands or your eyes. We will have need of your services after we win. Then we shall need statues and paintings dedicated to the fight—for what is a country without art to express its soul?"

"I am also a man," Koelman said, "who believes in independence and unity for this beautiful country. It has nurtured my talents and I owe it my fealty."

Unsure how to argue that point, Giuseppe conceded with an invitation for Koelman to don a red shirt and join the Legion. "You may be a foreigner, but I sense you love this land almost as much as I do—and I was born here."

"Italy may be the land of your birth, but it's the land of my inspiration," Koelman said. "And that is perhaps a more important pull on my heart."

On April 30, 1849, these new men of the new republic's army, fully under Giuseppe's command, marched into battle against the numerically superior French. In preparation, Giuseppe called for the fortification of three villas on the outskirts of Rome, including the Villa Doria Pamphili. Aguyar saw to the task himself, knowing how much these reminders of Rome's ancient prominence meant to Giuseppe. Each villa had walls higher than the Porta San Pancrazio gate, the city wall they had come to defend, so fortifying and occupying those buildings was of primary importance.

Then, to hinder the French troops further, Giuseppe ordered his men to cut down trees and scatter the logs and any other natural obstructions they could find across the road. This would create a hazard for troops accustomed to advancing by marching in lines. While the Villa survived the battle, sadly, the Porta San Pancrazio gate was destroyed by French bombings, as was the prominently sited neighboring Villa Corsini.

Still, Giuseppe's regiment of nearly 2,300 troops including Father Bassie and Count Livraghi, who had become friends, prevailed with the aid of local students. Soon they were joined by the Bersaglieri regiment of the Army of the Kingdom of Sardinia, led by Luciano Manara, who had driven the Austrians from the streets of Milan with new tactics of house-to-house fighting. Then, fighters from the Trastevere district of Rome, a section that had housed an important Jewish center dating to the Middle Ages and was still one of the most multicultural areas, completed Giuseppe's legion.

These men were as fiercely defensive of their homes as Giuseppe was of the whole of Italy. Together, these regiments forced the French back from their invasion, but political considerations infringed on their chance to crush the French.

Mazzini called a hasty meeting with Roselli and Giuseppe, asking him not to follow up their advantage. "It is my fervent hope that our Roman Republic can befriend the French. It is the only way forward," Mazzini said.

"We will hold a higher advantage if we hold the military might," Roselli said.

Mazzini pointed to a letter he had sent to the French diplomat Ferdinand de Lesseps, quoting their very own French constitution: "France respects foreign nationalities. Her might will never be employed against the liberty of any people."

"They do not yet think of us an equal and separate foreign country," Giuseppe said. "They believe us to be a rogue section of their own country, quite the way the English viewed the Americans during their revolution. We have to strike while they are weak, before they regroup."

Yet even as Mazzini ignored Giuseppe's advice, General Oudinot welcomed reinforcements sent by Louis Napoleon and allowed his own men to rest. Thus, the French continued to bombard the city and send troops to weaken the Italians' morale over time, the true purpose of any siege.

Giuseppe and the other Italian commanders continued to counterattack, and by May 19, the French abandoned their positions in the Alban Hills to retreat southeast through Velletri. By now, troops sent by King Ferdinand II of the Kingdom of the Two Sicilies to aid the French had arrived.

Giuseppe's Black Lancers headed the charge against Ferdinand's men but found themselves up against a cavalry that was equally well-trained but better supplied, more numerous, and eager to attack. A pack of enemy riders converged on Giuseppe, riding amidst his men. In the fighting, Giuseppe's horse collapsed and pinned him underneath without his weapon. As enemy riders loomed nearer to trample the leader, the newest of his volunteers, Achille Cantoni, led a charge that repelled them. He dismounted hastily and dragged Giuseppe out from under his wounded horse as other Legion men beat back the attack. Cantoni offered Giuseppe his own horse to ride off the battlefield.

"I can stand," Giuseppe said, marveling that none of his bones had broken.

"We must get you to safety," Cantoni insisted.

"Clearly, with such brave men around me, I will always be safe," Giuseppe said, mounting one of the horses captured from the retreating French. Together they rode back to their troops, who were driving the enemy off into the hills around Velletri. The advance guard held their own for several hours and even managed to push the French back toward Velletri by evening.

Giuseppe desperately wanted to follow up this rout and finish off the invaders. But Roselli, who resented the love Giuseppe's men showed him, arrived on the scene and refused to authorize an attack on the town. Roselli couched it with the excuse that Giuseppe had been reckless. It became clear he had begrudgingly accepted Giuseppe's men, for he needed as many as possible, but he did not believe any of them to be equal to his own disciplined charges.

"Though you call yourselves the Italian Legion, your men do everything in the American fashion," Roselli said condescendingly. "You ride like Americans, and you even groom your own horses, like Americans. I have seen even you, their leader, bending down to clean the ass of a horse. Is this the behavior of Romans?"

"They ride like Americans because many of them are from the Americas," Giuseppe said in defense.

"But they fight like Italians—for Italians, for freedom," Count Livraghi shouted.

"That is all the behavior I require," Giuseppe said. "Now, will you give the order for attack while the enemy is weakest, or shall we lose the town?"

"You may have Mazzini on your side in Rome, but we are not in Rome right now," Roselli said. "Here, I give the commands. If you do not obey, you and all your troops will pay the price of defying orders."

Defeated, Giuseppe returned to grooming his horse. Preparations were made to invade the town come morning. But when it arrived, as Giuseppe had predicted, the town was empty of enemy soldiers. There was no one to fight.

Chapter 10

LOVE, LOSS, AND LEARNING TO LIVE AGAIN

Angry but still committed to the cause, Giuseppe yearned to make his own decisions. The one he could make immediately involved promoting his dear and trusted friend Andrea Aguyar to lieutenant in recognition of his abilities and his willingness to share them with Giuseppe's native country.

"I don't deserve this," Aguyar protested when Giuseppe tendered the promotion.

"You do more than so many others," Giuseppe said. "I only wish I had the power to raise you above my own title for all you have done for me—traveling from Brazil, protecting me and my family. Why, the children love you like a *padrino*."

Together, the two rode back into Rome to face another force of French reinforcements. The siege of Rome had begun. Aguyar was with him. Cantoni was with him. Count Livraghi and Father Bassi were with him. Giovanni Ossili and Jan Philip Koelman were with him. Giuseppe marveled at the loyalty and love men from such differing lands could show for his home country. Then he remembered how Anita, four months pregnant, and Margaret, with a toddler in tow, helped staff a makeshift hospital, though they had not been born in Italy either.

Loyalties among the citizens changed hands daily based on each victory and loss. Those who favored Mazzini's push for diplomacy and negotiation with Napoleon one day would support Giuseppe's push for hard fighting the next. Once again, Giuseppe's instincts proved prescient. On June 1, 1849, General Oudinot warned all French civilians living in Rome to leave before his planned attack on June 4. Giuseppe, Mazzini, and Roselli met to debate their next step.

"There is every chance of success if we push forward audaciously," Giuseppe said to Mazzini, frustrated that he could not find agreement with his former mentor.

"But what will Rome be without a friendship with France?" Mazzini said.

"You think like a politician. I think like a soldier. The French consider themselves at war with us. Now is not the time for talk," Giuseppe said.

"Against these superior forces, I do not believe we can win," Roselli said vehemently.

"We can't win if we wait for them to march into the heart of Rome," Giuseppe insisted. "We need to defend the outer city now!"

While the question remained unresolved, General Roselli, who held rank above Giuseppe, visited the troops billeting at the Villa Doria Pamphili, the key to the outer defense of Rome. He allowed them to stand down until June 4 to be better prepared for the announced assault. On Roselli's orders, Giuseppe and his troops spread out and took up a position on Janiculum Hill to the west of the Tiber River and also covered the east bank of the river. On the evening of June 2, General Oudinot proved Giuseppe right by staging a surprise attack on the Villa, taking it over and claiming all four hundred of the resting troops who did not have time to escape over the walls.

At 3:00 a.m., Aguyar woke Giuseppe with the news.

"The fool!" Giuseppe thought, but there was no time for recriminations nor for showing fear to his men. "Gather the men and have them meet us at Piazza San Pietro immediately."

"What more can you do?" Anita asked. She too had been awakened.

"We can fight," he answered as he began to dress.

Anita also began dressing. "Then it will be a busy day at the hospital," she said. Soon, they had left their lodging with a kiss and a prayer that they would reunite by evening.

No matter how she traveled that day, Anita saw the many women of the city offer housing to the hundreds of soldiers, bring food to those stationed at the barricades, and carry the wounded away from the scene of fighting. At the hospital, Anita found several women wounded from taking part in the fight themselves, either beside husbands, brothers, and sons or in place of those who fell.

She grew tired quickly, though the work seemed no harder to her than it had in the past. Still, she found herself out of breath. Margaret noticed a difference in Anita too.

"You need to rest," Margaret said. "The coming child needs your strength to bring him into this world."

"So long as Giuseppe is out there somewhere, and so long as the wounded keep arriving, I will be here," Anita said.

Among the other women helping at the hospital, Anita worked with Cristina Trivulzio di Belgiojoso, a noblewoman from Milan and her twelve-year-old daughter, Mary. Like both Anita and Margaret, Cristina had this child out of wedlock, an act that scandalized her upper-class society. So, the three older women bonded over many things, beside witnessing the ongoing carnage caused by the siege. Cristina had been supporting Mazzini with funding from the beginning. Then she used her words by publishing articles describing the Italian struggle for independence in French magazines, such as the influential *Revue des Deux Mondes*. Now she offered her hands-on support.

"Money is cold," she told Anita. "Hands are warm." Cristina laid her hand on Anita's arm to demonstrate that warmth, only to find Anita radiating her own heat.

"Have you a fever?" Cristina asked.

"It's nothing," Anita said. "Carrying a child always warms me up." She changed the subject by asking Mary to care for the random children who were appearing at the hospital, lost and wounded and unsure if their parents had died.

"Thank you for giving my daughter some way to contribute," Cristina said to the request. When Mary left, the noblewoman confessed to Anita and Margaret, "It is better she see to the children and not to the carnage this war creates of all these men, who were once someone's babies."

"Sometimes the saddest work is not the nursing, but the lying," Anita said. "Telling men who won't see tomorrow's sunrise that they are fine is the work of the many mothers who cannot be here with their sons."

"Or of the many wives who cannot be here with their husbands," Cristina said.

"Or of the poets," Margaret added.

Anita nodded and said, "Sadly, there is poetry in telling lies."

"Yes, but shall the angels ever forgive us these lies?" Cristina asked.

"For him whose striving never ceases, we can provide redemption," Margaret said.

Cristina thought she recognized the quote. "Faust?"

"Exactly!" Margaret said. Then she saw a sadness pass over Anita's face.

Anita noticed the question come into her friends' eyes and quickly clarified, "You are both so well educated and well read, as is my Giuseppe. Sometimes . . ." She faded off and focused on rolling a bandage.

"Sometimes," Margaret said, picking up the thread of the conversation, "people who are marvelous do not require formal education."

Anita smiled at the kindness she had found among such elite women.

As the day wore on, the hospital provided the most up-to-date news of the fighting, which had spread from Villa Doria Pamphili to Villa Corsini to Villa del Vascello. Each location changed hands during the day as Giuseppe's men fought with more passion and fewer rations and the French fought with more fresh rations and weaponry. Working within the regular army, Giuseppe relied on Roselli's instructions. As before, the general tenaciously refused to permit the Italian Legion to continue certain battles. Each such pause resulted in the French receiving reinforcements while Giuseppe and his men, typical of those inside a besieged city, worked with whatever was on hand.

Through wounded man after wounded man, word

traveled to Anita of how Giuseppe gave orders from the center of the battlefield as he raced between sets of his soldiers astride his horse. Aguyar was always right beside him, making sure the orders were carried through. Over six thousand men fought valiantly that day against the sixteen thousand sent by the French.

That night, Giuseppe and Anita returned to base camp and talked of the future.

"Can you win against such a force?" Anita asked earnestly.

"Perhaps not," Giuseppe said. "But what I have seen in the faces of the men today, men who volunteer and could leave at any time but do not—what I have seen is a love of country and a dedication to destiny that surpasses even my own."

"That means no matter what happens in this battle," Anita said, "someday there will be a unified Italy for our children."

"And for the children of all the men who fought today," Giuseppe said.

"And all the men who died today," Anita concluded, content that they were once again united under this roof, albeit temporarily. "I hope all who do not make it to the end of this struggle know they contributed to the dream others will enjoy."

The morning of June 4 broke with the French troops destroying some ancient aqueducts to inhibit the city's water supply, then firing a barrage of shells into its most densely populated areas. After listening to a newly appointed officer suggest a frontal attack, Giuseppe found himself instead agreeing with Roselli. Having lost so many officers to the earlier surprise attack, Giuseppe's style of guerilla fighting was no longer practical. Instead, they kept on the defense and rested their men whenever they could to try to inflict damage via their own surprise attacks, one on the night of June 11 and another on June 21.

For the latter attack, against his previous stance, Mazzini ordered Giuseppe and his troops to aggressively retake the villas lost to the French. Giuseppe refused—it was a suicide order. "When action holds no possible outcome but annihilation, it makes no sense," he said.

Instead, Giuseppe insisted on trying a tactic from his Brazilian campaign. He offered to lead a thousand troops behind enemy lines to attack from the rear and draw the French out of the city. Roselli vacillated, saying yes then no until he finally quashed the plan.

By June 28 and 29, after much consultation with Count Livraghi, Aguyar, and Luciano Manara, who was now his chief of staff, all that was left to Giuseppe was to take his legion under his own command again, follow his instincts, and use them to defend the Aurelian Walls.

Marching through the city toward Janiculum, wearing their red shirts proudly, the Italian Legion drew cheers from those citizens out in the streets celebrating the Feast of Saints Peter and Paul, one of the greatest feasts of the Catholic calendar. Attendance at mass on such days was a must, and fervent believers braved the streets to reach their local churches. Because the French were passionate Catholics too, fighting to return the pope to Rome, they held their cannon fire the whole day, allowing the citizens to celebrate mass safely and Giuseppe's men to reach their destination.

Giuseppe begged Anita to stay at the home of a private citizen to avoid random fire, but she insisted on reporting to the hospital, this time in the makeshift one set up at the Church of Santa Maria della Scala, about three miles from the Aurelian Walls.

"Margaret will be there, and Cristina," Anita insisted. "How can I not be?" She also knew Santa Maria would be the closest place to the hard fighting Giuseppe was about to engage in and she wanted to be as near as possible. In case.

"We all have our obligations," Aguyar said with a wink to Anita.

So the day passed in relative peace. From the Aurelian Walls, Giuseppe's men watched the local citizenry come out at night carrying torches and dancing in honor of the saints. The women brought some wounded men out to see the festivities and to raise their morale, but all were back inside when, at 2:00 a.m., after a day of respect, the French began their final assault. A combination of infantry, cavalry, and cannon fire descended upon Giuseppe's remaining troops. He ordered a bayonet charge, which retook the Villa Spada, but the French took it back later that day when reinforcements arrived.

In the midst of the day's second battle, while fighting off soldiers via horseback, Giuseppe kept an eye on all the loyal followers around him. Father Bassi, who had brought the Bologna volunteers to Giuseppe on the march to Rome, risked his life many times while tending to the wounded under fire. To keep as close to his priestly vows as possible, he tried not to inflict pain but to alleviate. Giovanni Ossilli fought valiantly, luring French soldiers away from Legion members whenever he could, all the while dodging shells as they dropped from the sky. Count Livraghi seemed to be everywhere, always almost overtaken and somehow always avoiding capture.

Finally, Giuseppe saw the thing a soldier most dreads: Luciano took a bayonet to the chest and fell. Moments later, mere feet away from Giuseppe, a shell landed on Aguyar, his dearest friend. Giuseppe jumped off his horse and cradled Aguyar's gashed head in his lap. "Long live the republics of America . . . and . . . Rome!" Aguyar whispered as Giuseppe carried him into the Church of Santa Maria della Scala.

"Save your strength, my friend," Giuseppe insisted. But when Anita rushed to him and saw Aguyar's eyes, she could not hide the look on her face, flushed from days and nights of working nonstop. "Please, not him too," she pleaded as she washed the blood from Aguyar's face. But there was nothing else any of them could do. Their friend, her countryman, and *padrino* to their children was gone.

Both sides called for a cease-fire to tend to the wounded and bury their dead. Luciano's funeral was held at the church of San Lorenzo in Lucina, and Father Bassi gave the homily and Giuseppe and Count Livraghi served as pallbearers. Luciano's mother begged the Austrian authorities in Vienna for permission to take her son's body home to the family vault in Milan, but to no avail. His body would remain in Rome until many years after the Second Italian War of Independence.

Giuseppe and Anita waited to see what both the French and the new Roman Republic would choose as their next move. Would the French honor the cease-fire and leave the Legion to minister to the wounded, or would they take this opportunity to crush them forever? After their deceit on June 2, no one was sure. Equally unclear was whether the Roman Assembly would send new orders, or new troops.

The answer to the first question came with a request for Giuseppe to speak at the Roman Assembly on June 30. He arrived wearing a dusty uniform, stained in the blood of his fallen men, his sword at his side. The Assembly met in the midst of the cease-fire and debated three options: fully surrender, continue fighting in the streets, or retreat from Rome to continue the resistance from the Apennine Mountains. Naturally, Giuseppe's speech urged them to live to fight another day by continuing the resistance outside the city.

"All further defense across the Tiber would be useless, as the French control the Heights," Giuseppe said. His voice rang loud and clear. "Let us leave Rome with every armed volunteer willing to accompany us! *Dovunque saremo, colà sarà Roma*," he promised. *Wherever we may be, there will be Rome.*

Instead, the Assembly followed Mazzini's advice and negotiated a truce on July 1. The French army entered Rome and reestablished the pope as leader of the Papal States The American Chargé d'Affaires, ambassador John Rowan of Kentucky, offered Giuseppe space on his sloop, docked at the Port of Rome. Instead, Giuseppe withdrew from Rome with four thousand of his troops. A flood of goodbyes followed. Cristina fled, accompanied by her daughter, Mary.

"Where shall you go?" Anita asked.

"To Malta," Cristina said as she and Mary kissed the Garibaldis goodbye. "I have people there, and if it is not safe, we'll move on to Constantinople. Promise me you'll take care of my friend," Cristina beseeched Giuseppe. "Anita is worth a hundred of your soldiers."

"A thousand," Giuseppe agreed. He and Anita watched the mother and daughter mount horses and disappear into the hillside.

Next, Margaret and Giovanni readied to take their leave. "We will return to Margaret's home in the United States," Giovanni said as he kissed Anita goodbye on both cheeks.

"Come with us," Margaret and Giovanni invited as Anita

cradled their eleven-month-old son, Angelo, for perhaps the last time.

"We can't leave now," Giuseppe said. "I can't leave all these men who have followed me so far."

"I understand," Giovanni said, but Margaret seemed less understanding. She hugged Giuseppe stiffly.

"Worry more about your wife," she whispered in his ear. He and Anita watched yet another set of friends disappear, hoping to meet again someday.

On July 12, 1849, the Roman Assembly members broke up. Fearful of retribution, they claimed their right to rule a city they had lost, but left Giuseppe and Roselli in charge of the armies. Mazzini set out for Switzerland by way of Marseille. Count Livraghi joined Giuseppe, his family, and his forces—now hunted by Austrian, French, and Spanish troops—headed for the shelter of Venice. "It's the last beacon of liberty in all of Italy," he said. Anita agreed. They bid goodbye to Rome, knowing somehow that they would once again return. But how and when were questions even Giuseppe could not contemplate.

To travel safely, Anita cut her hair and dressed in the Legion uniform so she would not be conspicuous riding at Giuseppe's side. By then, the men had taken to calling her their American Amazon. But their retreat was scattered and tattered at best, as many of the four thousand men broke rank to return to their own homes and families far afield.

"Cowards!" Anita called as they peeled off from the group.

"Even I can't blame them, my beloved," Giuseppe said sadly. "I feel I have let them all down."

"No," Anita said. "They win nothing for their families by leaving, nothing by giving up their dreams."

The march continued until they reached the Adriatic Sea. In

the middle of this beleaguered escape, with only 250 men still following, Giuseppe requisitioned thirteen small fishing boats in the port of Cesenatico to take his followers to Venice by sea. It took time to talk those cavalry men left among them into leaving their precious horses behind, but haste was the priority. Yet the sight of Anita, lifelong horse trainer that she was, patting her horse goodbye hurt him most.

"All I have given you is a life of leaving," Giuseppe said as she handed the horse off to the head fisherman in exchange for his boat.

Anita laid his hand on her pregnant belly. "What you have given me is a life of love. Menotti. Rosina. Teresita. Ricciotti," Anita said, listing their children. Then she took his hand and headed toward the first boat. "Neither I nor they would have a life without you."

Despite choppy seas, most of the fishermen managed to keep up with Giuseppe's boat, even Count Livraghi who had only sailed for sport and Father Bassi, who had never manned a ship of any kind. They sailed the entire day unobserved from the coast and accompanied, almost escorted, by a school of dolphins that danced in the waters ahead. They made Anita laugh in the midst of her badly concealed pain and Giuseppe loved them the more for it.

Some eighty kilometers from Venice, when night fell and the moon rose, they were spotted by an Austrian brig near a small island on the Comacchio Lagoon. Giuseppe piloted his boat toward the sandbar to make a hard landfall, one he knew the brig could not copy. Few fishermen piloting their own boats chose to ruin them by copying that maneuver; instead, they allowed the Austrians to board and capture more than half the

Legion members left, including the boat carrying Father Bassi and Count Livraghi.

Giuseppe saw all this as he struggled to carry Anita, pregnant with their fifth child and sick from the malaria she had been trying to hide, to shore. Most of his remaining men scattered into the woods, on the run from the Austrians. One man, an infantryman Giuseppe only knew as Leggero, stayed behind to help carry Anita and lay her in a cornfield out of sight. Then Leggero went in search of help. Giuseppe waited for nearly a day with Anita, going in and out of consciousness. He prayed he could take her pain away. She woke when Leggero returned with Colonel Nino Bonnet, who had lost a brother in the siege of Rome and maintained his allegiance to Giuseppe's cause.

"Nino," Anita whispered in welcome.

Giuseppe could barely speak. Looking at the grief in his eyes, Nino realized his leader would not be able to manage alone the loss of so strong a helpmate. He guided what was left of the group, which amounted to Giuseppe and Leggero pulling Anita along in a cart until they reached a different beach on the lagoon.

"You must go," Bonnet said to Giuseppe. "We can get you to Tuscany if we leave now."

"I can't leave her," Giuseppe said. "Not here. Not alone."

"We'll be with her," Nino promised. He stopped himself from saying "until the end." Instead he said, "You can't risk capture."

As Giuseppe attempted to understand Nino's point, Anita, rallying for the last time, woke and pleaded with Giuseppe not to leave her.

"I can't do this alone," she said hoarsely, trying with what strength she had left to hold his arm. Her touch reminded

Giuseppe of the first time the infant Teresita had wrapped her tiny hand around his smallest finger. Struck deeply by the gesture, he instantly understood so many imponderable things: he was soon to lose the love of his life; she would never see her children again; they would never see their mother again; he would have to tell them, if he survived himself. It was almost too much to digest at once—yet he had to or he would fail her in her final moments.

Giuseppe looked at Nino with a face that said he had made up his mind. "You cannot imagine what and how many things Anita has done for me," he said. "I owe her the most immense debt of gratitude and love."

So the two men carried Anita to yet a different boat, but even this boatman was too afraid of capture by the Austrian army, and he stopped far short of the goal. So, Giuseppe and Nino placed Anita on a mattress on a cart they pulled away from the coast.

Reaching refuge at the Ravaglia Farm in Mandriole, Italy, owned by a local Garibaldian follower, they called for a doctor. Over the next couple days, overwhelmed with caring for Anita, Giuseppe barely digested the news that came through a messenger from the city. Louis Napoleon had issued a manifesto asking the reinstalled Pius IX to establish a liberal government. Pius refused, then promised his own set of reforms, claiming them to be to the benefit of his people and not in answer to the French. The rebellion Anita had given her life to had failed.

On the evening of August 4, 1849, at the age of twenty-seven, Anita Garibaldi died holding Giuseppe's hand. She spent her final moments alternating between murmuring "I am my beloved" and "Love the children as I have loved you" as if they were prayers. All Giuseppe could say over and over through his tears, hoping she heard and understood, was "I obey."

Chapter 11

1850
LONELY IN A NEW LIFE IN THE NEW WORLD

Yet another blow came four days later, though word would not come to Giuseppe for several days after that. The papal governor had turned Father Bassi and Count Giovanni Livraghi over to the Austrians for a military tribunal in Bologna.

"I am guilty of no crime save that of being an Italian like yourself," Bassi said in his defense.

Count Livraghi asserted, "I have risked my life for Italy, and your duty is to do good to those who have suffered for her."

The Austrians convicted both men of bearing arms against the state and sentenced them to death and on August 8, 1849. Father Bassi and Count Livraghi were executed by firing squad. While the loss of his beloved Anita and the brutal murder of his friends seemed like the end of the fight for Italian independence, those losses instead fueled the fire of a new generation. Yet it would be ten more years before Giuseppe could return to finish the fight. In the meantime, he had a family to care for and a life to rebuild.

By then, Giuseppe and Leggero had been smuggled out of the area in hunters' clothing after burying Anita in an unmarked grave on the Ravaglia farm. Traveling both on land and on water whenever possible, the two made it to the home of Father Giovanni Verità, a parish priest in Modigliana. Don Verità made it his personal goal to see them safely across the Apennine Mountains via the lesser paths, not likely to be guarded by the Austrian or French armies, though it sometimes required clearing brush to make their way. Leggero worried Giuseppe had sapped his physical strength on the earlier march and his emotional strength at Anita's deathbed, but the vigorous work of chopping through the foliage seemed therapeutic to the newly widowed man.

On the other side of the mountains, they continued traveling through several small towns. Finally, they reached Cala Martina, where a boat aptly named *Madonna dell'Arena* awaited them.

"We've made it," Leggero said, hugging Giuseppe in joy. But he could tell Giuseppe was torn about embarking. "Why are you hesitating?"

"I have known the waters all my life," Giuseppe said. "So I trust them to take me home in safety."

"But," Leggero prodded as he watched Giuseppe stare off into the gulf.

"But these waters," Giuseppe said. "These waters I have not sailed. I do not know if I can trust them." Giuseppe continued staring until, as if from the far back regions of his mind, words long forgotten came to him:

"Old age and youth, manhood and infancy,

Mixed in one mighty torrent did appear,

Some flying from the thing they feared and some

Seeking the object of another's fear."

Leggero looked at Giuseppe questioningly, waiting for his grieving leader to explain. "Percy Shelley drowned in these waters less than thirty years ago after writing those words . . . and nearly losing the love of his life," Giuseppe said.

"I am not the reader you are," Leggero said, gently trying to move Giuseppe toward the boat.

"On the verge of death, Shelley called that poem 'The Triumph of Life,'" Giuseppe said. "Did he know? Do we ever know?"

Leggero nudged Giuseppe forward, but he was still too pensive.

"It is the sea, laughing at me. To travel such waters so soon after . . ." He couldn't yet bring himself to say her name. "It seems ominous."

"But this boat—our boat—is named for the most blessed Madonna," Leggero said, trying to use Giuseppe's poetic mind to sway his movements, but Giuseppe did not move. Leggero did not want to hurt his friend, yet he knew he was the only one who could convince Giuseppe to move. "You promised you would tell the children," he added.

It was the kind of brutal honestly Giuseppe admired. He took one last look back down the coast, toward where he imagined Shelley was as he embarked, never to see land again. But the pull of his children drove Giuseppe forward, and finally he followed Leggero onto the *Madonna*.

With the love of his life gone and his revolution a failed goal,

Garibaldi returned to civilian life to earn money and support his children. But first he had to face them. Menotti was now ten, Teresita five, and Ricciotti three. When he arrived at his family home in Nice, the two oldest ran out to meet him. Nicoletta stood in the doorway holding Ricciotti, who squirmed and squiggled to get free. Giuseppe could tell by the look on her face that she knew everything, but had not told the children.

"That's your job as their father," Nicoletta said to Giuseppe, the first words out of her mouth.

"Papà! Papà!" all three children shouted as Ricciotti broke free of Nicoletta and ran to wrap himself around Giuseppe's left leg. Teresita hugged his other one. Their chorus continued as Giuseppe stood silently, not yet ready to say the words that would end their childhood. Then Teresita looked beyond her father to where his horse stood still, and looked up into his eyes with the question he had dreaded all these days.

"When is Mamma coming?" she asked. Giuseppe held his breath and looked to Nicoletta for help.

"There is nothing to it but to tell the truth," Nicoletta said.

"Mamma is gone. And I must go," Giuseppe said, forcing the words from his lips.

"When will she come?" Teresita asked.

Giuseppe kneeled down in the dirt beside his daughter and hugged her tight. "She has gone to visit the saints in heaven. In fact, I believe they are inviting her to be one of them herself. Won't that be wonderful for her?"

"But when will she come back?" Ricciotti asked.

Before he could drum up the words to explain to his youngest, Teresita used her five-year-old understanding of the world to soothe her little brother.

"She won't," Teresita said with authority. "Saints only send their statues back."

Menotti watched them all quietly. "Why can't we come with you, then?" he asked.

"Because you are safer here," Nicoletta said.

"Your *nonna* is right," Giuseppe said.

"But you're a hero," Menotti insisted. "No one would ever hurt you. All of Italy must love you."

"Not all," Giuseppe said. The tiny corners of his mouth turned up for the first time since Ravenna. *If only children ran the world*, he thought as he hugged them all to him.

So the children remained in safety with Giuseppe's mother as he traveled the regions. He was looking for a city that would allow him to settle, but most local governors feared his presence would escalate tensions with Austria or France. As Giuseppe traveled, he found himself taking Margaret Fuller's advice and writing his memoirs. He had learned that newspapers in England and the United States were spreading his story far and wide, and he hoped a publisher would pay for his story. For this he had precedent; Giovanni Battista Cuneo, his old friend from Montevideo who now lived in Turin, had published a biography of Giuseppe in 1850. Likewise, Cristina Belgiojoso—who was now traveling through Syria, Lebanon, and Palestine—published an account of the Roman Republic and its fall in the French magazine *Le National*. Finally, that same year, Alexandre Dumas published *Montevideo, or the new Troy*, a historical novel about the Uruguayan Civil War that focused largely on Giuseppe. Clearly, Giuseppe's story proved popular.

So he sent his manuscript to Francesco Carpanetto, a wealthy Italian in Tangier. But Carpanetto felt only a sensational version of the most recent events would be worth publishing and Giuseppe was not ready to recount that last year with all its losses. Still interested in helping Giuseppe find work, Carpanetto financed a merchant ship for Giuseppe to command. Soon, the widowed Giuseppe had returned to a life at sea, sailing to New York City to oversee the building of the ship and to hopefully come to grips with his grief.

New York City in 1850 was a hodgepodge of some seven hundred thousand peoples from all over the world. Giuseppe silently thanked Nicoletta every day for making him read the poems of Percy Shelley in English as a child, for it made his transition easier. He watched many other immigrants struggle with communicating in such a strange language. If anything, despite the accent he carried, his command of the language showed off his education, which helped some people accept him more easily than others of his countrymen.

On news of his impending arrival on June 30, 1850, a committee of Italian immigrants who had read those other biographies planned a great welcome. When word came to Giuseppe aboard the ship, he asked that his arrival not create such a scene, as he felt his life mission was yet unfinished. "I am lamenting the overturning of my country's liberty," he wrote, and was planning only to "follow a career that will allow me to earn my living and await a more favorable occasion to free my country."

Times were tumultuous in this new world. President Zachary Taylor, himself a general and hero of the Mexican-American

War, would die only a couple weeks later, on July 9, leaving Vice President Millard Fillmore to ascend to the presidency. A lack of medical consensus as to the death lead to rumors that Taylor was poisoned by pro-slavery Southerners, though Taylor himself was a Kentuckian slaveholder. But he had made preserving the Union one of his campaign promises, which angered the South. The American Civil War was another decade away.

Rather than a formal welcome, a group of supporters met Giuseppe at the dock. Even surrounded by so many countrymen, he still felt alone. While many other authors held readers in awe of his activities, Giuseppe felt himself far from his children and separated from Anita forever.

"Thank God for friends," his new employer, Antonio Meucci, said as they clinked glasses at Antonio's home one night. "*Cent'anni*!"

"Why would any man want one hundred years?" Giuseppe asked.

"It's a saying, my friend," Antonio explained. "All it means is God is not finished with you yet."

"Italy is finished with me," Giuseppe said.

"Not yet, I think," Antonio said. He was a strong believer in Italian unification, even though he had been living abroad for fifteen years, first in Havana, Cuba, and only recently here on Staten Island. A trained engineer from the Florence Academy of Fine Arts, Antonio supported himself as an inventor; his wife, Esterre Mochi, designed costumes for stage plays.

"Things take time," Esterre said, pouring more wine into their glasses. "Look at my Antonio. He began as a stagehand and now, because he likes to solve problems—"

"And I didn't give up," Antonio said.

"He is the inventor he was meant to be," Esterre finished proudly.

"And an investor," Antonio added.

It was all true. So far, Antonio's inventions included a system for water purification and an electromagnetic voice transmission able to send sound through wires, though he would lose the patent for his telephone years later to Alexander Graham Bell. As far as finances, Antonio's investments in Cuba did so well that Antonio already owned the first tallow candle factory in America, though he had moved to New York just two months before Giuseppe. Such a business allowed him to employ several Italian exiles, including Giuseppe, who needed work because Carpanetto's funds had not yet come through and the promised ship had not yet been built. In the factory, Giuseppe learned a new form of toil and shared in the immigrant experience that would define America.

Meanwhile, while Carpanetto's promise of publishing faded, Antonio continued to raise funds to support Italian unification. To Antonio, Giuseppe's arrival in New York was a sign.

"Now, with the champion of liberty of both hemispheres here at my side, I can raise yet more funds for the unification of Italy," Antonio said, raising his glass again.

"You seem to think the dream is not dead," Giuseppe said.

"You think it too," Antonio said.

"You just need time to rest," Esterre said.

To that end, Antonio and Esterre asked Giuseppe to live with them while he worked at the factory, and to participate in dinners meant to add to their fundraising. They even arranged an evening at the opera to see a performance of Giuseppe Verdi's *Nabucco*. They were joined that night by Giuseppe's older brother, Angelo, who now lived in Philadelphia. Angelo had become a counsel for the Kingdom of Sardinia. The two brothers had not spoken in a while and Giuseppe thought Angelo disapproved of his actions, as Angelo had grown into a diplomat and Giuseppe into a general.

Business brought Angelo to New York, and Antonio and Esterre brought them both to the opera house. There, they heard "Va, Pensiero" performed professionally for the first time. The lyrics brought tears to their eyes as they sang along:

Go, thought, on wings of gold;
go settle upon the slopes and the hills,
where, soft and mild, the sweet airs
of our native land smell fragrant!

As the music died down, Angelo whispered to Giuseppe, "I hope you understand. I work for the future of Italy too, just in a different way."

"You each have separate talents," Antonio said. "By uniting them, you will unite Italy."

"As long as we have your talents as well," Giuseppe said. "I have found that money is necessary to the success of an army or a country. Even Napoleon knew the world is governed by its belly."

"At least all that reading you've done has taught you something," Antonio teased.

"Funny how the reader became the general and the athlete became the diplomat," Giuseppe said. For a moment, it was as if they were back on the beach with their mother, chasing the waves of their childhood.

Over the next weeks, many things became clearer to

Giuseppe. Tensions were rising in the United States—things such as the 1850 Fugitive Slave Act passed Congress and provided for the return of slaves brought to free states. This angered Northern abolitionists but did not completely placate Southern slaveholders. Giuseppe knew he would have to decide if he should use his talents to help preserve the union of these two factions, or find a way home—yet his exile seemed destined to keep him from home.

Working in the candle factory was a gift from Antonio, but Giuseppe missed the life of the sea. He often wandered down to the docks and offered to help mend sails for the chance to borrow a boat for fishing or hunting ducks. On his way, he would encounter other expatriates sure he was resting for another chance at uniting Italy when he himself was still unsure.

In their evening gatherings, Antonio and Esterre and the other expatriates kept assuring Giuseppe their dream of a unified Italy was not lost. Finally, though, it was Pope Pius IX who helped Giuseppe understand, even from so far away, that he had effected change. Giuseppe read that Pius IX had officially reformed the governmental structure of the Papal States and its finances on October 28.

"It means that if those things could change, then other things can too," Giuseppe said over coffee with Antonio and Esterre one morning.

"Meaning the cause has not yet died," Antonio said.

"Meaning I need to find my way back to Italy. And that can't be done while working in a factory," Giuseppe said by way of resigning. "I need to win back my original trade. It's the only way to find passage back home. I have to finish what Anita and I started, or else my children have lost their mother for nothing."

Chapter 12

Upon learning of Giuseppe's intent to return to sailing and journey back to Italy, Carpanetto invited Giuseppe along on a ship set to sail to Central America called the *San Giorgio*. Giuseppe traveled under his old pseudonym Giuseppe Pane, so they would not encounter problems due to his fame. On the *San Giorgio*, the men and their crew traveled to Nicaragua, then to Lima, Peru, where the large Italian immigrant population knew and supported Giuseppe's exploits. There, word reached them of the California Gold Rush, and Carpanetto saw an opportunity.

"Men from this area are sailing to San Francisco as fast as they can," Carpanetto said one day over dinner with Giuseppe. "Captains who have managed to return here tell me whole ships lay in dock, stranded by crews who had no intention of serving on the return trip."

"They merely signed on for their own free ride to the gold fields," Giuseppe said. "Not very honorable."

"No," Carpanetto agreed. "But we will turn their dishonor into our opportunity. Whole ships are being sold for impossible discounts just to clear the docks for trading vessels."

True to his word this time, Carpanetto joined forces with several Italian exiles who had done well at business in Peru. Together, the men purchased a ship from the dock in San Francisco and Giuseppe returned to the sea, though on this first trip he and his cargo headed not to Italy, but back to Lima.

"It seems I must take the long way around once again," Giuseppe joked to his first mate.

"What matters the path as long as you arrive?" the mate said. "You can't punch your way into heaven. We all have to take the long route."

"You spout proverbs like my mother," Giuseppe said, remembering all the times he had listened to Nicoletta. He wondered how she and his children were faring on their own back home in Nice.

Any thoughts of his children naturally brought about pain. This manifested most when, in his travels in South America, he came to meet the exiled Manuela Sáenz, who couldn't help but remind him of his lost Anita. Like Anita, Manuela had left the husband she had been forced to marry when she fell in love with Símon Bolívar, a man known as El Libertador for having helped liberate Venezuela, Bolivia, Colombia, Ecuador, Peru, and Panama from the Spanish Empire. Manuela aided the revolution early on by gathering information from military officers she met at parties and by secretly distributing pro-revolution leaflets.

More famously, she had saved Símon's life during the September Conspiracy of 1828.

Giuseppe found Manuela living as an outcast in northern Peru, because those in power in her home country of Ecuador had revoked her passport due to her earlier revolutionary activities. The two shared tea and war stories one afternoon.

"But how did you save Símon?" Giuseppe asked.

"I was checking on bread rising in the kitchen when the assassins snuck in," she said as she expertly rolled him another cigar. Since her exile, she had been making ends meet by selling tobacco and translating letters for North American whale hunters who wanted to write to their lovers in Latin America but did not speak Spanish.

"I snuck back into the bedroom, woke him up, and told him to flee," she said. "But Símon had such pride in his machismo. He wanted to fight. I told him it would not be a fight among men but among guns, and I had seen the size of their guns. So, he left."

Giuseppe smiled. "So, when they entered your room—"

"I could honestly tell them I had no idea where he was. From that point on, he called me Libertadora del Libertador." Manuela said.

"My friends tell me, like my Anita, you were his protector more than once," Giuseppe said. In her voice, he heard the echo of Anita's.

"True, true. Just a few weeks earlier, my maid told me these same men were plotting to attack Símon at a party—to which I had not been invited." Manuela added the last part delicately. She had never divorced, so she and Símon had never married, for which she was frowned upon in society. Knowing the same was true about Anita too, Manuela felt safe with Giuseppe.

Being a gentleman, he picked up on her point and ignored it in favor of urging her to finish the story. "So, how did you get word to him?" he asked.

"First, I dressed in one of his old military uniforms. But the guard turned me away, so I came back dressed in my maid's work clothes and banged pots and screamed his name until the hostess begged Símon to come outside, quiet me down, and escort me home. When the assassins arrived . . ."

"He was nowhere to be found," Giuseppe said. "Bravo, Madame Libertadora."

"If only more men understood, as you do, the value of having women in their ranks. In the military, in politics, in all seats of power," Manuela said. She had dedicated the end of her life to the fight for women's rights to property, position, and safety from abuse.

"I can only imagine how far we might have gone if I could have made my Anita the true general she deserved to be," Giuseppe said.

"It is too late for Anita," Manuela said, "but not for her daughters. Or granddaughters. Or great granddaughters, if you work toward such a goal with as much passion as you bring to the goal of unity."

"If unity itself were still possible for my beloved Italy," Giuseppe bemoaned.

"It is," Manuela said. "As long as you remember that not until all women are equal in society will there be true unity."

Manuela sent Giuseppe back to his ship with a box of cigars and her thanks. Recounting her stories that day went a long way toward helping her heal from the loss of Símon. Sadly, physical decline would take Manuela just a few years later when she died in a diphtheria outbreak.

~

Shortly after meeting Manuela, another local Italian merchant and supporter of unification, Pietro Denegri, gave Giuseppe command of his larger ship, the *Carmen*, for a trading voyage across the Pacific. "Each coin we earn funds the future revolution," Pietro had said as the ship set sail. It was to be the first of many voyages to faraway lands.

On January 10, 1852, Giuseppe sailed from Peru for Canton, China. Arriving in April of that year, the widower traveled through Xiamen, an area only opened to foreign trade ten years earlier by a treaty between China and Great Britain at the end of the First Opium War in 1842.

Next, he visited Three Hummock Island, off the south coast of Australia, then traveled to New Zealand. Birds and marine animals Giuseppe had never seen swarmed the port in Otago Harbor. Looking through his binoculars in disbelief, he watched albatrosses fly over the boat and estimated their wingspan at nearly eleven feet. He saw them land on the nearby hillside, where they fed their chicks in huge nests more gently than some people he knew treated their own children.

In the evening, after the crew unloaded the cargo, they stood on deck and watched scores of tiny penguins swim ashore and toddle up another hillside. The scene brought back memories of the lost Rosita as a child. When the tiny creatures dove headfirst into their burrows and began singing as they met the mates they had missed all day, it brought an even lonelier melancholy to Giuseppe. He went back below deck to read and fell into a restless sleep.

While that exotic island had been "found" by Dutch seamen in 1642 and steadily inhabited by more and more Europeans over the decades, the British Parliament had only the year before passed the New Zealand Constitution Act of 1852, which set up a central government with an elected general assembly and six provincial governments.

Visiting the young island nation gave Giuseppe a firsthand view of a nascent government and made him wonder if this system could work once Italy reunited. *If* Italy united. He knew many people still believed in his dream—patriots such as Pietro who were willing to stake their fortunes on that future. And he knew he had never lost the dream, even though it had become buried deep inside him, perhaps because it was so intertwined with the pain of losing Anita. But his mother always used to say, "*Ogni mali nun veni pri nòciri.*"

"Your Sicilian confuses me," said his first mate who had come to check in on Giuseppe.

"Have I spoken aloud my thoughts?" Giuseppe asked.

"Yes," the mate said. "And it's hard enough trying to translate your Italian into Spanish, I can't begin to know how to serve your orders if you speak Sicilian."

"It was an old saying of my mother's," Giuseppe said. "'Not every pain comes to harm you.'" Hearing it out loud again made Giuseppe even more pensive. As he navigated the waters of the Indian Ocean and the South Pacific on his way back to Peru, he pondered whether even this pain was meant to give him the strength to return to the fight.

On the *Carmen's* second voyage, laden with raw copper and wool from Chile, Giuseppe returned to the United States via Cape Horn. Docking in Boston for business, he went on to New York to visit Antonio Meucci and ask his advice about returning to Italy. Instead, he learned some news.

"I am sorry it is I who must tell you, but the letter came six weeks ago," Antonio said. "It was marked urgent, so I opened it hoping it was a business matter for which I could be of service." Giuseppe could tell his friend was hesitating before handing over the letter. "After the loss of your beautiful wife, you have now lost the second dearest woman in a man's life."

The letter was from Giuseppe's younger brother Michele, himself now a sea captain sailing around the Italian Peninsula. Their beloved mother, Nicoletta, had died on March 19, 1852, leaving Giuseppe's children in Michele's care.

The only happy news in the correspondence, something Michele knew would help Giuseppe heal, was about his dear friend and fallen comrade Luciano Manara, leader of the Bersaglieri regiment who had taken a bayonet to the chest at the Battle of Villa Spada. It seemed Manara's mother had been offering continued prayers and supplications. Finally, the Austrian emperor Franz Joseph had granted permission for Luciano's body to be taken and buried at Barzanò, where the Manara family had a villa, so long as the reburial was kept private.

"I must go home to see my children and say a prayer at Luciano's grave," Giuseppe said.

"You must end your legal exile first," Antonio advised. "A father in prison is no father to his children."

"Sometimes I feel like the whole of Italy has been imprisoned for years," Giuseppe said. "Like my father, I have now sailed into many ports. I have studied the governments of many countries. Why can't Italy be whole again?"

"Look at all the arguing it took for this country to grow from English colonies along the coast into what it is today," Antonio said. "Even during America's war against England, not all those who lived here supported the idea. Like them, you need a consensus for unification."

"I thought I had one then," Giuseppe said. "Perhaps I have one now."

"You won't know until you go back," Antonio said. "And that means flooding those still in power with letters of appeal to your exile."

"That could take years," Giuseppe worried.

"Only if we start now," Antonio said with a smile. "But your friends on both these American continents have been in correspondence over this idea for some time. While you were off meeting penguins, we were writing letters. The duke is willing to hear your appeal—in person."

Overjoyed, Giuseppe went to Pietro and resigned his command. Antonio introduced Giuseppe to another Italian who had just come to the States to buy a ship. Giuseppe bought the *Commonwealth* in Baltimore, and left New York for the last time in November 1853, headed for the United Kingdom.

When he arrived on March 21, 1854, he was greeted enthusiastically by local working men and women who had read about his exploits in newspapers and those several rushed biographies that were sold in shops. They presented him with an inscribed sword in thanks for his work for freedom fighters around the world. He soon learned that many of them admired Anita as much as they admired him, a flame Giuseppe fed whenever he could. It felt healing to hear her name uttered with such love and admiration, even by Mazzini, who had been living in exile in England. They had each been following the news from Italy closely and had watched newspaper owner Camillo Benso, Count of Cavour, rise via election to the Parliament that Giuseppe had walked away from. Now, Cavour had reached the pinnacle of politics. On November 4, 1852, Victor Emmanuel II, who had succeeded his father Charles Albert as King of Sardinia three years earlier, entrusted the formation of a government to Cavour. Giuseppe and Manzini felt this was the time to return home and began writing their own letters of appeal. Giuseppe stressed that he needed to return for his children too. The two men talked often of returning to reengage in the revolution.

Buoyed by the hope that all these appeals would sway the hand of the king, Giuseppe stayed in South Shields in England for over a month. Then he departed at the end of April 1854 to sail to Genoa, where his five years of exile ended on May 10, 1854.

Giuseppe immediately traveled to Nice to see his children: fourteen-year-old Menotti, now a man; nine-year-old Teresita; and Ricciotti, who had just turned seven. The three ran to his horse as soon as they heard it riding up the road.

"You came back," Ricciotti said in awe.

"I told you he would," Teresita said.

"But Mamma never did," Ricciotti said firmly.

"I told you," Teresita said, already taking over the nurturing role left behind by Anita and Nicoletta. "Saints only send their statues back."

"Are you saying I am no saint?" Giuseppe teased as he picked her up and swung her around in big circle, just as he had when she was much younger. How much time he had missed with them—regret hung in the air around him. He had nothing to show for all his time away except the beautiful sword from the English supporters. He pulled it out of his pack and handed it to Menotti.

"This was given to me in memory of the sacrifices made by your mother and I," he said. "Now I give it to all of you."

Menotti accepted the gift solemnly as Teresita ran her fingers along the inscription that bore her mother's name. Ricciotti looked on, holding back tears.

Michele appeared in the doorway of their childhood home. "That'll bring a good sum, should they ever need to sell it," he said. Giuseppe could not tell if his brother's tone carried empathy or anger.

After dinner that night, Michele gave Giuseppe one more bit of sad news that had not reached Giuseppe's ship. Their older brother, Angelo, had died. "Happily, mother did not live to see it," Michele said. "She was so proud of his achievements in America."

Again, having not seen his brother in many years, Giuseppe could no longer tell if the man liked him or not. Was the comment meant to insinuate their mother had disliked Giuseppe for all the burdens he laid upon her? He went to bed that night wondering if accepting the sword represented the end of his revolutionary career; if, for his children's future, he ought to lay down roots and begin creating a legacy. When he awoke the next day, he knew that before he could leave again to build a homeland for other Italians, he first had to give his children a home of their own.

Using the financial legacy left by Angelo, Giuseppe purchased half the Italian island of Caprera, north of Sardinia. The island came cheap, as it had been deserted since Roman times. Its only occupants were a revolving collection of shepherds who used the area to graze their goats (*capra* in Italian, hence the name). Giuseppe knew he would feel at home on such a small island, surrounded by the sea and the remains of the many Roman cargo ships found there by current sailors. To establish this as their family home, Giuseppe and the children spent their first weeks building what he dubbed the *casa blanca* in honor of his time in America, and planting their own forest of pinewood trees.

As he helped Teresita pat the ground down around one of the saplings, he smiled. "*A ogni uccello il suo nido è bello*," he said. As in the days of studying with his mother, he asked, "Can you translate that into English?"

The little girl knitted her brows together, thought for a moment, and said, "To every bird, his own nest is beautiful."

"Well done!" he praised her. Then he told her the story of the oak tree his mother used to show him, and of the calandra larks and the crickets it housed.

"She told us that story too," Teresita said with a smile. There and then, Giuseppe planned to create the same kinds of memories on this island for his children while he nurtured a farm that would nurture them. Over the next few years together, they began raising goats for cheese and milk and gradually became the family they had never had the chance to be.

As another step toward healing them all, Giuseppe arranged to have Anita's body moved from Ravenna, where she had been so hastily buried after her death, to the Garibaldi family cemetery in Nice. There, she could lay beside Rosita, the beloved baby daughter they had lost so young.

Chapter 13

1854–1860
SECOND ITALIAN WAR FOR INDEPENDENCE BEGINS

As seemed par for the course of Giuseppe's life (or was he cursed?), he had but these few years of peace and tranquility with his children on Caprera. To keep himself and others working toward a united Italy, Giuseppe spent the evenings writing his first memoir, *The Life of Garibaldi Written by Himself*. He hoped it could aid the friends who were supporting a return to that fight, including Antonio Meucci, to whom he sent the manuscript so that it could be submitted for publication in New York. There were still forces in Italy who would suppress those ideas in order to maintain their territorial power.

Meanwhile, Mazzini had been busy fomenting revolution as well. In 1856, after returning to Genoa, he organized a series of uprisings, none of which succeeded in anything other than earning him a condemnation to death, which could not be carried out once he again escaped the country. In London,

Mazzini started *Pensiero e Azione* (*Thought and Action*), another journal devoted to Young Italy.

With this kind of unrelenting pressure, a Second Italian War of Independence (first called the Austro-Sardinian War) broke out in 1859. This time, the Kingdom of Sardinia, ruled by Victor Emmanuel II and his prime minister, Cavour, sent messengers to Caprera announcing Giuseppe's appointment as a major general in the Sardinian army.

"I did not think to leave you so soon," Giuseppe told the children after he read the letter.

"We can manage, Papà," Menotti assured him. By now, Menotti was nineteen, Teresita fourteen, and Ricciotti twelve. They could tend to the farm on their own.

"We love working with you, but if you give up now . . ." Ricciotti said, his young voice fading away.

"If you give up now," Teresita said, "then Mamma will have died for nothing."

With that new mission in mind, Giuseppe reported for duty, but first he had to recognize the role politics would play in the success of the unification movement. So, he accepted the added political position as deputy for Nice in the Piedmontese Parliament at Turin. In April 1860, he took the floor and vehemently attacked Cavour for several acts of which he disproved. First, in pursuit of France backing Italy against the Austrian occupation, Cavour had sent his cousin, Virginia Oldoini, Countess of Castiglione, and her husband to Napoleon to plead for Italian unity. Instead, the countess had become Napoleon III's mistress and caused a scandal that led her husband to demand a marital separation. Second, and far worse in Giuseppe's eyes, Cavour had betrayed him by ceding his beloved home county of Nice (and Savoy) to Napoleon. Cavour argued it was the only way, but this act angered Giuseppe, turned him against Cavour, and further fueled his desire to succeed at uniting his country this time.

To that end, Giuseppe formed another volunteer unit, again named the Hunters of the Alps. Understanding the importance of raising awareness of their success, he enlisted a photographer to take photos and to spread word of their victories via telegraph so those in other places would stop fighting and accept the unification movement. He then proceeded to win unexpected victories over the Austrians at Varese and Como, two cities of the Lombardy region in Northern Italy.

At the Battle of Varese, Giuseppe and the Hunters occupied the town on the night of May 23, 1859. Despite heavy pouring rain, many inhabitants lined the winding mountain roads as they arrived, shouting, "*Viva Garibaldi! Viva Italia!*" The locals offered the soldiers refuge in their homes and inside the many frescoed chapels along the Via Sacra, which gave the men the feeling that they could prevail. Taken aback by Giuseppe's audacity, the Austrian Field Marshal-Lieutenant Carl Baron Urban sent his division on the march, but it took three days for them to arrive. That delay provided Giuseppe enough time to prepare to defend the town by digging trenches while also resting his men on a rotational schedule.

At dawn on May 26, Urban arrived with superior firepower but was repulsed by a battalion commanded by Giacomo Medici, another by Nicola Ardoino, and yet another by Gaetano Sacchi. By scattering his other battalions around the city, Giuseppe succeeded in convincing Urban that he commanded a larger force, which caused Urban to retreat toward Como, some thirty kilometers away, to await reinforcements. Medici, Ardoino, and Sacchi attacked the retreating Austrians, causing them deeper losses. Then Giuseppe called for his men to continue toward Como as well, despite knowing he had only three thousand men while, if their enemy's reinforcements arrived on time, the Austrians would have nearly eleven thousand soldiers.

In Como, again, a combination of Giuseppe's bold tactics and Urban's mismanagement aided the Italian soldiers. Giuseppe marched his men along the main road toward where Urban had stationed the majority of his forces. Along the way, he insisted they use "Fratelli d'Italia" as their marching chant to announce their presence:

> Let us unite, let us love one another.
> For union and love,
> Reveal to the people the ways of the Lord.
> Let us swear to set free the land of our birth:
> United, by God, who can overcome us?

Giuseppe started the song himself as he rode beside the troops and urged them along. It reminded him of other comrades who had once sung with him but had been silenced by death in the many battles of the past.

In truth, Giuseppe had sent more of his men stealthily through the local hillsides under cover of the chestnut woods and cypress trees. In this way they took control of the hillsides, making Urban's forces both in and on the outskirts of the city and those approaching through the mountain road targets for torrents of fire from the Hunters who overwhelmed the Austrians from on high.

Again the Austrians retreated into Como and Giuseppe followed, aware that on even ground Urban would realize the disparity among their forces. Early on the morning of June 1,

1859, a local priest rode out to Giuseppe's lines to offer information on the movements of the Austrians. Yet while he spoke with Giuseppe, all the general could concentrate on was the beauty of his passenger, Giuseppina Raimondi, who kept her eyes focused demurely in her lap. Being on the march as they were, Giuseppe had no time to learn more than her name before bringing this small army into the battle for Como.

But once the Italians reached Como, they discovered Urban had evacuated the city, having fallen for Giuseppe's strategy to convince Urban he held inferior numbers. Giuseppe not only took the town, but all the stores of weapons and food Urban left behind in haste. Inhabitants of the city came out in droves that night to celebrate the heroes of their independence. He found Giuseppina in the crowd and asked her for a dance. Again, her eyes demurred, but she moved forward and allowed the general to take her in his arms in the mood of celebration.

"I must move on with my men," Giuseppe whispered in her ear as they waltzed. "May I send you letters from the front?"

"Of course, General," she said.

"Call me Giuseppe," he insisted. "And may I address you as *cara* in my letters?"

Agreeing to such an endearment gave Giuseppe hope she might welcome his interest, and perhaps, these many years after the loss of his lovely Anita, there might be love in his life again.

The next morning, however, the two were too soon separated as Giuseppe and his men marched toward Milan to help take that city. They were quickly met by a courier, however, with news that at first seemed exhilarating but quickly became distressing. A fierce battle had already been fought, and the Austrians had retreated out of the entirety of Lombardy.

"Except for the fact that we had no chance to join our

countrymen in this success, this is news to celebrate!" Giuseppe shouted to all his men who had gathered to hear the news.

"It was," the currier said, "until this news came from Villafranca." He handed Giuseppe a dispatch. Scanning the contents, Giuseppe's heart fell.

"What news, General?" his men shouted. "What news?"

Giuseppe could almost not speak the news to this loyal soldiers, yet as their leader he knew he had to. "The Austrians and the French . . . they signed a treaty," he said. A few men raised their fists in the gesture of victory, but Giuseppe motioned them to stop. "The Austrians won."

The men stood silently until one asked, "What's to become of us?"

Giuseppe took a moment to respond. "Rather, we should ask what's to become of Italy," he thought to say, but he could not form the words for perhaps the first time in his life since the day he lost Anita. This day, this news struck the same place in his heart.

Then the words of his only daughter rang in his ears: "If you give up now, then Mamma will have died for nothing." These brought both tears and guilt to him. He felt he had doubly let down his beloved Anita, having lost this battle yet again, and for writing so many love letters to Giuseppina. While his letters carried stories of camp life and his growing love for her, her responses stayed detached but interested, as best befitted a single woman. Later that night, he would write to share his deep feelings of being let down yet again by those in power.

"Would that such a lady could be with me tonight to help take the sting from this loss?" Giuseppe said as he handed the letter to Luigi Cairoli, a cavalry officer who would serve as his messenger, delivering the letter while scouring the local area for more horses and volunteers.

"You are a blessed man, General," Cairoli said, "to have had two such women in your life."

As Cairoli rode off, Giuseppe's mind wandered. Was he blessed to have lost one such wonderful woman? Could he ever hope not to lose another whom he loved? He shook off such fears to focus on learning all he could about what this treaty and this new armistice meant for his cause.

When terms of the treaty became public, those now known as Garibaldini—the men who followed Giuseppe, as well as the townspeople who still celebrated him—knew the fight had not ended. But what form could their protest take if there was no more appointed army and no more official battles? To continue fighting would make them mercenaries, not soldiers. Yet, to end the fight so suddenly when they had come so far seemed wasteful. This question absorbed Giuseppe and his men for a while.

Some small movement forward came when the Piedmontese army needed to defend itself against the armies of the King of Naples. The king threatened the newly formed Central Italian League (comprised of Tuscany, Modena, Parma, and Romagna), which had declared its own freedom. General Manfredo Fanti asked Giuseppe to become his second in command and bring his men to the defense of Romagna, as the King's army was on its way to that region first.

Giuseppe wrote to Giuseppina that he thought this Risorgimento, this resurgence of passion for a united Italy, should be the moment that brought Rome and the Papal States into the Central Italian League. Fanti disagreed vehemently, fearing that would draw Austria back into the fight. This time it took the advice and efforts of King Victor Emmanuel II to persuade Giuseppe that waiting would be the better strategy. "Patience is the better part of valor," the king wrote in a letter requesting Giuseppe to meet with him about his next moves.

"He misquotes Shakespeare," Giuseppe said to Giacomo Medici, who had been with him since the Anzani Battalion. "The king means to say, 'Discretion is the better part of valor.'"

"Perhaps he is not as well read as you," Medici teased. "But even I can read between the lines. The good king means to say we need to save our courage for another day, when we have a better chance at winning. When you meet with him, that is what he will ask."

"But how much longer must we wait?" Giuseppe asked. Neither he nor Medici knew the answer—or that the answer would become known much faster than they imagined. He packed his saddlebags for the trip to see the king.

"You must let us protect Romagna," Giuseppe argued respectfully after being ushered into the king's office and making his ritual bow.

"I would like to," King Victor said, "but in conference with my advisors, even I came to see that an attack on the Papal Territory would invite France back into the fight—or Austria, or both."

"But the people are ripe for revolution now," Giuseppe said, but he was trying to explain this to a man who had never spoken to his subjects the way Giuseppe had when he walked among them during this campaign.

"This plan to push the revolution southward too soon is pure folly," the king said. He came from behind his desk bearing a shotgun, which he handed to Giuseppe. "Take this in gratitude from a great nation in the throes of birth. And I would like to offer you a generalship in my army of the Kingdom of the Two Sicilies."

The king walked back to his desk and dismissed Giuseppe, but Giuseppe did not exit. The king looked at him questioningly.

"I am sorry, my king," Giuseppe said, "but I cannot accept this title, as I do not accept your plan. I will return to my home on Caprera, and to my children. I will do my best for the many men who have followed me across oceans, and we will never stop hoping for the right to free the Italian people."

But life—and love—go on. In October, Giuseppe sent a letter of proposal to Giuseppina and in November she responded yes. So, he traveled to her family home in Fino Mornasco, north of Milan, to ask her father's permission and to arrange the wedding. Giuseppina greeted him with more emotion than had appeared in any of her letters.

"I can't wait until we are wed," she said shyly at their first embrace. Giuseppe agreed that there was no reason to wait. He wanted to bring her home to Caprera to meet his children and see the land they would share together. But that evening in a ride around the villa's lands with her father, he fell from his horse and required a few weeks of recuperation. During that time, Giuseppina and her parents showered him with care and concern, making Giuseppe feel he had finally found a new family to unite with his children back on Caprera. Sadly, Caprera proved too far for them to travel to attend the wedding, and Giuseppina did not want to wait.

"I promise I will love your children," she said one day as she delivered a breakfast tray to Giuseppe. "I will love them as Anita would have loved them."

"You are a treasure," Giuseppe said. "Few women would be comfortable naming their predecessor with such love and honor."

"The name of Anita Garibaldi means much all across Italy," Giuseppina said. "I feel I knew her before I knew you."

As soon as Giuseppe could put weight on his leg again, they wed at the Villa Raimondi on January 24, 1860. Her family's prominence in the region, and Giuseppe's prominence in the minds of so many Italians, drew witnesses to the event as important as the newly elected governor of Como, Lorenzo Valerio, and Count Giulio Porro-Lambertenghi, the son of politician and essayist Luigi Lambertenghi and nephew to a local Cardinal.

When Giuseppina's father passed her hands to Giuseppe before the local parish priest, and before the eyes of all those present, Giuseppe gulped back one last feeling of betraying Anita and turned his heart toward his and Giuseppina's future together. As he stood beside her when she knelt to pray to the statue of the Blessed Virgin Mother, Giuseppe silently vowed to be a good husband and father to any children they would have.

As they left the ceremony and stood in the receiving line to embrace all the guests, one passed a piece of paper into Giuseppe's hand with a look of such sadness that Giuseppe excused himself. He went back into the chapel alone, sat in a pew, and read news that destroyed him perhaps more than that of the Villafranca treaty. He went to the door of the chapel and looked out over the sea of guests still moving through the line. Giuseppina glanced back, saw the stricken look on his face, and excused herself as well.

"Is this true?" Giuseppe choked, showing the letter to his bride.

She didn't even have to read the words scrawled across the page before she nodded slowly and raised her tear-stained face to his. "If I did not marry soon, this child would be born with no claim to land or title . . . or love," she said.

"It is not my child," Giuseppe said. "It can't be."

"It is not," she said. "But it will be now . . . now that we are married."

A fury overcame Giuseppe that he had never known before. Whereas the pain of losing men he had loved on the battlefield had brought tears to his eyes, this pain brought only anger.

Before he could speak, Giuseppina tried to bring him to her side. "You are doing a service to save the child of one of your loyal men. Isn't that the work of a general?" she said. There was no apology in her voice, but the phrase "one of your loyal men" rang in his ears. Giuseppe could not form the words to articulate his anger.

"Who?" he croaked.

"Luigi Cairoli," she said, "of the cavalry." When she spoke the name, her eyes glowed with the emotion Giuseppe now realized she had never truly shown to him. He knew he had the right to make a scene, to rant and rage about how he had been tricked, about how unkind she and her whole family had been to him. But he also knew he was tired.

By now, the guests still standing in the halted receiving line were looking in on the new couple and sensing the emotions on display were not compatible with the occasion. Giuseppe looked at them and back to Giuseppina. Then he simply walked away, leaving Giuseppina to explain things to her father and her guests.

He did not have long to mourn this new loss. In April 1860, he retreated to Caprera, where his children and his farm had some power to soothe him. But due to uprisings in Messina and Palermo in the Kingdom of the Two Sicilies, Giuseppe was needed to gather over a thousand volunteers. This revival of the Redshirts, who would soon come to be known as the Expedition of the Thousand, included some who had been following him from Brazil, as well as others newly invigorated with the fight. One of his newest recruits had even been born in the midst of battle—his son Menotti.

"I cannot be a farmer while my father fights in other men's fields," Menotti said the day he volunteered. "Was I not born to the red shirt? Is it not the legacy of my father and my mother?" So, Giuseppe conceded and allowed his eldest to join the Expedition, openly proud but secretly worried about whether he could survive the loss of someone so connected to Anita and her memory.

He turned his attention back to the true dream of his life.

"If I cannot unite your family . . ." Giuseppe said to Teresita one evening over dinner.

"You can unite my country," Teresita finished. "You can and you will."

"You sound so like your mother," Giuseppe said with a touch of melancholy. If only Anita could see the way their daughter had become a young woman. "I look into her eyes every time I look into yours."

He would unite his country. It was what he had promised Anita and what he now promised her daughter—and her sons. Perhaps it would be enough.

Chapter 14

1860
THE EXPEDITION OF THE THOUSAND LANDS IN SICILY

In the early months of 1860, uprisings in Sicily were occurring on an island that had been home to continuous invasion and foreign ownership from ancient times. Since the time of the Phoenians, Sicily had been invaded and owned by the Carthaginians, the Greeks, the Romans, the Saracens, and the Byzantines. At this point in its history, the Bourbons, a branch of the Spanish royal family, claimed the kingdom under the leadership of Francesco II, who had only been in power less than a year. No one had dared to militarily challenge his father, Ferdinando II, as he had commanded the largest army and navy in the Italian states. The sulfur mines in Sicily and Basilicata kept his military supplied with gunpowder, though the children of the poor mined most of that sulfur.

Had Francesco any foresight, he might have joined with Giuseppe and his revolutionaries, as their goal was never to destroy the monarchy. In fact, Giuseppe believed a superior form of government came from having a king, a prime minister, and a parliament. The Expedition of the Thousand carried the same goal Giuseppe had from the start: unite the country under one such government. Most of the then-kings of Italy did not bother listening to Giuseppe's philosophy, and therefore missed the chance to prosper at his eventual victory.

For now, though, the beginning of 1860 brought a surge of interest in an independent and unified Italy, fueled largely by patriots in Sicily, so Giuseppe heeded their call and headed to the island in hopes of realizing one dream after the failure of his marriage. Mazzini had begged Giuseppe to go to Sicily twice in the past, but Giuseppe had declined each time.

"Why now?" asked Giacomo Medici, who had held commander status in any military organization Giuseppe formed since the Anzani Battalion of the Hunters of the Alps. The evening of May 5, 1860, found the old friends standing in a remote corner of the port in Quarto, Genoa. Beams from the eastern lighthouse circled the waters as the men stared off to sea. Awaiting the arrival of two ships—the *Lombardia* and the *Piemonte*—the men, together with nearly a thousand others, readied themselves to embark on yet another expedition.

"Yes," Menotti, who served as adjutant to Giacomo, said. "Why now, father?"

"Because now the Sicilians have begun their own rebellion," Giuseppe said. "Because they have called for me—for us—to help. Because now they have the spirit to succeed."

"If what Crispi says is true," Giacomo warned.

Newly dedicated to uniting Italy, Francesco Crispi was a journalist and friend to Mazzini who had traveled around Italy under various disguises for months. Twice in the past year he had gone to Sicilian cities, supporting insurrectionist thought and action to make sure the Sicilians would join Giuseppe's forces once they arrived. Then Crispi had helped persuade Giuseppe to gather men and go to Sicily, despite all of them knowing the project was a risky venture.

"I trust Crispi," Giuseppe said.

"Why?" Giacomo asked.

Giuseppe could not articulate why, even to such a friend as Giacomo. It would mean mentioning things better left to the recesses of his mind. Crispi had lost a wife too. The lovely Rosina D'Angelo had died in childbirth ten years before Anita's death. In fact, Rosina died the year Giuseppe and Anita met. There was something about that shared grief that caused Giuseppe to trust Crispi.

Giacomo felt he had to ask a question no one else had broached with their beloved general: "How can one conquer a kingdom with a larger regular army and a more powerful navy, especially when we have been provided only a thousand men— and less than a thousand surplus, possibly useless, guns? Why did Crispi not provide more?"

Overheard by several nearby newcomers to Giuseppe's brigade, the question created murmurs among the men, especially as midnight approached with no ships yet in sight.

"Silence!" Giuseppe ordered. The many men accustomed to his leadership listened; others followed suit, though they were not acquainted with proper soldier etiquette. Half were artisans and common laborers. Many were intellectuals or small urban bourgeois. These various groups participated in the expedition for a variety of reasons. While the original Redshirts were as loyal to the idea of a united Italy as they were to Giuseppe himself, the Sicilian bourgeoisie wanted to free Sicily and make it an independent part of a new Kingdom of Italy. The many farmers among them merely dreamed of fairer land distribution. All wanting to acquit themselves well, they listened. Together, they watched until the shout went up as the first man spotted the oncoming ships. Men quickly clambered aboard a collection of small rowboats donated by local fishermen to take them out to the ships. By morning, the Expedition set sail on the open sea.

Supporters had raised enough money to supply only fifty red shirts as uniforms. Menotti claimed one almost immediately, but most men wore their own plain clothes. Even without the tradition of matching uniforms, the next five days on the Tyrrhenian Sea helped the men form an alliance from the excitement of the cause. Giuseppe tried to join in some of their bonding conversation, but each night his mind went back to the last time he sailed so secretly following a battle. The memory of Anita was never so strong as when his new ships passed by the coastline where, on that miserable night in August 1849, he had watched his beloved die in his arms. It was as if the schools of dolphins that followed the ship mourned with him, for their lonely moans seemed to match his mood.

One night, Menotti joined Giuseppe as he stood near the rails.

"You are thinking of mother," Menotti said.

"Yes," Giuseppe said. "She loved dolphins. A girl of the mountains who never thought she would see the sea . . ."

"I like to hear stories of mother," Menotti said. "It's one of the things I've loved about these men. Many have stories to share."

Giuseppe realized he had not told his children much about their mother. Perhaps the pain had kept him from speaking, but from this point on the father and son spent their evenings in conversation. Telling stories of Anita seemed to bring her back to life for them both.

Giuseppe kept busy by day, organizing the men into eight companies of infantry, artillery, staff men, and scouts. He ordered frequent drills for the men with their new (yet old) rifles and supervised as the artillery commander, Giordano Orsini, taught the men how to cast bullets and manufacture cartridges.

Other passengers, eager to take this ship with Giuseppe, included an Englishwoman named Jessie White, the first female journalist in the empire. Though she had come ostensibly as the wife of a member of Giuseppe's staff, Alberto Mario, her real purpose was to write about the revolution. Giuseppe welcomed her aboard, despite his rule that no women should join this invasion force.

"You made an exception just for me?" Jessie asked.

"In order to succeed, this mission requires aid from other countries," Giuseppe said. "Some who simply believe in freedom and unity, and others who may want only to create problems for the French."

"True," Jessie said. "That is something England has relished dating back to the Battle of Hastings. I promise to write articles that will thrill the hearts—and pry open the purse strings—of my countrymen."

Alberto stood beside his wife with pride. "She is also a trained nurse," he said. White had been the first woman in England to apply to medical schools—multiple ones—only to be turned away each time due to her gender. Instead, she had studied Florence Nightingale's book, published a year earlier, about nursing on the battleground of the Crimean War.

"I hope we shall need more of Jessie's first profession than her second," Giuseppe said.

After five days of sailing south along the western coast of Italy, the Expedition reached the Sicilian port of Marsala on the morning of May 11. Local fisherman saw the boats arrive and, guessing they belonged to Giuseppe based on rumors that had been bandied about for the last month, rowed out to help disembark the Thousand. Soon encampments dotted the landscape.

"The men can only be so ready," Menotti said one night over the rations they shared with Giacomo in Giuseppe's cabin.

"Yes," Giuseppe agreed. "Their rifle skills are what they are. I cannot make them more. But their morale can be fed by feeling they are getting better each time. In the coming battles, morale may be the only weapon we can have in abundance."

"I wondered when you would broach the subject," Giacomo said with a sigh. "Nearly a thousand men against what reports tell me can be—" He could almost not speak the number of royal army men they knew to be stationed in Sicily.

"Nearly twenty-five thousand men," Giuseppe said. "Hence, much depends on the outcome of our first battle. They must feel they are winners from the start."

"How can any man instill such a feeling in another?" Menotti asked. He wanted to learn as much from his father on this expedition as he could.

"By winning," Giuseppe said. "And they will. These men will. I know they will."

"You sound like you are convincing yourself," Giacomo said.

"If I don't believe in them, how can they believe in themselves?" Giuseppe asked.

"Would that it were enough," Giacomo hoped out loud.

Francesco Crispi met the various landing craft, accompanied

by an aide. He and the local municipal board had drawn up a document for Sicily similar to America's Declaration of Independence, but with a different form of government at its core.

"You are to be the dictator of all of Sicily!" Francesco declared solemnly.

Giuseppe immediately read the full document. "This is a title I have never considered, and frankly do not want," he said.

"But it is your title, and needs be in order to bring the locals to our side," the aide said.

"I am not in the habit of taking orders from aides," Giuseppe replied, impressed by the audacity but not wanting to encourage mutiny.

"Excuse him," Francesco said. "He is new to the uniform but quite devoted to the cause."

Giuseppe stared at the aide for a long beat, knowing something was off but not sure what. He focused back on the mission and accepted the title with a sigh. "I will be reigning in the name of Victor Emmanuel II until such a time as this Expedition expels all enemies and the king can safely rule," he said.

Then he sent the men to rest in preparation for the string of battles he knew would be required to take the island. His mind was still perplexed by the young aide's attitude.

Marching through miles of corn fields and under olive trees for the next couple of days, Giuseppe stayed on foot as much as possible—better to engage the men in conversation, to take the lead on singing songs of patriotism and valor, and to keep the mood high in general. It required him to play the part of an indefatigable leader, when in fact all his strength was focused on hiding the limp caused by his increasing rheumatism. At night, he slept under a small covered tent, nothing extravagant, while his army slept in the open surrounding him.

In the hours before sleep, Giuseppe made sure those who could read and write, including Menotti and Jessie, assisted those who could not in writing letters to their families back home in the North of Italy, which was still controlled by others. As much as Giuseppe wanted the men to be proud of their experience and to consider their work a legacy they were leaving for their sons and daughters, he also wanted word of their movements to reach other supporters. To be sure, some of this was designed to keep up the camaraderie and morale, but much of it came from Giuseppe's genuine love for the men who had followed him so far for so long with so little guarantee.

"And so little success," Giuseppe concluded, writing in his own nightly journal. He was trying to erase the melancholy memory of their past failed campaigns in his own mind as much as in the minds of his men.

"This time will be different," Francesco said as they sat around their small campfire, drinking wine offered by locals as they had marched that day.

Almost too tired to speak but not wanting to be found out, Giacomo agreed with a nod.

"It has to be," Giuseppe said. "For them. For me. For Italy."

"For Sicily," added Father Pantaleo, a local Franciscan friar who joined Giuseppe's staff when Giuseppe took the calculated risk of alerting the locals of his approach. As he had hoped, the friar led nearly three thousand peasants, armed with their own older flintlocks and blunderbusses, to join the march. Pantaleo reminded the general of his old friend, Father Bassi, who had once brought more men from the region of Bologna to join Giuseppe's cause. By way of welcome, Giuseppe shared the story of how Bassi had been captured by the Austrians in their dire escape on the Comacchio Lagoon the day Anita died.

"How can I be expected to live up to such a man?" Father Pantaleo asked.

"No one can," Giuseppe said. "I merely wanted to explain to you why your presence both motivates and comforts me on this campaign."

Pantaleo proved to be a gifted storyteller, sharing tales of the ancient Sicilian peoples that soothed not only Giuseppe but also his officers and any of the men who gathered near their fire. The view of the beautiful ancient Temple of Segesta in the distance gave the stories even more strength and power.

"We couldn't ask to fight in a more glorious battlefield than in the shadow of Segesta," Pantaleo said, nodding respectfully to Giuseppe as he continued to mesmerize the group. "In his history of that war, Thucydides, himself a great general of the Peloponnesian War, tells us that a fighting spirit and a yearning to be free began here when the Trojan warriors arrived and laid claim to what belonged to the Elymians. They were one of the three indigenous peoples of Sicily."

"I take it they fought not to lose their land?" Menotti asked.

"If you believe Thucydides," teased Pantaleo. "I have learned in all my reading that history belongs to those who tell it—and Thucydides told it well to his conquering Romans. Yet Virgil told another story in his *Aeneid*, that of King Aegestus, who was said to be the offspring of a maiden named Segesta and the river god Crinisus. And evidence tells yet another."

Pantaleo took a small, hand-carved coin from his pocket and passed it around. "My father gave me this coin, a gift from his own father and I don't know how many fathers before him."

"What does it say?" asked Francesco's aide, once again speaking without permission, against most military custom. "I can tell it's Greek, but that's a language I do not read."

"Despite what the conquerors or poets like Virgil wanted to prove, real evidence tells a different story—that of Greek civilization shown here by this coin, inscribed with Greek characters and bearing the unquestionable influence of Greek art long after the Romans came," Pantaleo said. "It would suggest they were equals for a while. But then the Syracusans took them. And then the Carthaginians. And then the Muslims fled here during the Norman conquest."

"You tell stories like my mother," Giuseppe said, complimenting Pantaleo.

"Stories strengthen faith, and faith fuels life," Pantaleo said. "My poor island needs all the faith and fuel it can get in order to survive and thrive."

Jessie, who attended these evening gatherings with her husband, nodded to Giuseppe. "And it needs a leader to bring it back to its real home," she said. "Sicily was never so safe as when it served as the summer home to the emperors of ancient Rome."

"To unity!" Crispi said, lifting his wine glass.

"*Cent'anni!*" the others said in unison as they clinked glasses.

Four days later, Giuseppe's Expedition proved in their first battle at the nearby town of Calatafimi that belief in and love for country—as well as a fierce bayonet attack—could win out against a superior force. With Giuseppe in the lead, dressed in the red shirt inspired by Anita, his thousand men threw back a three-thousand-strong detachment of Bourbon troops.

The first move that went in their favor was when Giuseppe observed the enemy on the hill using terraces to hide. He quickly discovered that he and his men could use those same terraces as shelter for their advance. So, he ordered a charge against the first line of terraces, took them and then the next line, and the next.

Giuseppe stayed in the lead as often as possible. Morale meant more to him than his own safety.

He admitted only to himself that having Menotti join him was a two-edged sword. He relished seeing his son become a leader, but feared how quickly he could lose him. On one such fearless terrace attack, Giuseppe watched as an enemy soldier captured the Garibaldian flag from one of the thousand and killed him. But Menotti, who was nearby, grabbed it back up. Giuseppe's mood swung from fear and shock as the enemy soldier stabbed wildly at Menotti, wounding his hand, to pride when the youth refused to drop the flag and scrambled onto another terrace. Relief flooded Giuseppe. But he had little time to register any of those emotions, as he battled his own sword fight throughout it all.

"You worry for your son," Francesco's aide said, staring at Giuseppe while engaged in a nearby swordfight. Before Giuseppe could respond, the aide's hat flew off and revealed a mane of long, dark hair.

The shock made Giuseppe's eyes stray a beat too long off his own opponent, who lunged in, but the aide stepped in and parried his thrust. As the two dove behind a terrace to regroup, the aide confessed to being Franceso's wife, Rosalia Montmasson. By disguising herself in men's clothing, she had defied orders that no woman board a ship bound for the battle in Sicily in order to stay with her husband. Giuseppe had been fooled all along.

"I should send you away immediately," Giuseppe said.

"But you won't," Rosalia said. "You can't."

He knew she was right. Something in Rosalia and her determination to aid the man she loved reminded him too much of Anita, and the memory gave him solace in the midst of such chaos.

"You love Francesco this much?" Giuseppe asked.

"I love Italy this much," Rosalia said. With a smile, she retied her hair, replaced her hat, and reentered the fight. Giuseppe was right behind her when Nino Bixio, an officer, rode up on his white horse to warn Giuseppe of incoming soldiers.

"If you die, the campaign is lost!" Bixio shouted. He advocated for retreat, but Giuseppe would have none of it.

"Here we make Italy or die!" Giuseppe shouted as he led yet another group of men toward a terrace.

He continued fighting for so long, he began to entertain Bixio's advice about retreat. But then Giuseppe noticed the Neapolitan enemies had begun throwing stones. "They have run out of ammunition!" he shouted, realizing the changed situation. His men were low in numbers as well, but were reinforced by the many locals who had joined their side of the struggle.

With Pantaleo and his peasants in the mix, this relentless push continued, while on the other side his counterpart, General Landi, a seventy-year-old regular army general, was used to relying far too heavily on his heavy artillery in battle. He had marched his men to Calatafimi, but after hearing rumors that Giuseppe might have more men than expected and feeling he could do more good at his home base in Palermo, Landi opted to retreat without risking losses. This allowed Giuseppe to claim the full victory his men needed to claim in Calatafimi.

"This victory refuels all our men," Francesco said enthusiastically. He looked over the hillside, now free of enemy fire, with the disguised Rosalia once again at his side.

"Not all our men," Giuseppe said. Instead of focusing on the lack of fire on the hillside, he saw only the many dead and wounded men scattered across the landscape. Father Pantaleo moved from man to man, offering last rites. Soldiers helped

Jessie bundle the wounded onto makeshift gurneys or over the backs of those horses that had miraculously survived, preparing to transport them to the city in hopes there would be bandages and comfort. It seemed the prophecy had proven true, and her nursing skills were more in demand than her journalism.

Giuseppe looked in sadness at the many mangled men who had put their trust in him. Rosalia stood beside him and said, "Of course, military victory always comes with a price." She moved to join Father Pantaleo and Jessie in bandaging those wounds she could and comforting those whom she knew would not survive the night.

"I am growing tired of paying that price with the blood of men who consider themselves my brothers," Giuseppe said to Francesco, who was looking at Rosalia with pride mixed with fear for her safety. Giuseppe couldn't help thinking yet again of Anita. "Not to mention the blood of our women."

Francesco understood Giuseppe now knew his and Rosalia's secret. "Aren't we all Italians?" he asked. "Don't we all have the right to fight?"

Once they had buried their dead and delivered the wounded to the grateful locals for care, Giuseppe ordered a hidden march through the mountains. Relying on the previous experience of many of the men who had been part of his Hunters of the Alps proved wise, as the victorious men approached Palermo unseen by the enemy. Still clad in torn and bloodied clothing, with many sporting bandages over slowly healing limbs, they marched through a cleansing downpour of rain. Bixio urged his battle-weary battalion on with a promise: "We shall soon be in Palermo or in the center of Dante's *Inferno*. You choose!" he said.

To Giuseppe's amazement, almost all the men kept marching, the gleam of success in their eyes. As if a gift from above, their march took them through groves of oranges and olives, planted by the Arabs who had once resided there, which this day fed the Thousand. Giuseppe rode beside them, his poncho soaked through but his spirit soaring.

Chapter 15

1860
THE BATTLE FOR THE HEART OF PALERMO

Without rest, the Thousand arrived in the hills above Monreale, some ten kilometers outside Palermo, on May 19, 1860. Knowing that Landi's forces outnumbered his and would be further filled by those locals who disagreed with his mission, Giuseppe also knew he could not attack the city directly. So, he sent scouts to locate Landi's forces and in doing so discovered that a large contingent already lay in wait at the Cathedral of Monreale.

"To use such a holy place as a site of carnage seems a sin in itself," Father Pantaleo said.

"I'm guessing you know a story about this cathedral too?" Giuseppe asked. After what they had seen of the wounded in Calatafimi, it was important to keep the men's minds focused on things other than the impending battle and its expected losses while he planned their best avenue of attack.

"Of course," Pantaleo said. He looked down into the valley

at the beautiful Norman architecture. "It was dedicated to the Nativity of the Virgin Mary by William II of Sicily. As the story goes, after a long day of hunting, he fell asleep under a carob tree and the Holy Virgin appeared to him in dream. The most holy of all mothers asked him to build a church here in her honor. So, he dug up the tree and found a treasure of golden coins buried in its roots, proving her presence."

As Pantaleo occupied the soldiers billeted in the hills above the city with his stories, Giuseppe talked over strategies with his command team.

"We will need to look like we are attacking at the cathedral," Giuseppe said.

"With 'look' as the key word, yes, General?" Menotti asked.

"Yes," Giuseppe said. "They will expect such an attack, so it must come—but rather than racing down to their location, you will take a company into the hills and rain fire down upon them, forcing their retreat without exposing your men to much return fire."

Menotti accepted the assignment instantly. "Yes, General," he said.

Giuseppe turned to Rosolino Pino, another commander. "Then Pino and I will each take the hills closer to the city as they focus attention on you," Giuseppe said. "Finally, when you rout the men at Monreale, you will circle around to our position and join us. It will appear to Landi that reinforcements have arrived."

Before dawn, however, the opposition unexpectedly went on the offensive rather than the defensive, and attacked Pino's forces relentlessly. As Pino huddled behind a rock to write a quick update for Giuseppe, a bullet took him before he could sign his name. The messenger fled with the note and most of Pino's men followed haphazardly. Missing their leader and wanting to reach

Giuseppe for further instructions, they clambered over rocks and under tree branches in a race away from the city they were supposed to take.

Thanks to the messenger's loyalty to Pino and Giuseppe, Giuseppe received the note and the news on time for him to break camp and bring his remaining men around to the other road leading into Palermo. Along the way, they gathered yet more men with fresh ammunition no matter the age of their firearms, thanks mostly to the work of scouts sent ahead to announce the coming battle and to inspire recruits. One was so successful in the town of Termini that the citizens provided his Thousand with more men, more food, and as many rifles and ammunition as they could smuggle from behind the backs of the enemy officers who thought they were holding the town.

Over camp dinner that night, Menotti brought up a talent his father had been hiding. "The men you sent ahead—they aren't very good as fighters," he said.

"But they are very good at recruiting fighters," Giuseppe said. "It takes many talents to make an army."

"And to make a general," Menotti said.

"Everyone has something to offer and it is your job to find that talent and put it to its best use." During talks like these, Giuseppe remembered how he had felt as a young man on his father's ship, learning about the astrolabe and trying to master his navigational skills. He looked across the fire at his son with an expression only Menotti could recognize.

"You're thinking of mother, aren't you?" Menotti asked.

"Yes," Giuseppe said. "And of my mother and my father and all they taught me."

"Isn't that what we are fighting for in the end? Our heritage?"

"And your future," Giuseppe said.

~

They spent the next nights digging trenches around their new encampment on the summit of the Cozzo di Crasto, a natural fortress against any enemies coming from Palermo. But for all their marching, the Thousand were still some thirteen kilometers away from the city. They had marched in a semicircle to avoid being overtaken by Landi's larger forces but had now arrived at a stronghold—if they could hold it with this ragtag collection of largely untrained soldiers. They knew they couldn't, but they could continue to regroup and retrench. On the evening of May 24, stationed on the Piana dei Greci, Giuseppe succeeded in diverting the enemy enough to allow his men some room to rest.

Scouts reported that Landi and the other army leaders assumed the Thousand had been spent. Giuseppe decided to feed their assumptions by ordering the sick and wounded men to make a visible retreat away from Palermo, dragging five cannons with them. The infantry followed along behind, but when they were out of sight of the city, they doubled back through the woods and pastures until they reunited with other scattered divisions. While Giuseppe had been uniting his army, Landi had depleted his by sending many away from the city on the wild goose chase of Giuseppe's creation. Meanwhile, the bulk of Giuseppe's Thousand, now down by nearly three hundred lost in previous battles, approached Palermo in surprise. In the early hours of May 26, Giuseppe and his officers talked yet more strategy while his men slowly woke from the good night's rest he knew they needed before pouncing on Palermo.

Opinions varied as to where to focus the attack, but scouts pointed to weak defenses at the southeastern gates to the city, which had only two heavy cannons and a few companies of infantry on guard. Then the question turned to timing: Would tomorrow be the right day?

"These men have marched hungry and hunted through these hills," Bixio said. "Many have sailed with us across vast oceans, all for this chance to complete the task they laid at your feet. Need I remind you, you are now dictator of all of Sicily."

"Only so long as need be," Giuseppe said. "I long to pass this title back to men who master politics. I would prefer to master farming or sailing—"

"Or writing about this grand adventure once it is completed," Crispi said.

"So let it be done," Menotti said.

At 6:00 a.m., Giuseppe gave the order for the whole of the Expedition to attack Palermo directly and immediately at Porta Termini, where navy ships from several countries—including England, Hungary, and the United States—were moored merely to watch the drama unfold. Rather than march into town via the road, which would be watched, they opted to descend their mountain hideaway through a rocky gorge and approach Palermo through an olive grove that skirted the grounds of the Castello di Maredolce.

Riding beside Giuseppe, Father Pantaleo looked up at the castle's dome and crossed himself.

"How can such an abandoned old castle count as a church, Father?" Giuseppe asked.

"Though built by a Muslim emir in the days when Arabia owned Sicily," Pantaleo said, "it holds a chapel dedicated to the apostles Filippo and Giacomo. It is to them I offer prayers and homage if they allow us to claim victory today."

"I can't decide if your value to us lies more in your being a man of religion or a man of history," Giuseppe said.

"As long as I am a man of value," Pantaleo said with a smile. Together, they rode in silence, contemplating what the day would bring and how best to use their individual talents to help those venerable saints help them.

Giuseppe's surprise attack seemed to be working until, just around the bend from the city gates, some of the newest Sicilian peasant recruits who were excited by the impending battle shot off their rifles in celebration and thereby announced their approach. The city guards bolted from their positions and began firing into the Thousand. Giuseppe saw some peasants, those not trained or seasoned from past engagements, scatter in fear of actual battle while his most reliable men were picked off by the guards. Chaos was moments away and knew he had to make a move.

Giuseppe rode to the front, shouting "*Avanti!*" so loud that the men behind him took up the cry of "Forward!" The call rippled down to those who had not seen this initial blast of defense and to those more accustomed to the carnage of real warfare. In the closest they could come to unison, squads fell in behind their leader, chanting along with him all the way. In moments, Bixio rode by with his cavalry, hopping low garden walls as if he were in an equestrian contest. When they approached the bridge over the river, the men swarmed it like a school of salmon swimming upstream.

There was no gate at Porta Termini, but the defenders had created a barricade wall out of whatever they could once they realized the Thousand had targeted this entry. The barricade's ramshackle construction allowed Bixio's men, who crossed the bridge first, to begin dismantling it with all speed. Dangerous work, it placed the men in the line of fire from the cannons of Landi's artillery division, and men began to fall. Those left standing continued to attack the wall, knowing it was the only way into the city and that failure meant all the men stacked behind them on the bridge would be wounded if they could not flow into the city and find places to shield themselves from fire.

Again fielding the lesser force, Giuseppe knew he and his men would have to rely on street fighting the enemy, often via one-on-one matches. This proved powerful, however, as they were joined by many local peasants with no military training who helped turn the tide by following the lead of the Thousand. With his soldiers and their new compatriots thus engaged, Giuseppe rode hard through town to establish a command center for the battle. When he arrived at the ancient market Fiera Vecchia just before dawn, he took a moment to relish the place where the earlier fight for independence had flared but extinguished. He promised himself that this time would be different.

Under his feet lay ancient volcanic rock formed into the cobblestones of the roadway, and above him loomed the waters of a city fountain stripped of its decorative statue. Giuseppe had read about how, in the failed uprisings of 1848, citizens had rallied around the statue of a man feeding a snake that had sat in the middle of this piazza fountain. Called *The Genius of Palermo*, it represented an equally ancient superstition of the old Roman religion dating back to the era of Emperor Augustus that dealt with . . .

Giuseppe's thoughts were so scattered, he could barely remember when the question "Where is Father Pantaleo?" flooded his brain. He knew his friend would have a readymade lecture on the subject if he were nearby. Giuseppe took a second to pray for the safety of such a man among the violence of this action.

From Fiera Vecchia, as they had in 1848, citizens gathered to ask how they could help their liberators. Giuseppe told them his men needed food and water and any weapons or ammunition available, and the citizens responded with fervor, though their wares consisted of any such swords and sticks they could lay their hands on. Gisueppe welcomed them all, knowing that taking part in their own liberation made the cause all the more precious and worth defending, even when he and his men would inevitably move on. Those who could not fight began taking the wounded into their homes for safety and care, creating make-shift hospitals. Bixio balked at being dragged off to dress the bullet wounds in his shoulder.

"We need to attack the Royal Palace. Landi and his cowards are harbored there!" Bixio shouted. He was struggling to get free of a local baker attempting to staunch his blood flow and bandage his wound.

"We will, my friend," Giuseppe assured Bixio. "But you will not be with us. What good is a broken Bixio? We need you whole, for this battle is the beginning of the end, not nearly the end itself."

Though Giuseppe's efforts were aided almost immediately by the peasants, the mismanaged strategy of Landi's superior, General Ferdinando Lanza, helped even more so. Threatened, he had ordered his men to now sack the town and burn the homes of anyone who aided the Thousand. If any citizens had hesitated to join Giuseppe's men, their minds changed as their homes burned.

Instead of heading to the Royal Palace, Giuseppe instructed

his senior officers to rendezvous at the Piazza Pretorio, home of the city's now-abandoned municipal buildings. Here he had to put his political hat back on and organize a ruling body that would hold the city when he took the soldiers on to the next battles, as he knew he would have to in order to finally unite south, north, east, and west into one Italy.

Though aides asked if they could help him settle down for the evening, Giuseppe insisted on behaving as he always had. He removed the saddle of his own horse and prepared to use it as a pillow. As he bedded down for the first night of what would become a three-day battle for control of this corner of Sicily, Giuseppe couldn't help but think about Anita.

"She should be here," he mumbled aloud in his exhaustion.

Billeting beside him, Menotti overheard. "Mother?"

"Yes," Giuseppe said. Memories flooded his brain at the sound of his son's voice: the night of Menotti's birth and the fear the accident would harm him; the day of Giuseppe's wedding to Anita; the night of Anita's death and the fear that he would be alone forever. He fell hard asleep wondering if she would be proud of their son or angered that Giuseppe was risking such a precious creation to the capricious nature of war.

This night and for the next few days of May 27 and 28, Giuseppe never slept more than a couple hours at a time between strategizing for the battles scattered across the city, organizing the new government, and fighting.

"But you can't risk being wounded," Bixio insisted, even as he went in and out of his own wounded fever. Jessie and Francesco changed his bandages and kept rags soaked in cool water on his chest and forehead.

"There's no use telling him to stop," Menotti said, though he knew his father would never stand aside while the others fought.

"You can't win this battle alone on one horse with one sword," Father Pantaleo said.

"No," Giuseppe agreed. He sheathed his sword and mounted his horse. "But these men have been following me and fighting with me for as long as we all can remember. Most came out of loyalty to Italy, but many came out of loyalty to me. I can't leave them out there alone."

So, once again, they all followed Giuseppe—except for Bixio, whose fever overtook him and kept him in his makeshift bed during the day's history-changing battle for control of Toledo Street. Because it led to Lanza's and his men's station at the Royal Palace, which was believed to be the place to make their strongest stand, taking the street could take the battle. This time, Giuseppe's men weren't merely fighting hand-to-hand in the street; they were dodging cannonballs. The enemy's warships in the harbor sent a constant barrage of cannon fire into the area, haphazardly cutting down their own men nearly as often as damaging Giuseppe's troops. This chaotic waste of men contributed to Lanza's losses that day, which Giuseppe sensed brought morale down among their opponents.

As the day wore on and Lanza's men stationed around the city lost their individual battles, they retreated to the Royal Palace for safety until some eighteen thousand men collected there. This only made it easier for Giuseppe's smaller force to wear them down. Lanza's forces quickly began running out of ammunition, and food and care for their wounded. They also had no ability to communicate with the warships in the harbor thanks to an ingenious idea resurrected from the last yet lost battle for independence back in 1848: citizens and soldiers strung huge cloths in the sightline between the palace and the ships in port, cutting off their view so the warships had no way of knowing when the palace was in need.

But Lanza wasn't done yet. He sent men to the rooftops to transmit semaphore messages above the cloths via flags. But that system was vulnerable to anyone who understood maritime codes—including Giuseppe and his son, who had known since their early sailing days with their respective fathers.

Giuseppe ordered Menotti to a nearby roof to display a semaphore message for the last battalions stationed at the port and in the local garrison. "Retreat to the palace!" Menotti spelled out in flags over and over again. Lanza's lieutenants took the order as intended and evacuated their areas, marching through back alleys toward the palace. To clear their way, Giuseppe purposefully kept his men from guarding at least one road leading to the palace. Likewise, the squad guarding the local garrison abandoned their posts to follow the nefarious order, allowing the collection of prisoners to break free and join the liberators. While many of those men had been jailed for petty crimes, among them were also some accused of murder and other violent acts. This worried Giuseppe, but there was little he could do to separate them out when all were under fire.

A stalemate stood on the evening of May 28 and further harsh fighting resumed at dawn the next day. Giuseppe determined to take the palace, which meant also taking the cathedral, whose height could be used to bombard the bishop's residence with a barrage of fire. Knowing the damage the loss of the cathedral could cause, Lanza ordered his men to retake it. They did, yet they lost it again hours later. This back and forth tired and mangled the morale of both sides.

Giuseppe called for a meeting with Lanza to offer him a

chance to surrender the city before losing any more men. He waited anxiously for a response. Hours later, a young soldier rode into Giuseppe's encampment at the Piazza Pretorio under a British flag, recognized as neutral by both sides. Giuseppe tore into the letter as his officers anxiously watched.

"Lanza refused to recognize my authority or position," Giuseppe announced.

"He is too strong a man to give up," said Bixio, who was now able to sit. While recuperating from his wounds, he had been handling correspondence for his general.

"Fighting to the end is no real strength," Giuseppe snapped. "Unity is strength. Diversity is strength." The words came back to him from those long ago days lost in study with his mother. "We are always stronger together than apart. Why can't he understand?"

No one had an answer, so Menotti asked the next question on all their minds: "What happens now?"

"The carnage continues," Giuseppe said with a reluctance and melancholy Menotti had never before seen. It worried him. It worried them all, largely because of what they knew but only Jessie could put into words.

"And we are running out of provisions, not just for the wounded men, but for the able-bodied. If they are to recover and have the energy to fight, they all need more to eat," she said.

"But Lanza does not know that," Giuseppe said. "And he mustn't find out, or he will hold out until his reinforcements show up."

"And that will be the end of our advantage," Father Pantaleo said.

"But we *are* low on ammunition," Menotti said.

"Have our men stop firing, stop shooting," Giuseppe ordered. "The quiet will unnerve Lanza."

It was a bold move, but Giuseppe backed it up by sending messengers out to the port to ask for the loan of more ammunition from vessels sympathetic to their cause.

"In case this doesn't work," he said.

But it did. By the morning of May 30, Lanza broke. He not only sent Giuseppe a letter requesting a meeting, but he addressed it to "His Excellency, General Garibaldi."

"Quite a change from his attitude of the other morn," Father Pantaleo said. He almost smirked at the idea of besting a famed general such as Lanza.

But Giuseppe's face still held that touch of melancholy. "It means he's grown tired of watching men die all around him. As have I."

"You should be happy," Bixio said.

So, after these several days of fierce fighting, Lanza was forced to conclude a truce. He immediately left the site of his unprecedented failure, granting Giuseppe dictatorship of the area.

A week later, on June 7, Giuseppe and what men were still ambulatory witnessed two things they could not have imagined a month earlier. First, peasants dragged the statue of *The Genius of Palermo* out of a warehouse and situated it back on display in the Fiera Vecchia, which had since taken name of Piazza Rivoluzione. Then, at Porta Termini, where it all began, Giuseppe sat tall on his horse, dressed in his last—and best—uniform, beside Menotti.

A dozen of the longest serving members of the Thousand, all dressed in the red shirts of Anita's design, flanked the father and son and watched the nearly twenty thousand enemy troops march out of the city. Several other columns of Giuseppe's men had been sent to the city of Catania to clean out any remaining enemy soldiers. Giuseppe could not help but take pride in this long dreamed-of accomplishment, though in his heart he knew winning this one battle was still the beginning of unity, not nearly the end.

"We'll keep fighting, won't we, father?" Menotti asked.

"Yes," Giuseppe said wearily, hanging on to one thought. "Liberty does not fail those who are determined to have it."

Chapter 16

1861

MARCHING FROM MILAZZO TO NAPLES

Giuseppe and the Thousand, now winnowed down to 490 soldiers, rested in Palermo for a few days. Jessie and Rosalia organized the local women into a nursing corps for the wounded while Giuseppe and his officers planned the next move. Politics had intervened again. A series of dispatches from supporters on the mainland informed Giuseppe that King Francis II of the Kingdom of the Two Sicilies did not want to lose Sicily, as it would weaken his hold over Naples, the other half of his territory. Yet the Thousand had proven so successful that Francis's generals did not believe the island could be reconquered. To assuage Giuseppe's followers and keep them out of mainland Italy, King Francis declared the country now a constitutional monarchy, effectively cutting back his own sovereign powers.

"We've made them fear us!" Bixio said with pride. He advocated for crossing the straits at Messina, marching straight to Naples, and taking the whole nation.

"While I agree with you in principle," Giuseppe said, "this latest missive says they have sent troops to halt our passage across the strait."

Francesco said what was weighing on all their minds: "We need more men."

"We always need more men," Father Pantaleo said.

"Ask and ye shall receive," Giuseppe said, handing a letter he had been reading to the priest. Soon, Pantaleo's face broke into a broad smile.

"The Scots?" he said in shock.

"And the Americans," Giuseppe said, handing a different letter to Menotti. "All those letters you wrote, my son, sending word of our movements to the families of our brave men, they traveled much farther than you thought."

True to Giuseppe's hopes, their call for more men had reached followers as far as Scotland and the Americas, where newspapers hungry for sales and newsboys in need of dimes spread Giuseppe's fame as a liberator with every extra edition they could print. Likewise, the South Americans had not forgotten Anita and had been following her husband's and son's progress in detail. Now in the Milazzo harbor sat several ships sent to aid their cause. The *City of Aberdeen* from Scotland, the *Carlo Alberto* from Piedmont, and the *Amazon* from Genoa all arrived stuffed full with new volunteers. Before they could disembark, Giuseppe and a delegation rode to the port to share plans for transporting the men to the mainland for the larger battle he predicted must take place, though its location was still up in the air.

Meanwhile, to hold the island, he arranged to split his army into three columns. The southern column with Bixio in the lead crossed the island heading along the south coast toward Syracuse. Another column continued along the inland roads towards Catania, and Giacomo Medici took the northern column toward Messina using the opposite coast toward Milazzo. Giuseppe knew another battle on Sicily would make the difference between expanding the push for unification or trapping it on the island to starve it out. He hoped to set sail for the mainland before such a battle could take place.

General Bosco of the Bourbon forces had another plan. He and his three thousand men had been sent across the Strait of Messina to hold at bay Giuseppe's volunteer army of less than two thousand, with Medici in the lead, and to keep them from reaching the mainland.

"We have reinforcements too," Menotti told his father when the first scouts of the Sacchi Brigade, the brothers Bortolo and Antonio Marinello, rode up to announce their brigade had landed at Palermo and was on the march to Milazzo.

"How many?" Giuseppe asked.

"Two hundred men led by Gaetano Saachi," Antonio said proudly.

Giuseppe remembered Sacchi had served well in the Hunters of the Alps, then entered the regular Piedmontese army, only to leave it to support this Sicilian rebellion. "I told him the regular army would never suit him," Giuseppe said.

"Nor I," said Antonio with a wink toward Bortolo. Giuseppe wondered what secrets the brothers carried, but there was no time for questions. He immediately put the two to work acting as sentinels because they would know the difference between their own arriving brigade and any enemy soldiers attempting a surprise attack.

On July 20, battle lines were drawn between Bosco's highly trained military force with its cannons and modern rifles and

Giuseppe's men, who started the day with two cannons, a tiny cavalry, and a haphazard mixture of the Thousand and some locals. But this time, many of his locals were trained army men who had finally seen the possibility of a united Italy and had left their posts to join the revolutionaries. Their passion and drive, perhaps even their belief that this was their last chance, propelled them to push Bosco's forces back outside the city.

Still again, Bosco posted two of his eight heavy guns along the beachside road, bombarding Giuseppe's troops and keeping them from advancing. No longer tethered to the stringent rules of warfare, several of Giuseppe's newer men captured one gun. When Bosco ordered his cavalry to retake the lost gun, the power of their charge scattered Giuseppe's foot soldiers. This left Giuseppe, who insisted on riding at the head of his small cavalry, isolated with only one of his aides, Missori. Suddenly, a set of enemy horsemen surrounded them. Missori shot the horse out from under the group's captain, who tried to jump off his horse before it fell. The captain managed to slash at Giuseppe on his way down. Giuseppe parried the attack, then pulled his sabre from his sheath and struck the fatal blow.

Meanwhile, Missori used his revolver to shoot two more riders. Soon, the Marinello brothers rode back in search of the missing general, scaring and scattering the rest of the enemy riders. Bortolo leaped to his general's aid, as did Antonio, but as the younger brother did so, a scene much like what Giuseppe had experienced with Rosalia recurred. Antonio's hat fell off and with it a thick mane of curls flew about her face. In the confusion, Bortolo managed to thrust his sword into the side of the last lingering enemy soldier, thereby freeing the group from their potential captors. They all escaped.

"How many women are hiding among my troops?" Giuseppe

asked as they rode hard toward the sea, where the *Tüköry*, a ten-gun paddle steamer, had deserted the Neapolitan navy and joined their rebel forces. The Marinellos rowed Giuseppe and Missori out to the ship while, with no enemy on which to focus their attention, Giuseppe learned their story.

"Like you and Anita," Bortolo said proudly. "Or Francesco and Rosalia."

Antonio, who could now be called Antonia, nodded. "We even left our daughter home in Genoa with her nana so we could come to your service," she said.

"Why?" Giuseppe asked.

"For the future of our children," Bortolo said. "For the same reason you fight."

"For the same reason Anita died," Antonia said. "We too remember Anita and we love Italy."

While Giuseppe could accustom himself to women in battle, he still could not allow a woman to row his boat, so he took the oar from Antonia and helped Bortolo guide them all to the ship. On board, he kept Antonia's secret and went to work ordering the *Tüköry* to open fire on Bosco's forces, which were now holed up in the castle.

Bosco's losses were considerable and his pleas for reinforcements were ignored, which demoralized his regular army men further. On July 23, instead of reinforcements, the leaders in Naples sent a ship to evacuate Bosco's surviving men and ship them to Messina. They marched out of the area, leaving half their mules, their cannons, their ammunition, and all their horses behind in the castle.

Before allowing his men to enter, Giuseppe and a few of his trusted lieutenants approached the castle carefully. "I would not leave such a prize so easily to my enemy," Giuseppe said.

True enough, Giuseppe detected a trail of gunpowder attached to several detonators under the hay. "We were never meant to gain these supplies," Bixio said. They disarmed the explosives and moved to the outer enclosure, where most of the horses Bosco could not take with him ran wild.

"It will take hours to catch and calm them," Father Pantaleo said.

"Not necessarily," Giuseppe said. He smiled for the first time in a long while and took a leather lasso from his belt. Using skills he'd acquired in South America, he began catching the first few horses. "There are men among us who have traveled with me from Anita's homeland. Have them gather these horses. The rest of the able-bodied men might scavenge for whatever foodstuffs Bosco was so kind as to keep for us."

The new supplies rallied the Thousand and they carried or dragged them as they marched to Messina, taking that city without a fight on July 28. After resting and reorganizing their forces, the Thousand set sail for the mainland on August 18 and 19 in several ships, some commandeered and some that came voluntarily to join the revolution.

Giuseppe arranged for Bortolo and Antonia to share an officer's cabin so the lady could hide her gender for as long as she saw fit.

For the bulk of the voyage, Giuseppe and Menotti stood beside the ship's captain, a scene that reminded Giuseppe of his days aboard the *Santa Reparata* with his own father, but also of his mother and her love of language. He recited from memory:

"Treacherous in calm, and terrible in storm,

Who shall put forth on thee,
Unfathomable Sea?"

"I've never heard that poem," Menotti said. "Did you write it?"

Giuseppe smiled. "No, son. 'Time' belongs to Shelley, a poet who died on the water. Your Nana Nicoletta often read it to me as a child. I think she wanted to warn me off a life at sea like my father."

"*Grazie mille* it didn't work," Menotti said with his own smile.

"True," Giuseppe said. "I trust the sea. I love the sea. It has always soothed me. It has always saved me."

"Now you sound like a poet yourself," Menotti said carefully, always afraid of crossing the boundaries from soldier to son at the wrong time. The captain ignored the comment. Giuseppe said nothing, but he hugged his son for the first time in a long time, regretting as always that Anita would never know how strong and tall he had grown.

On August 19, between 3:00 and 4:00 in the afternoon, their ship landed near Cape Delle Armi, about a league away from the city of Reggio-Calabria on the mainland of Italy. Behind them came the rest of the invading force in whatever manner of small sailing boats they had been able to commandeer from the Messina coast. As the men disembarked, along with three heavy guns, they speedily gained the neighboring heights while under fire from a frigate in the King of Naples's service. Now, four thousand Calabrians joined the Thousand, strengthening Giuseppe's efforts over the next two days. On August 21, 1860,

Mayor Bruno Antonio took to his balcony and proclaimed that Giuseppe's dictatorship had replaced the monarchy of Francis II as the legitimate government of Reggio-Calabria.

Having conquered Sicily and Reggio-Calabria, Giuseppe's progress was met with much celebration as he and his men marched to Naples, the capital of the Kingdom of the Two Sicilies. To take this city would win them both to Giuseppe, who hoped to wed them to Piedmont and create a completed Italy. Well aware of this possibility, and of the fact that the loyalty of his own subjects was stronger for unity than it was for him, King Francis prepared to retreat with his queen, Maria Sophia of Bavaria. The monarchs boarded the *Messagero* and sailed north to Gaeta, halfway between Naples and Rome.

Meanwhile, Giuseppe received a telegram in his camp. "Naples awaits your arrival with the greatest impatience to salute you as the redeemer of Italy," it said.

"Can we trust this, father?" Menotti asked, again dancing between his roles as son and soldier while the others among Giuseppe's advisors split their opinions.

"It could be a trap," Bixio said.

Always more trusting of his fellow man, Father Pantaleo voted to believe the missive. "Someone has to trust someone someday, or nothing will ever change," he said.

Before Giuseppe could decide, what many of the men later defined as a miracle occurred. The local mayor and the commander of Italy's national guard arrived at camp and invited Giuseppe and his men to enter the city to triumphal parades of thanks.

"Many of my men have yet to arrive," Giuseppe said. "Entering the city at less than our number might leave the wrong impression on those garrisons the king left behind to guard his four castles." He was testing them out to weigh the truth of their invitation.

"Some twenty thousand of our loyal men are scattered across the roads and mountains between Calabria and here," Menotti said, agreeing with his father and demonstrating the strength of their army to these unknown men.

"We must wait for them to arrive," Bixio said. "Both for the support we may need and for the honor they deserve as the conquering army."

The mayor countered, pleading that a town without a leader is a recipe for chaos and anarchy. "And you are the only leader they will accept," he said.

That made up Giuseppe's mind. "Naples needs me and I obey."

"But—" Bixio began.

"It is worth the risk to show them we have no fear," Giuseppe said. Slowly, his inner circle came to agree and made preparations for their arrival. The mayor had outfitted a special train to hold as many of the Thousand as could attend at the moment, and soon they were all rolling along the Italian landscape, many seeing the hills of Salerno for the first time. Those who had come all the way from South America marveled at how similar the terrain was, with houses hugging the hillsides and overlooking the sea.

For Giuseppe and Menotti, the vista reminded them of the only home Menotti had ever known on Caprera. Giuseppe recognized the look in his son's eyes as he watched the terrain fly by the window. "You're missing home," he said quietly, so the other officers, many who were singing to pass the time, wouldn't overhear.

"Yes," Menotti said. "I had a letter from Teresita yesterday."

At this, one of the younger officers, Stefano Canzio, looked up from the seat behind them, where he was changing Bixio's bandages. "What does she say?" Stefano asked.

Giuseppe noticed the lilt in the young man's voice and smiled. "Yes, Menotti," he said. "What does our lovely Teresita say?"

"She wants to come help," Menotti said as his eyes ran over Teresita's smooth, Catholic-school cursive. "She has heard of the other women who are helping. Signora White, Signora—"

"And how has she heard these stories?" Giuseppe asked.

Menotti paused. He never knew how to lie to his father. "I wrote to her about them."

"Then tell her to come," Giuseppe said. "We are near the end."

"Soon it will be time for celebrating," Canzio said.

"Or for burying me," Giuseppe said quietly.

"Do not curse yourself," Father Pantaleo piped in as he made the sign of the Cross to counter any bad omens Giuseppe might have conjured. "The mayor assured us that the city wants us. They await our arrival with open arms."

"Nothing is guaranteed in war," Giuseppe said under his breath, so as not to affect the excitement coursing through the train car among the Thousand, many who had been with Giuseppe since South America, who were finally seeing the fruits of their labor near at hand. As the train neared Naples, they were buoyed by the sight of hundreds of local citizens, from fishermen to priests to shepherds to midwives, lining the tracks in welcome.

They disembarked at the equally packed Naples station on September 7 to the citizens of the city hailing Giuseppe as their new leader with chants of "*Viva Italiano! Viva Garibaldi! Viva Liberta!*" They followed his caravan of carriages to Castel Nuovo, a medieval castle that had housed monarchs from its design and construction in 1279 by Alfonso V of Aragon. It now served as a military garrison due to its location. What had turned into a victory parade for a battle not fought had followed Giuseppe and demanded a speech. From the windows of the Castel, Giuseppe happily capitulated, declaring the day holy.

"You have a right to exult in this day, which is the beginning of a new epoch not only for you, but for all of Italy," he said. "It is indeed a glorious day and holy. I thank you for this welcome, not only for myself, but in the name of all Italy, which your aid will render free and united!"

Then he and his Thousand, together with the citizens, celebrated this triumph with a mass at the town's cathedral. Father Pantaleo joined the local priests and gave the homily. It was perhaps the greatest gift his connection to Giuseppe had given him and he relished it, ending by quoting Giuseppe's speech. At this, the general smiled.

The cool, calm feeling that fell over them in the beautiful stone cathedral made many feel the fight was over. The Bourbon troops in the city had been told not to resist the entry of the Thousand, because the citizenry would turn on them in too many numbers to fight. But Giuseppe knew there was more ahead. France would not give up so easily, though for these few moments during the benediction he permitted himself to join in the dream. It provided the rest he needed to face the final battles.

Chapter 17

EQUAL OF A KING

In the end there was only one more battle that mattered. On September 30, 1860, Giuseppe and the Thousand fought the largest battle they had ever fought. The Battle of Volturno, at the Volturno River between Capua and Caserta, finally involved an equal match. Now that Sicily was part of Piedmont, the Piedmontese army joined thirty thousand of Giuseppe's men to fight against nearly that many Neapolitan troops. The Garibaldinis were headed by Giuseppe, joined by Menotti and Bixio. For the enemy Neapolitans, the presence of Francis himself helped force the first retreat. But Giuseppe and Giacomo Medici intervened, reversing the situation.

Defending the road to Maddaloni, Bixio needed the support of two Bersaglieri battalions, which arrived just on time. Together, they took Caserta and lost it within the same day. News came that Naples was under threat of being lost, but Giuseppe's troops rallied and regained both the next day, October 1.

On October 2, the citizens voted for the Kingdom of the

Two Sicilies to join the Sardinia-Piedmont region. All that was left to Giuseppe was to hand the leadership back to his chosen monarch, King Victor Emmanuel II.

Teresita arrived on time to help her father prepare for the momentous occasion. Canzio met her at the train station and brought her immediately to Giuseppe in his tent.

"Thank you, Officer Canzio," Giuseppe said as he helped his daughter from the carriage.

"Yes, sir," Canzio said, but his eyes followed Teresita rather than his general. Giuseppe smiled.

"Perhaps later you can join us for dinner in our tent," Giuseppe said.

Canzio snapped to attention, clearly wanting to take up this invitation. "I would love to, but—" he began.

"I know," Giuseppe said. "The wounded need you more than my daughter and I need your company. Mrs. White would flail me if kept any pair of hands away from helping heal our men."

"I would like to help Mrs. White too," Teresita said.

"Are you sure?" Giuseppe asked. He had seen far too many men mutilated by the rain of rifleshot or the random landing of a cannonball. He wasn't sure she should be exposed to such carnage.

"Yes," Teresita said. "If Officer Canzio will offer to escort me to the hospital—"

"Of course," Canzio said, then apologized for interrupting. Giuseppe sent them both off so he could prepare his remarks for the following day.

The next morning, Teresita helped Giuseppe pull his gray poncho over his head.

"You are lost in thought this morning, Papà," she said as she tied a black scarf around his neck. "Are you thinking of Mamma?"

"Of my Mamma," he said, remembering. "And of yours. And you. I have been sustained by women my entire life. I look into Anita's eyes every time I look into yours. This was to be our shared triumph."

His only surviving daughter kissed him on the cheek. "This day still belongs to both of you," she said.

"'I am my beloved,'" he said. "That's what she said to me." He had never shared Anita's last words with their children. "Now I say it of her. Forever."

The words brought a smile to Teresita's face, brightening his mood as he stepped from the tent and mounted his horse, groomed so meticulously, its coat shined like a mirror. Teresita watched him ride off, then busied herself with organizing his clothing for tomorrow.

Escorted by his most trusted aides, Giuseppe rode to a nearby hillside, arriving first.

"Where's the king?" Menotti asked, eager to be of assistance.

"Even a temporary dictator knows to arrive before a king," Giuseppe answered.

"Etiquette dictates you never keep a king waiting," Father Pantaleo said.

Then a contingent of riders came over the hill to the music of the Royal March. As they parted, King Victor Emmanuel II rode his elegant Arabian horse out from the security of their circle.

Giuseppe approached, taking off his hat and giving a

practiced cavalryman's bow. "Your majesty," Giuseppe said. "I hail the first king of Italy!"

The king nodded, then extended his palm for a handshake.

From their vantage point on the outside of this moment, Father Pantaleo whispered to Menotti, "Such a simple gesture to seal such a historic transfer of power. Would that men could learn that all wars lead to these moments."

"If we skipped the lead-up, then I would have no profession," Menotti whispered.

"Would it be such a loss?" the priest asked.

Giuseppe saw the men's exchange and wondered about the content, but his own moment with the king drew his focus.

"I am told you wear the attire provided by your lost Anita," the king said, looking over Giuseppe's poncho, red shirt, and scarf.

"It keeps her close," Giuseppe said.

"But nothing will bring her back," the king said with a tinge of melancholy. Giuseppe knew the king too had suffered deep loss. Two of his children died in infancy only five or six years earlier, both young boys whom he had hoped would inherit his throne. "Do not fool yourself, my friend. The loss of those so close creates a hole that can never be truly filled."

"Perhaps," Giuseppe agreed half-heartedly. "But I need something still to hope for."

"A new Italy," the king suggested.

"Once we gain Rome," Giuseppe said.

Here, the king's magnanimity reached its peak. "This I will not condone," he said with finality.

Giuseppe knew Rome, still under the Papal States, was under French protection, but he had hoped these recent successes would propel them all forward. It was not to be. Now that he had ceded rule to the king, he had to obey or risk all his men rebelling.

"Then, if you are no longer in need of my services . . ." Giuseppe began.

"The kingdom thanks you. The Italian people thank you. But, yes," the king said, "your service is done."

The king turned his horse toward Naples. Giuseppe rode beside him with his major officers, including Menotti, also side by side with members of the king's army. Equals at last.

To ensure the locals transferred their loyalty from Giuseppe, whom they saw as their leader, to King Victor, the king decided the two men would enter Naples together, which they did despite a horrendous downpour of rain on November 7, 1860. As they rode, they made plans for the disbursement of the Thousand. Those of lowest rank who came from Italy would be sent home with payment for services rendered; those of low to middling ranks who were from elsewhere could either join the king's army or return home; and the officers, men such as Bixio and Medici, could join the regular army with the hope of reaching the rank of general and receiving a generous pension.

"Many of them hoped to form their own regiments, to be available for the coming wars to unite Venice," Giuseppe explained. "And Rome."

"I said we will not advance on Rome," the king said.

"Not now," Giuseppe said. "Now I will retire to my home and family. But you will see the eyes of the people—*your* people. They want a united country. They will find a way to take Rome someday, with or without me."

"Our hold is far too tenuous to risk right now," the king

said. He shared with Giuseppe missives he had been receiving for the last few days. Leading monarchs from Austria, Russia, and Prussia had met in Warsaw to discuss overtaking Italy at its moment of triumph. But the king also had a dispatch from the British Foreign Minister Lord John Russell announcing England's support for an independent Italy.

In Giuseppe's disbelief at such support, he had to read the words aloud to believe them: "'Her Majesty's government must admit that the Italians are the best judges of their own interests.'"

"You and I have known that forever," the king said.

Giuseppe continued, loud enough for the carriage driver to hear. "'Her Majesty's government will turn their eyes to the gratifying prospect of a people building up the edifice of their liberties, and consolidating the work of their independence.'" The carriage driver sat a little higher in his seat as Giuseppe read.

In the following months, the missives kept coming. Even the United States, where he had once been no more than a poor immigrant, showed interest. In December of that year, the *New York Times* hailed the unity of the Italian people and made a point to remind readers that Giuseppe, a Northern Italian, had led his army across the southern regions of his country; as such, the paper had nicknamed his Thousand followers the Yankees of Italy. At a time when America's unity had been torn apart by the issue of slavery, Giuseppe's achievement shared space on the pages of the paper with the unprecedented news that, upon the election of Abraham Lincoln, the state of South Carolina had seceded from the union. South Carolina would shortly be followed by Mississippi, Florida, Alabama, Georgia,

Louisiana, Texas, and Virginia, creating the Confederate States of America.

Yet during the buildup to these destructive moves, many in the United States still had time to raise money to support Italian unity. New Yorkers formed a Million Rifles Fund and contributed an estimated $100,000. Now that he had accepted King Victor's terms for retirement, Giuseppe wrote a public letter to his former friends and neighbors to thank them for all they did.

Giuseppe filled his days with such correspondence—and with the happy planning for the wedding of Teresita and Stefano Canzio. On May 25, 1861, the two wed on Caprera, surrounded by local friends and family. Later, they confirmed their vows for Canzio's relatives in Genoa at the church of La Maddalena, where Teresita received a beautiful jeweled necklace from King Victor in thanks for all she contributed to the kingdom he now ruled.

The final triumph, though Giuseppe turned it down, came from Abraham Lincoln. When Virginia became the last state to secede from the Union, the new president lost his favored choice for general of the Union Army. Then Colonel Robert E. Lee, who had graduated West Point second in his class without ever earning a single demerit, turned down the promotion to general in order to lead the Confederate Army. So, Lincoln offered the position to Giuseppe.

"What an honor," Menotti declared upon receiving the letter. It had arrived from Secretary of State William H. Seward on July 17, 1861.

"But I cannot accept," Giuseppe said.

"Why?" Menotti asked, shocked. "You helped in South America, you helped here at home, why not help the Union? I will go with you. And Ricciotti is ready for such a responsibility."

"Take up your pen and I will tell you as I tell Secretary Seward and President Lincoln," Giuseppe instructed, then he began to dictate. "The only way in which I could render service, as I ardently desire, to the cause of the United States as commander-in-chief of its forces . . ."

Giuseppe thought slowly and deliberately about his declaration and Menotti wrote each word down carefully.

"I could only go with the additional contingent power of declaring the abolition of slavery in the areas of the South that I conquer; I would be of little use without such power, and without such a declaration, the world at large could have little interest or sympathy in your civil war."

"The president will do so immediately," Menotti said, certain.

"Would that politics were that simple," Giuseppe said. "I would have stayed in government, but the constant compromise is not a skill I possess. Lincoln cannot lose any more states to this Confederacy, and so far, not all the slave states have seceded. But if he truly declared slavery as the reason for this war, he would lose them too."

"I agree, politics is not my forte," Menotti said.

"Take another letter, this one to the king," Giuseppe said.

"Why must he know of this offer if you are declining?" Menotti asked.

"I want him to know I stay committed to the full unification of Italy," Giuseppe said.

"Ah, you still hope to take Venice."

"And Rome. I have to believe the king hopes so too," Giuseppe said.

With Lincoln's offer off the table, Giuseppe focused on completing his dream. He had supported King Victor because he believed in the theories of the English philosopher Thomas Hobbes. After reading Hobbes's *Leviathan*, Giuseppe agreed that people thrive best under monarchy.

"Why?" Teresita asked one night over dinner. Now that Canzio was like a son to Giuseppe, they sometimes argued over ideas, which made many dinners more like political meetings.

"Because Signor Hobbes recognized that people are, by nature, selfish," Giuseppe said. "They require a strong leader to keep them in check."

"But John Locke was right to note that people can govern themselves," Canzio responded, supporting his belief in Locke's philosophy that, if provided with the right information, people could make good decisions. It was a debate both men had had in battlefield campgrounds for years.

"You are not likely to settle this over *insalata*," Teresita said as she sat down. "So, eat and talk of nicer things. *Sì*, Menotti?" She roped her brother into the conversation knowing he tried not to take sides.

"Someone has to keep the union in a family always fighting for unity," he said with a smile.

What the men did agree on was that, despite Giuseppe's choice to support King Victor, they were all frustrated at the king for bowing to the desires of the pope and not moving on Rome.

"Italy can never be truly free until the ancient seat of the Empire once again becomes the center of this civilization," Giuseppe declared both publicly and privately whenever he could.

By October, his two sons, Menotti and Ricciotti, helped

create an International Legion out of volunteers from France, Poland, Switzerland, and Germany. The countries all hoped that once Italy was liberated, their own lands would follow suit. Giuseppe's movement was beginning to influence the world in ways he had never imagined.

Chapter 18

By June 1862, Giuseppe found himself aboard yet another war ship. This one was sailing from Genoa to Palermo, gathering volunteers along the way for a campaign he had named *Roma o Morte*. Once again, an enthusiastic set of volunteers quickly joined him, and the ship was soon loaded with over two thousand men.

Reports flew back and forth at every port. Giuseppe's proclamations that Italians would overthrow the pope by military action mobilized French emperor Napoleon III.

"He's stationed a new garrison in Rome," Menotti reported one morning as he and his father walked the deck discussing their troops and deciding which men should lead which regiments. "And the king is making proclamations against anyone who joins any revolutionary activities . . . especially ours."

"King Victor naturally has to show wariness of all possible international repercussions of our actions," Giuseppe said. "In public, at least. But I know in his heart he feels the hole Rome leaves in this union. A man who sent such a beautiful gift to Teresita . . . he was signifying his support of our cause."

Menotti hoped his father was right. But when their ship turned toward Messina, hoping to cross to the mainland via the eastern tip of Sicily, the garrison proved loyal to the king's instructions and barred their advance.

On Menotti's suggestion, the captain turned south and set sail for Catania, where they were received. There, Garibaldi declared to the press, "We will enter Rome as victors, or perish beneath its walls." Yet more volunteers scrambled aboard the ship, and they sailed from the Ionian Sea through the Strait of Messina and into the Tyrrhenian Sea, paralleling Italy's west coast. They landed at Melito, near Naples, on August 14 and marched at once into the Calabrian mountains.

Again Giuseppe's scouts, trained by Menotti, gathered intelligence that the King had ordered General Enrico Cialdini to dispatch a division of the regular army, under Colonel Emilio Pallavicini, to fight against the volunteers.

"There's no turning back now," Giuseppe said. "These men came to fight. So, we fight."

No one knew where the fight would take place as each set of combatants moved ever closer to the other's position. Finally, on August 28, Giuseppe and Pallavicini's soldiers met in Aspromonte.

"These are our countrymen," Giuseppe told his followers. "I believe many support our cause but can't disobey their commanders, so we must prevail with as little loss of life as possible."

"How can we manage such a thing?" Menotti asked.

"As all things are done: by order," Giuseppe declared. Then he forbade anyone to return fire on these fellow subjects of the

Kingdom of Italy. Despite being a collection of many men (and women) with many dialects (and desires), Giuseppe's soldiers listened to his orders and did their best to follow his mantra of obedience.

The standoff broke early in the engagement when one of Pallavicini's soldiers fired—whether accidentally or on purpose, no one knew—setting off a volley of several others.

Giuseppe tried to keep the bloodshed down by standing on his order until the man beside Menotti fell. While Father Pantaleo ran to offer medical aid, Menotti looked to his father for the next move, only to realize Giuseppe had been shot in the foot and was losing consciousness from blood loss.

Menotti ran toward his father. The army men began taking many of Giuseppe's volunteers prisoner. Others began running deeper up the mountains to avoid capture. In the confusion, Menotti lost sight of Giuseppe and had to take charge of his men, ordering swift retreat.

Meanwhile, Pallavicini ordered that Giuseppe be taken to a local prison. Though surgeons there operated on his foot and saved his life, all Giuseppe could focus on was the fact that he had failed to add the jewel of Rome to his dream of a fully united Italian empire. Was it ever to be so? The thought agonized him, especially when he was forcibly sent back to Caprera, once again in defeat, because his captors thought keeping him far from others would keep his ideas jailed as well.

Teresita and Canzio helped his recovery both in body and in spirit. It was Teresita who gave him the idea that revived him. She had read that on August 6, 1863, still in the midst of a Civil War, President Abraham Lincoln had announced the Emancipation Proclamation. "He took your advice," Teresita said.

Giuseppe misunderstood her point. "It is far too late for

me to join his cause. Besides, many others were advocating for the same thing. And those who understand politics will see that this is only a half measure. It only frees slaves in areas conquered by the Union Army, not in all areas everywhere in the United States."

"Is it not enough that he is trying? Like you?" Teresita said gently. "One step at a time."

Recognizing her wisdom and generosity, Giuseppe wrote to Lincoln. "Posterity will call you the great emancipator, a more enviable title than any crown could be, and greater than any merely mundane treasure," he said.

Teresita persisted in aiding her father's recovery, first by fashioning for him a traveling suit that included a white poncho lined with red silk, an embroidered red shirt, and a colored red tie. When he ran the fabric through his fingers, she could see the reverence in his eyes. Second, she showed him coverage of his activities by so many varied international newspapers. In this way, she showed him his future.

"Much as my son wants more time with his *nonno*," Teresita said as she had already had the first of her eventual sixteen children. "Much as we'd all love to have you with us, you don't belong only to us anymore." She pointed to a front-page article in a London newspaper. "You belong to the world."

With Teresita's encouragement, Giuseppe decided to tour Europe to revive his spirits, though secretly he also hoped to gain support for the taking of Rome. In London, British Prime Minister Henry John Temple, 3rd Viscount Palmerston received Giuseppe as an equal. The citizens lined the streets with enthusiasm wherever he traveled in their city. At dinner one night, he told the prime minister that he held great affection for the people of England. "The English nation is by no means exempt from imperfections, yet the English are the only people who can be compared with the ancient Romans," Giuseppe said. Together, the men discussed the eventual complete liberation of Italy as well as a range of occupied nations, such as Croatia, Greece, and Hungary.

Giuseppe proudly told the prime minister that his own son Menotti had organized the Garibaldi Legion, a unit of Italian volunteers led by General Francesco Nullo, who, during the January Uprising of 1863, had also fought for Polish independence.

"A son who takes after his father is a blessing," Temple said, raising his wine glass. "A salute to a true Italian."

"Ah, yes," Giuseppe agreed, clinking his glass. "But Menotti is also the first son of Anita, a proud Brazilian," he said, and almost choked up at mention of her name. "A salute to Anita and to Menotti—Brazilian and Italian through and through."

Giuseppe's travels included a tour of the Britannia Iron Works, where he planted a tree, and of the small town of Fowey. As small towns are not visited by international heroes every day, merchandise commemorating his visit immediately clogged store shelves. Giuseppe's visit became so entrenched in the lore of the city that when local author Kenneth Grahame wrote *The Wind in the Willows* many decades later, he included a statue of Giuseppe in the garden of his main character, Mole.

In his own time period, Giuseppe met the British poet laureate Alfred Tennyson on a visit to the estate of Charles Seely in Farringford. Crowds on horseback or in carriages lined the roads leading to the estate so thickly that it took Giuseppe two hours to reach the front gates.

Over a lavish catered meal, the men discussed their mutual admiration for poetry, especially the work of Percy Bysshe Shelley, which reminded him so deeply of his mother. From memory, Giuseppe recited: "'I pass through the pores of the ocean and shores; I change, but I cannot die.'"

Tennyson smiled and said, "For me, the lines that resonate best have always been: 'Like a child from the womb, like a ghost from the tomb, I arise and unbuild it again.' Words last forever, my friend. They have the power to connect continents—and people."

"Are you saying words are more important than deeds?" Giuseppe asked.

"Of course," Tennyson said. "I wield the pen. You, the sword. In a generation we shall see whom our grandchildren remember more."

It was an idea that stayed with Giuseppe for a long while, even as he savored the flavors of the bountiful brunch provided to all the visitors that day.

During his time with Tennyson, Giuseppe received a letter from the mother of Luciano Manara, the comrade he had lost on the first attack on Rome in 1849. She wrote to thank him for his support in properly burying her son. It had taken nearly twenty years, but now that the bulk of Italy called itself united, she had been able to move his bones from where he fell to the family plot and erect a monument surrounded by a small park of cypress trees and a chapel.

To his traveling companion that night, he read the inscription: "Luciano Manara, leader of the illustrious legion of valiant men, gave his blood for the fatherland, claiming the honor of

Italian arms against foreign mockery. His mother, worthy of envy and pity, places his beloved bones in this monument on which stands written a name, the boast and glory of Italy. He died fighting in Rome on June 30, 1849, with a hero's smile on his lips, an everlasting example to posterity."

"Might that be its own bit of poetic license," Tennyson said.

"About Luciano, no," Giuseppe said. "He was one of our bravest men. About his mother, I do not know. But having lost a child myself, I have no argument with her need for pity and memorial."

On his return through London, the crowds so thronged the streets that the prime minster shared a message from Queen Victoria as their carriage stood at a near standstill in the sea of people hoping to see the famous general.

"You have succeeded in a way I have yet not," Temple said with a smirk, nodding toward the telegram in his hand.

"In what fashion?" Giuseppe queried. Rather than recognize the success that was Venice, his one-track mind focused on the failure that was Rome. "Rome still belongs to France."

"I meant here in my country," Temple said. "You have shaken my queen, the great Alexandrina Victoria. She desires me to urge my visiting revolutionary general to return home, lest he foment rebellion here."

"She doesn't understand me," Giuseppe said. "I am not against monarchy. I am for union under whatever form of government the citizens desire."

"That is where you and I differ, my friend," Palmerston said. "A republic is the only form of government for the future."

Giuseppe did not want to be rude to his host, so he avoided noting that, while the prime minister hailed the concept of a republic, he was riding in an extremely expensive carriage and wearing extremely expensive clothing, while barely deigning to notice the many poor citizens who stood in the rain to praise them both. In his heart, Giuseppe hoped his work would create a better world for such followers. He made sure to turn his attention to those around him as the carriage made its way toward London.

Across Europe, Giuseppe found that most citizens shared his desire for unity, not only in individual countries, but for the entirety of Europe. Repairing his relationship with Mazzini, Giuseppe began to advocate for a European union modeled on the United States but without losing each country's individual status. He wrote about this idea to German revolutionary Karl Blind in April 1865:

> *The progress of humanity seems to have come to a halt, and you with your superior intelligence will know why. The reason is that the world lacks a nation which possesses true leadership. Such leadership, of course, is required not to dominate other peoples, but to lead them along the path of duty, to lead them toward the brotherhood of nations where all the barriers erected by egoism will be destroyed. We need the kind of leadership which, in the true tradition of medieval chivalry, would devote itself to redressing wrongs, supporting the weak, sacrificing momentary gains and material advantage for the much finer and more satisfying achievement of relieving the suffering of our fellow men. We need a nation courageous enough to give us a lead in this direction. It would rally to its cause all those who are suffering wrong or who aspire to a better life, and all those who are now enduring foreign oppression.*

This role of world leadership, left vacant as things are today, might well be occupied by the German nation. You Germans, with your grave and philosophic character, might well be the ones who could win the confidence of others and guarantee the future stability of the international community. Let us hope, then, that you can use your energy to overcome your moth-eaten thirty tyrants of the various German states. Let us hope that in the center of Europe you can then make a unified nation out of your fifty millions. All the rest of us would eagerly and joyfully follow you.

Clearly, Teresita had been right. Travel revived her father, a fact she noticed when he briefly returned to Caprera to organize the recruitment of men for another assault on Rome. Prime Minister Temple had promised support for such a venture, as had other leaders along his travels. In fact, it became the reason most wanted to meet him.

Back on his home island by 1865, something else began to brew. Teresita by now had three sons and had hired a young woman named Francesca Armosino to nurse them. When Giuseppe and Francesca met, he could sense a strength in this young woman that reminded him so deeply of Anita that he was immediately drawn to this new presence on the island.

"Francesca?" Teresita questioned him over dinner one night. "How could she ever replace mother?"

"I never said she could replace our Anita," Giuseppe said defensively as he reached for his daughter's hand, "but I see my mistake. By making such a myth out of the love I had for your mother, there can never be another you will allow to take a place at my side."

"Certainly not this slip of a thing," Teresita said.

"I am not asking that you accept Francesca as a mother to you. She could never be that. I am only asking that you allow me some comfort in my old age, should the lady find herself interested in such a war-worn specimen."

"But, father—"

"Not now," he said. "I have no place in my heart right now for other thoughts when the dream of winning Rome before I die lives there so largely."

So, he left Caprera yet again as Italy joined Prussia against the Austrian Empire in the Austro-Prussian War, hoping to remove Venice from Austrian rule. For this Third Italian War of Independence, Giuseppe regathered his Hunters of the Alps, now some forty thousand strong, and led them toward Trentino with Menotti at his side. Together, the father and son orchestrated the only Italian victory in that war, defeating the Austrians at Bezzecca, before reaching Trentino to try to wrest it out of Austrian control.

Meanwhile, news came that the Italian regular forces had been defeated at the island of Lissa and suffered disaster inland at the Battle of Custoza. "I can't be everywhere at once," Giuseppe lamented as he headed ever more earnestly toward Trentino. On the eve of battle, as he sat on his saddle by the fire and planned the next day's strategy with his officers, a rider approached Giuseppe's tent and handed him an official order.

The look on his face as he read the missive told Menotti all he needed to know. "We are being told to withdraw," Menotti said in disgust. "But we can't. Not this close." Menotti had taken on his father's mission with perhaps even more energy.

"Austria has agreed to cede Venice to Italy," Giuseppe read aloud. "But they will never release Trentino, or so the pressure Prussia exerts is making them say."

"They haven't seen us fight yet," Menotti argued.

"And they won't," Giuseppe said. "I have received an order from my superior officers. I obey."

"But—" Menotti began.

Giuseppe waved his hand for silence. "Often it is better to recognize a victory when it is handed to you and remember you can return at a later day to extract another. You especially must learn, my son, that the job of an officer is to listen to *and* to accept the orders of your superiors, unless you know them to be morally corrupt. This order is not a corruption, but a compromise. You may not realize what it means—but be sure, due to discussions happening far, far away, that no matter what our soldiers did in Trentino, they would eventually be forced to withdraw for diplomacy's sake."

Seeing that Menotti still felt this venture had been a failure rather than a success, Giuseppe added, "Besides, leaving Trentino alone means we can turn our attention back toward other ways of winning Rome for what is now a more solidified Italian state. There are more than two ways to win the day."

Reluctantly, Menotti gave in to his own superior officer (and father) and relayed the order to stand down. As they all returned yet again to their homes, an armistice was signed. Austria's citizens had voted to cede Venice to Italy.

After the war, Giuseppe tried to follow the advice he had given his son. He thought blending politics with military strength was the key, so he created a one-platform political party focused only on the cause of capturing Rome.

In 1867, he marched on the city, but the French still defended the Papal State, and the battle resulted in one more lost friend, Cantoni; one more wound to his leg, during the Battle of Mentana; and one more lost chance to wrest Rome from papal control.

Once again exiled to Caprera, Giuseppe decided to see if Tennyson's philosophy could help. Was the old trope about the pen being mightier than the sword true? Instead of reading at night, Giuseppe found himself writing his own first novel, *Cantoni il Volontario*, as a kind of catharsis from the awful loss of young Cantoni's vibrance and gifts, of the many vibrant and gifted young people he had lost across his career.

"What are you writing?" Francesca asked one day when Teresita was away on a hike with her sons. Teresita's active family reminded Giuseppe of the many outings to the woods or to the sea that he had shared with his mother and brothers all those years ago.

"It's a memorial to those who have followed me," Giuseppe said, "and a call to service for those who have not yet." He found himself admitting to Francesca a truth he might not have completely accepted on his own yet, one he certainly had not shared with anyone else. Something about her inquisitive eyes and her kind, quiet manner soothed and settled him, but nothing yet could keep Giuseppe—or his many loyal followers—from continuing to pursue the larger dream of Italian unity.

When Francesca questioned this dogged pursuit of one life goal, Giuseppe answered with one of his mother's many proverbs. "*Chi cerca, trova; cui sècuta, vinci.*" *Who seeks, finds; who perseveres, wins.*

Chapter 19

1867–1870
WINNING ROME AND RETURNING
HOME FOR THE FINAL UNION

In 1867, Giuseppe felt compelled to travel to Geneva, for he had been elected honorary president of the first Congress of Peace in Geneva, founded by Charles Lemonnier, a French pacifist who hoped to end the pope's role as ruler of the Papal States. Lemonnier wanted a complete end to the role of the pope, whereas Giuseppe wanted only the annexation of Rome to his united Italy.

"But how will the two of you find common ground?" Menotti asked as Giuseppe prepared to meet troops who had begun gathering near Rome for another advance against the city. "You must oppose Lemonnier's extremism."

"It's insane to oppose when you can neither win nor compromise," Giuseppe said, falling back on another of his mother's proverbs. "If all my voice can do is counter his, then it is a trip worth taking. The volunteers will wait for me."

~

"As always, my father knows the heart of his men," Menotti told Bixio when they arrived at the outskirts of Rome, where they found several hundred men ready to follow wherever the senior Garibaldi would lead.

"They will follow you as well," Giuseppe assured Menotti. "You have proven yourself many a time."

This comment proved prophetic as, unbeknownst to Menotti, the king and commanders of the formal Italian army feared the power Giuseppe's popularity might wield. As he rode to meet Menotti and his many volunteers, Giuseppe found himself and over fifty of his followers arrested when they arrived in Sinalunga, barely two hundred kilometers from Rome.

Menotti and Bixio managed to escape and spent the night hunkered down with others in the local woodland.

"I'm not sure we can continue without him," Menotti said.

"Truth be told," Bixio said, "your father's health worries me. I believe he has reached the place in a man's life where his greatest power lies in the words he shares, not the weapons he wields."

Bolstered by the faith of his father's oldest surviving friend, Menotti made plans to continue to Rome and support the formal Italian army as they, in three columns, marched into the now unguarded areas around the Vatican.

Meanwhile, though imprisoned, Giuseppe smuggled out a note of support to those followers who had escaped arrest. He found that feelings for full unity swelled so wholly in the hearts of many of the men in the formal army, including those who served as guards at the prison, that soon chants of "To Rome with Garibaldi" rang out across the city. To avoid mutiny, the superior officers arranged for Giuseppe to be released and returned to Caprera under honor guard. But the general could not long be kept from his regiment. Under the disguise of an elderly local, Giuseppe openly took a packet boat back to the mainland, only to be recaptured and retaken home. Afterward, the king sent nine warships to watch over Caprera.

"That's how much he fears your name," Canzio proudly said to his father-in-law and former commander. "No matter what happens now and who rides at the front of the troops, when Rome is taken, it will be because of your efforts."

"And yours," Giuseppe insisted. "And all the men and women who came before you."

"It seems so unfair to deprive a man of the moment he has worked his whole life to see," Teresita said.

"They won't," Canzio said with a note of secrecy.

Late that night, the two men made their way stealthily to the beach under cover of the moon. They met a fisherman heading out for his early morning catch, trailing a second small boat behind him. Canzio helped Giuseppe into the smaller boat and covered him with a tarp. Then the fisherman sailed close to the nearest warship and began a shouting match over the idea that such large ships frightened away his fishes. This allowed Canzio to slide his small boat along the coastline unseen until he had rounded a bend and could move into more open water.

Though free of the warships, the weather refused to cooperate. Rain fell the entirety of the nearly fifty hours they remained onboard, until Canzio's rowing brought them to the western coast of mainland Italy. With the help of other rebels, Giuseppe reached Florence on October 25, 1867. There, he gave several speeches denouncing the lack of government support for the taking of Rome. Then he traveled by train to join his men in the town of Monterotondo on the outskirts of Rome on November 3.

Sadly, King Victor foddered away so much time that Napoleon III had had the chance to send reinforcements to the area. They were armed with the latest in weaponry, the Fusil model 1866, a bolt action military breech-loading rifle that could fire off twelve shots a minute due to its ammunition cartridge. In contrast, some of Giuseppe's men carried muskets while others relied on bayonet-style fighting in hand-to-hand combat. This mismatched battle left 150 of his men dead while only 32 French soldiers died. All Giuseppe and his officers could do was call a retreat, which led him back to Florence, where he was arrested yet again. Giuseppe spent over twenty days in jail before being banished back to Caprera.

When the Franco-Prussian War broke out in July 1870, Giuseppe's dream of unifying the nation was interrupted once more. Many Italians signed up as volunteers at the Prussian embassy in Florence with a new hope of finally wrenching Rome from the papal powers. When the French garrison was recalled from Rome to defend Paris against the Prussians, the Italian army knew it was their best chance to move in and claim the Papal States for Italy.

Even at the age of sixty-three, plagued by rheumatism and pains from his various wounds, Giuseppe could not hold from his desire to join Bixio and his other officers in this final fight. But King Victor's government again surrounded his island and thereby effectively imprisoned his energies away from his volunteers. So, Giuseppe turned to a new mode of battle as the physical limitations of his body took hold, providing support with words smuggled from his captive state.

"It is all I can contribute now," he told Teresita as she readied another letter for the packet boat to bring to the mainland. It was from this same boat that word finally reached them on September 20, 1870, that General Bixio's troops had entered the Porta San Pancrazio in Rome at the same time a separate force of Garibaldinis entered Porta Pia.

With this, Rome became one with Italy.

Despite being elected again to the new Italian parliament, Giuseppe spent much of his late years in Caprera, living in impoverished retirement in the house he had built years ago that reminded him of those Uruguayan ranches he had traveled with Anita. He sent the Uruguayan parliament a draft of legislation to include a salary for General Garibaldi in the national budget. So many back in South America appreciated his efforts that they forced their government to grant him the pension.

In 1880, he and Francesca married with all his children in attendance. Together, they would have three more children. Though no one ever could erase Anita from his mind, Giuseppe finally felt whole again.

Giuseppe never forgot the large number of female participants on his journey to unity—his mother, Nicoletta's, teachings; the nursing skills of Jessie White, whose ceaseless exertions saved many of his followers; the poetry of Margaret Fuller, who brought his name to far-off lands. In memory of them and Anita, he issued dozens of appeals and proclamations that supported the question of women's rights, which eventually took hold. In 1879, he founded the League of Democracy, which advocated for universal suffrage, free education, labor unions to aid the working class, and the emancipation of women.

On June 2, 1882, Giuseppe asked for his bed to be moved to a place where he could gaze at the sea he had so loved and lived on nearly all his life.

Memories of the men and women who had gone before him seemed to flood his brain all day as he whispered the names of people his own children barely remembered. Then a bird alighted on his window sill.

"Mamma, look," he whispered. "A calandra lark . . ." Francesca tried to chase it away, but Giuseppe stayed her hand. "He is free and must be allowed to go where he pleases."

Giuseppe Garibaldi died that day at the age of seventy-four. His surviving children buried him on his farm on Caprera alongside some of the children he had outlived. The country he loved had been reunited for just over twenty years, and Rome had served as its capital for just over ten of those years. Giuseppe's dreams had come true. He had made them come true for all his fellow Italians, who soon built monuments in nearly every major city in his honor. Those who emigrated to other countries carried his story with them, resulting in statues and other memorials scattering his name and fame around the world.

Epilogue

Of Giuseppe and Anita's children, Menotti remained in the military, rising to the rank of general and being named to the Legion of Honor in France for his service during the Franco-Prussian War. He retired and moved to Rome, where he served in parliament from 1876 to 1900. Through it all, he remained involved in agriculture, using the lessons learned from his father on Caprera.

Teresita eventually had sixteen children, twelve of whom reached maturity. Following her family's philosophy of respecting friendship, she found herself helping her father's old friend and employer Antonio Meucci, who had gone bankrupt in his battle to copyright his inventions. Teresita wrote many letters petitioning the Italian government to give Meucci a modest pension of $30 a month in his old age, which it finally did.

Ricciotti followed his father's and brother's footsteps, serving as a soldier with Menotti in the Franco-Prussian War, then as a politician in the Italian parliament from 1887 to 1890. He then returned to the military for the Turkish-Greek War of 1897. Five of his seven children also became soldiers, two of which served in World War I. He named his only daughter Anita in honor of the mother he barely knew but the world never forgot.

Thanks to Giuseppe's push for women's emancipation in memory of Anita, Ernestina Puritz-Manasse Paper became the first woman to receive a university degree in a united Italy in 1877. In 1907, Rina Monti became the first female professor at an Italian university.

In 1925, Italian women gained the right to vote, making Italy truly and finally united.

About the Author

Rosanne Welch, PhD, serves as Executive Director of Stephens College MFA in TV and Screenwriting. Her television writing credits include *Beverly Hills 90210*, *Picket Fences*, *ABCNEWS: Nightline*, and *Touched by an Angel*. For the Mentoris Project Welch wrote *America's Forgotten Founding Father: A Novel Based on the Life of Filippo Mazzei* (2018). She has also edited *When Women Wrote Hollywood* (2018), named runner up for the Susan Koppelman in feminist studies by the Popular Culture Association and co-edited *Women in American History: A Social, Political, and Cultural Encyclopedia* (named to both the 2018 Outstanding References Sources List and to the list of Best Historical Materials, by the American Library Association). She wrote *Why The Monkees Matter: Teenagers, Television and American Popular Culture* (2016). Welch serves as Book Reviews editor for *Journal of Screenwriting*; and on the Editorial Board for *California History Journal*. You can find her TEDxCPP talk "The Importance of Having a Female Voice in the Room."

NOW AVAILABLE FROM THE MENTORIS PROJECT

America's Forgotten Founding Father
A Novel Based on the Life of Filippo Mazzei
by Rosanne Welch, PhD

A. P. Giannini—The People's Banker
by Francesca Valente

The Architect Who Changed Our World
A Novel Based on the Life of Andrea Palladio
by Pamela Winfrey

A Boxing Trainer's Journey
A Novel Based on the Life of Angelo Dundee
by Jonathan Brown

Breaking Barriers
A Novel Based on the Life of Laura Bassi
by Jule Selbo

Building Heaven's Ceiling
A Novel Based on the Life of Filippo Brunelleschi
by Joe Cline

Building Wealth
From Shoeshine Boy to Real Estate Magnate
by Robert Barbera

First Among Equals
A Novel Based on the Life of Cosimo de' Medici
by Francesco Massaccesi

God's Messenger
A Novel Based on the Life of Mother Frances X. Cabrini
by Nicole Gregory

Grace Notes
A Novel Based on the Life of Henry Mancini
by Stacia Raymond

Harvesting the American Dream
A Novel Based on the Life of Ernest Gallo
by Karen Richardson

Humble Servant of Truth
A Novel Based on the Life of Thomas Aquinas
by Margaret O'Reilly

Leonardo's Secret
A Novel Based on the Life of Leonardo da Vinci
by Peter David Myers

Little by Little We Won
A Novel Based on the Life of Angela Bambace
by Peg A. Lamphier, PhD

The Making of a Prince
A Novel Based on the Life of Niccolò Machiavelli
by Maurizio Marmorstein

Marconi and His Muses
A Novel Based on the Life of Guglielmo Marconi
by Pamela Winfrey

No Person Above the Law
A Novel Based on the Life of Judge John J. Sirica
by Cynthia Cooper

Relentless Visionary: Alessandro Volta
by Michael Berick

Ride Into the Sun
A Novel Based on the Life of Scipio Africanus
by Patric Verrone

Soldier, Diplomat, Archaeologist
A Novel Based on the Bold Life of Louis Palma di Cesnola
by Peg A. Lamphier, PhD

The Soul of a Child
A Novel Based on the Life of Maria Montessori
by Kate Fuglei

What a Woman Can Do
A Novel Based on the Life of Artemisia Gentileschi
by Peg A. Lamphier, PhD

FUTURE TITLES FROM THE MENTORIS PROJECT

A Biography about Rita Levi-Montalcini
and
Novels Based on the Lives of:
Amerigo Vespucci
Andrea Doria
Antonin Scalia
Antonio Meucci
Buzzie Bavasi
Cesare Beccaria
Father Eusebio Francisco Kino
Federico Fellini
Frank Capra
Guido d'Arezzo
Harry Warren
Leonardo Fibonacci
Maria Gaetana Agnesi
Mario Andretti
Peter Rodino
Pietro Belluschi
Saint Augustine of Hippo
Saint Francis of Assisi
Vince Lombardi

For more information on these titles and
the Mentoris Project, please visit
www.mentorisproject.org

Printed in Great Britain
by Amazon

50973806R00152